The Day She Came Home

A desperate mother. An angry father. A family with dark secrets.

Emma Dhesi

Rowanbrae Press

Copyright ©2019 by Emma Dhesi

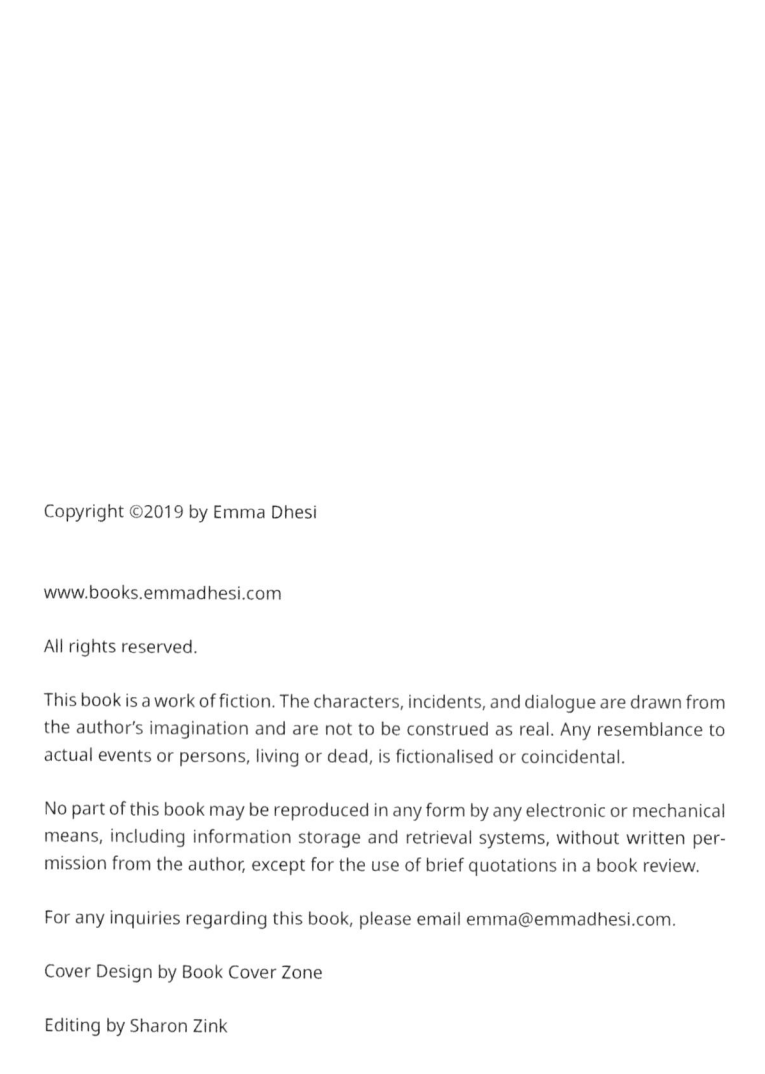

www.books.emmadhesi.com

All rights reserved.

This book is a work of fiction. The characters, incidents, and dialogue are drawn from the author's imagination and are not to be construed as real. Any resemblance to actual events or persons, living or dead, is fictionalised or coincidental.

No part of this book may be reproduced in any form by any electronic or mechanical means, including information storage and retrieval systems, without written permission from the author, except for the use of brief quotations in a book review.

For any inquiries regarding this book, please email emma@emmadhesi.com.

Cover Design by Book Cover Zone

Editing by Sharon Zink

Dedicated to PSD, with love

Contents

1. Chapter 1 — 1
2. Chapter 2 — 11
3. Chapter 3 — 16
4. Chapter 4 — 22
5. Chapter 5 — 30
6. Chapter 6 — 38
7. Chapter 7 — 44
8. Chapter 8 — 51
9. Chapter 9 — 56
10. Chapter 10 — 63
11. Chapter 11 — 69
12. Chapter 12 — 76
13. Chapter 13 — 83
14. Chapter 14 — 92
15. Chapter 15 — 100
16. Chapter 16 — 108
17. Chapter 17 — 117
18. Chapter 18 — 124

19. Chapter 19 — 131
20. Chapter 20 — 138
21. Chapter 21 — 143
22. Chapter 22 — 149
23. Chapter 23 — 156
24. Chapter 24 — 162
25. Chapter 25 — 170
26. Chapter 26 — 178
27. Chapter 27 — 185
28. Chapter 28 — 198
29. Chapter 29 — 206
30. Chapter 30 — 213
31. Chapter 31 — 219
32. Chapter 32 — 226
33. Chapter 33 — 236
34. Chapter 34 — 243
35. Chapter 35 — 251
36. Chapter 36 — 260
37. Chapter 37 — 265
38. Chapter 38 — 272
39. Chapter 39 — 278
40. Chapter 40 — 281

Acknowledgments — 285

About the Author — 286

Also By — 288

Chapter 1

From the master bedroom upstairs, I heard Ross's key enter the lock and the front door open. I froze. My heart thumped, my face flushed. I almost cried out in panic, but at the last moment put my hands over my mouth because this wasn't my home anymore. I wasn't supposed to be here. It was with trembling limbs I had made my way to the garden gate only half an hour before.

I'd stood at the gate, dizzy at the thought of what I was about to do. I had given myself the chance to back away, but curiosity compelled me to try my key in the front door. It turned. Ross hadn't changed the locks, he'd waited for me. Stepping over the threshold, it had felt wonderful to be inside our family home after an absence of four years.

I had come to the house simply to look around, to see and touch my former life, and remind myself of what I'd left behind. I was surprised that so little had changed—the same pictures on the walls, the same unread books on shelves—but it was in Ross's room, our bedroom, that the least amount had altered. My clothes remained hung in the wardrobe and still lay folded in the chest of drawers. I hated knowing I had created this time capsule inside my husband. Even our bed linen was the same and, when I lowered my face to the pillow and breathed in, was bombarded with memories of Ross cuddling me, of the sheets' coolness when I first got into bed and of how comfortable my pillow had been. I remembered the morning light in summer waking me too early because I'd never got around to upgrading the curtains. Thin and flimsy, they were no protection against even a Glasgow dawn.

I was relieved to see only two toothbrushes in the bathroom—Ross's electric one and Sam's Spiderman one. I picked up Sam's brush and examined its chewed bristles with tender sentiment.

Sam's bedroom had changed the most. It was no longer a nursery; it was a little boy's room. His drawings, pinned to the walls, had progressed from lines scribbled across a page to people, animals and objects, all identifiable. The toys scattered about the room were those of an older child, not the toddler I'd left behind. He didn't read simple word books any more, but story books, and I ached at the thought of all those missed bedtimes.

His clothes, which looked so big to me, were strewn over the floor and unmade bed. I had to stop myself from plumping the pillow and straightening the duvet. I looked at the photos of my son that were sellotaped to the wall next to his bed. His hair had darkened, his face had lengthened and lost its chubbiness, but he was still, unmistakably, my boy. I took a photo and tucked it into my bra.

The sound of Ross settling himself on the sofa in the living room brought me back to the here and now. Mortified at the absurdity of the situation, I wondered what I was going to do next. I also wondered why here was here at this time of day.

For three weeks now, I'd watched the house, embarrassing myself by lurking behind trees and cars, sure someone would report me to the police. Worried as I was, the temptation to glimpse my husband and son was too much, and I'd taken my chances.

It was early morning, the first time I saw Sam. He was running out of the front door in his school uniform. I thought my heart

THE DAY SHE CAME HOME

had stopped and I willed time to slow down so I could look at him properly, absorb every detail and be sure it really was my little boy. From the tree behind which I was hiding, I saw Ross follow him out and shut the front door. They both got into the car and drove away. It took only a minute, but what a magical minute. I'd wept at the joy of seeing him, and I was on a high for the rest of the day. I'd seen my son. He was six years old now, but still my baby. I'd have recognised him anywhere.

Seeing him became like a drug, and I visited as often as I dared. I still anxious a neighbour might recognise me. That was how I came to know their routine so well and why it was such a shock that Ross had come home early.

I stared out the bedroom window, not daring to move. The tree on the opposite side of the road had grown since I was last here. I could no longer see into the first floor of the house in front of which it stood. That was good, as it meant they couldn't see me, trapped and immobile. A noise downstairs brought my focus back to Ross and what the hell I was going to do now.

As quietly as I could, I made my way to the landing. I took a deep breath before, step by step, tiptoed my way down the stairs. The first I saw of him were his feet, solidly placed on the ground, his knees supporting a newspaper. As I got closer to the bottom, I saw his body, his shoulders, and finally his face staring at me in disbelief. I reached the ground floor and stopped, one hand on the balustrade.

Ross stood up, the newspaper falling to the ground, and walked tentatively towards me as if I were an apparition that might disappear if he moved too suddenly. I felt myself blush. I searched Ross's face, but I couldn't discern what he was thinking.

'Nicola.' He said my name simply, as if confirming I was who he thought I was.

'Hello, Ross.'

He put his hands on my face, then my shoulders, and then wrapped his arms tightly around me, happy and confused at the same time.

'Nicola, is it really you? I thought you were dead.' He held me at arm's length before taking my hands and leading me to the sofa, all the while looking me up and down. 'Where have you been?' he asked. 'What happened to you?'

'I don't know where to start,' I said.

For so long, I'd wanted to have this conversation with him, to explain myself and make him understand. I'd run it through my head umpteen times, and each time I'd been calm, coherent and rational, so much so that Ross could do nothing else but take me in his arms, kiss me and tell me he understood. In my daydreams he'd tell me all was forgiven and we need never talk about my disappearance again. All he'd ever wanted was to have me home safe and sound, and now here I was.

'Start at the beginning,' he said. 'We've all been so worried, I... I thought someone had kidnapped you. Were you?'

'No, no, I wasn't kidnapped.'

'That's a relief.' For a moment Ross's kindness overwhelmed me, his instinct to see the best in me was touching. 'So, what happened, where did you go?'

'I went to Shetland.'

'Shetland?'

'Yes.'

'As in the Shetland Islands?'

'I don't understand.'

I took a deep breath before saying, 'I wasn't coping here, with the baby.'

'Right.' Ross was cautious.

'I needed to leave. Not just for a week or two, or because I was having a bad day. I was struggling and couldn't see a way out. I was depressed.' Ross looked bewildered, but I could see he was absorbing my every word. 'It wasn't a case of feeling sorry for myself,' I blurted. 'Everything confused me. Every decision I made was the wrong one.'

'What do you mean?'

'I'd give Sam porridge for breakfast, but really I should have given him eggs. I'd hoover when really I should have cleaned the bathroom. At the supermarket I couldn't put anything in the basket so would leave empty-handed. What a bad, useless mother, I thought to myself, you're letting everyone down.'

I watched my hands twisting in my lap. 'Guilt compounded every negative thought because I had nothing to be depressed about. I had a husband who loved me and a beautiful, beautiful little boy I adored. My brain went around and around, circling between feeling miserable and then guilty for feeling that way.'

'Why didn't you tell me any of this? I'm your husband, you're supposed to talk to me.'

'I don't know why exactly, but I think I was ashamed. I didn't want anyone to know I was failing. What did I have to be depressed about?' I lowered my voice and said, 'Plus, you and I had grown apart.'

'Yes, but I didn't think it had got so bad you wanted to leave. I thought we were having trouble adjusting to Sam.' After the birth of our son, Ross and I had drifted apart. Like a leaky bucket, the love and connectedness we'd once felt for each other seeped away, drip by drip. Motherhood took its toll on my time and mind, and I subsequently wondered if Ross felt excluded as Sam and I tried to bond.

Cautiously, and with as little accusation as I could muster, I said, 'Ross, I know about your affair with Sinead.'

Ross sat back on the sofa, putting distance between us.

'You thought I was having an affair with Sinead? From work?' I nodded. He stood up, ran his hands through his hair, then was static for a moment, thinking about what to say. He came back to the sofa, sat down, and took my hands. 'Nicola, I did not have an affair with Sinead. I don't know why you thought that, but I didn't.'

I felt myself physically shrink. I could see he was telling the truth and was mortified. All this time I had pictured him with Sinead, but it seems it had been in my head and nowhere else. 'Is that why you left?' he asked. 'Because you thought I was having an affair?'

'It was part of the reason,' I half whispered.

'How could you think me capable of that?' I couldn't look at him. He moved through to the kitchen and out the back door to the garden.

After a few minutes, I gathered myself up and followed him. I watched him pace up and down the lawn, his fists banging against the sides of his head, rambling, as a mad person might.

At moments like this, my mother would automatically turn to the kettle and make a pot of tea. The much-repeated movements of putting the teabags in the pot, pouring the water and gathering the mugs gave her a task to hide behind as she worked out what to do next. I copied her example and switched on the kettle.

Everything was where I'd left it four years ago. The teapot next to the kettle, cups in the cupboard above. While the water boiled, I looked around the room and was struck again by how little had changed. He came back as I was pouring water into the pot.

With an evidently forced calm, he sat down at the table, his hands flat on the tabletop. I brought the teapot and mugs over and sat down opposite him.

'I'm sorry, Ross. I realise now it was crazy of me to think you would have had an affair, you're not that type of man.'

I took a deep breath, involuntarily shuddering because of the tension surrounding us, and poured the tea. The sound of the liquid as it hit the cups echoed loudly, emphasising our silence.

I got the milk from the fridge, all the while wondering what to say next. We sat in silence, taking tentative sips.

'Why did you go to Shetland?' he asked.

'I remembered watching a programme about a man who wanted to disappear. He didn't want to be part of society anymore. Instead, he wanted to be where nobody asked too many questions. He started over and made a new life for himself. I remember, too, how beautiful it looked. It always struck me as a place of sanctuary.'

I thought of my little studio flat on the edge of Lerwick and its view of the CalMac ferry pulling in and out of the harbour. It had been a sanctuary. I'd created a little world for myself there. A world of no stress and lots of space and time. The vast skies that watched over the Shetland archipelago and the powerful winds that chased away bad memories gave me the respite I needed to recover. My only regret was leaving Sam. That would always haunt me.

'What did you do there?'

'I worked in a hotel doing a little of everything. In the summer I sold small paintings to tourists.'

'I didn't know you could paint.'

'Neither did I.'

'Where are you living now?'

'I've got a small flat near my work.'

'You've got a job?' His tone was accusing, as if I shouldn't be able to work, not in my condition.

'The Strathclyde City Hotel, in the Merchant city.'

'You left us,' he said, suddenly furious. 'You dumped Sam and went off to the back of beyond. Have you any idea of the havoc you left behind? The police thought I'd killed you.'

'I'm sorry.' I was shocked. Not once did it occur to me that people would think I was dead.

'You should be. I had to get a lawyer. People were staring at me on the street, wondering if I did it. It was horrific.'

'I am so sorry.'

'And as for Sam, you dumped him—'

'I didn't dump him. I left him with Claire, our closest friend.'

'Claire felt guilty for months, thinking she should have known something was wrong.'

'Did you feel guilty?'

'For what?'

'For not seeing how unhappy I was?'

'Are you blaming me for this?'

'No, I'm not.'

'Well, it sounds like it.'

'No, I'm not blaming you, but didn't you see how much I was struggling?'

'Yes, I did, but I didn't know how to help you. You turned away from me.'

'What do you mean?' It was my turn to look confused.

'You wouldn't let me near you. Every time I touched you, you flinched.' He turned his head away. 'You didn't want me.'

'What do you mean, I didn't want you? I needed you more than ever.'

'Then why did you turn away from me?'

I broke down and wept at how much misunderstanding there had been between us and how much heartache might have been avoided if we'd been able to talk to each other. 'Ross, I'm sorry about this, about the whole mess.' My tears wouldn't stop. 'I genuinely thought you and Sam would be better without me because I couldn't look after him. I was going out of my mind. What if I'd hurt him?' Ross said nothing, and gradually my tears abated. 'I know I have a lot of big bridges to build with you and Sam.' Ross looked at me sharply.

'Why are you here?' he asked. 'What do you want?'

'I want you.'

THE DAY SHE CAME HOME

'What a nerve,' said Ross, more or less laughing in my face. 'You disappear for four years and expect just to walk back into our lives.'

'I'm still your wife and Sam's mother.'

'If I hadn't caught you snooping, would you ever have told me you were in Glasgow?'

'Of course.'

'When?'

'I don't know. When the time was right, when I had the courage.' I knew I sounded weak.

'This is too much. You need to go,' Ross said, his previous laughter giving way to panic. He stood up and walked towards the front door, trying to get me out of the house as quickly as possible.

'Don't be like that,' I said, trailing him. 'Ross, please, please give me a chance. I've never stopped loving you or Sam. I just want to be involved.' He opened the door and manhandled me out.

'Keys,' he said, holding open his hand. Reluctantly, I put them in his palm.

I stood, impotent, on the doorstep and Ross slammed the door in my face. My attempt to convince Ross I had left out of desperation, not cruelty, had failed miserably. I almost knocked on the door to try again, but knew it would be fruitless. I wasn't sure what else I could say to him, so instead scribbled my number on a piece of paper, put it through the letterbox and hurried to the bus stop.

As I waited for the bus, I thought about how optimistic I'd been on my journey back from Shetland to Glasgow, only three months before. I'd stood at the back of the ferry and watched the twinkling lights of Lerwick's tiny harbour recede and finally disappear.

The sky had been clear that evening and the stars shone vibrantly above me, almost as though they were lighting my path home. I was heartbroken to wave goodbye, but knew I would return one day, bringing Sam with me. I wanted him to see the place that saved me and for him to love it as much as I did. The crossing was calm, and the gentle rocking of the boat soothed me. I slept soundly in my berth that night.

The next morning my cabin was cold, and I hurried to get washed and dressed before heading to the restaurant for breakfast. It wasn't long before the tannoy announced our arrival and I headed up on deck to watch us dock in Aberdeen. I breathed in the bitter tang of seaweed and burning diesel, while watching the seamen move easily around the pier, unhurriedly throwing thick, rough ropes over the mooring bollards to secure the ship before we passengers disembarked. Their banter carried through the air, but I couldn't make out the words, only their laughter.

From the ferry quay, I staggered with my one, over-stuffed bag to Union Square and bought a ticket for the next bus to Glasgow. I was excited as I boarded, all too aware that in a few hours I'd be in my home city where a new job and a new flat waited for me. After what felt like an eternity, my National Express coach pulled into Buchanan Street Bus Station.

Stepping into St George's Square, I lifted my face to the sky and breathed in deeply. The ground was wet and moisture hung in the air, giving Glasgow its distinctive city smell of rain-diluted petrol fumes and damp concrete. This is my time, I thought. I'm not running away from myself anymore—no, I'm propelling myself forward. The next chapter of my life is beginning.

Chapter 2

After Nicola had left, Ross spent the rest of the day in a self-induced blur. He refused to think about her until later, when Sam was in bed, and he could allow himself to fall apart if he needed to. He let routine and habit take over as he tidied the house, ate lunch, collected Sam from school, made dinner, read bedtime stories, and said goodnight.

'Night, Dad,' said Sam, as his father tucked him up in bed. Ross stroked his son's face, wondering if he should tell him his mother was back in their lives, but the thought of explaining Nicola's sudden reappearance made his stomach churn, so he said nothing.

Returning to the kitchen table, this time with a beer, he tried to fathom that morning's events. Ross looked at a photograph of Nicola hanging on the wall. That was the Nicola he'd loved and married. The one before him today was a Nicola he didn't recognise; a woman who had chosen not to let him know she was alive and, in doing so, had taken away his right to be angry with her, to grieve and accept she'd left, or even start rebuilding his life.

He rooted around in a kitchen drawer for an already opened packet of cigarettes. Ross still enjoyed a smoke from time to time, and tonight he needed one more than ever. Outside, the cool night air felt good. He pulled hard on that first drag and felt felt the smoke fill his lungs and the slight feeling of suffocation as they reached capacity. He exhaled a long, steady stream of smoke, taking a moment to acknowledge and enjoy how light-headed it made him feel.

He re-ran Nicola's story, trying to see things from her point of view, but he kept coming back to the simple fact that she'd rejected him and Sam, that she preferred to run away to the back of beyond in Shetland, rather than turn to him for help and love and support.

Without embarrassment he let tears fall, tears not only of personal rejection, but of relief that she was alive. He felt foolish too now, humiliated. He needn't have cried all those tears for her when she first left, because she certainly hadn't been weeping for him.

Ross finished his cigarette and beer and went inside. He picked up the phone.

'Hi, Claire, it's Ross.'

Claire had been a close friend since his university days. After a brief dalliance, they realised they were better as friends than lovers and had remained close ever since. Claire, her husband Jamie, Nicola and Ross had been almost inseparable, even having their children at the same time, although Claire and Jamie had gone onto have a second while Nicola was missing.

'You alright?' she asked.

'No, I'm not. Nicola came to the house today.'

Ross sensed Claire's shock. She was silent for a few moments before asking, 'Is she okay?'

'I think so. She seems to be.'

'What happened to her?'

'She ran away. She ran away to Shetland of all places and didn't think to tell anyone.'

'Shetland?'

'That's what she says. She says she had a breakdown.'

'Oh, God,' said Claire. After a moment, she said, 'It's all my fault, I should have said something. I could see she wasn't herself.'

'Stop it. It wasn't your fault, and it wasn't mine. We have nothing to feel guilty about. She left, she ran away. We can't be blamed for that.' Ross ripped at the label of his empty beer bottle, slightly uncomfortable at saying something he didn't entirely believe.

'What happens now?' Claire asked at length.

'I don't know. I'm so angry with her I almost wish something had happened to her.'

'You don't mean that.'

'Don't I? At least then I could feel sorry for her, have some sympathy, instead of the blind rage I'm feeling now. Aren't you angry that she let you worry all these years?'

'I don't know, I suppose so. I think I'm still in shock. Why Shetland?'

'She said it was a sanctuary. Oh, God, I'm so angry with her. How could she do this to me, to Sam, for Christ's sake?'

'You're angry and I don't blame you, but listen, sleep on it. Things might feel different in the morning.' Claire paused. 'I can't believe she's really back. It seems so incredible. Did she leave a phone number?'

'Yes, but I'm not calling her.'

'Where is she staying?'

'She's got a flat near the Merchant City.'

'Is she well again?'

'I didn't ask.'

'How long has she been back?'

'I don't know, I didn't ask that either.'

'Jesus, Ross, what did you ask her?'

'I asked her where the hell she'd been.' Ross was embarrassed at how little he'd found out. Claire's questions made him feel he'd done the wrong thing by Nicola again. 'I'm sorry,' he said. 'I didn't mean to shout. There's a lot I didn't ask, it was so unexpected. She says she wants to come back, but I panicked and kicked her out of the house.'

'You mean she wants you back?'

'That's what she said, but I don't know what to think. She walked out on us. She gave up her rights to us four years ago.'

'Do you still love her?'

'I don't know what I feel. If I don't get back together with her, do you think she'll try taking Sam?'

'Surely no court would give him to her. Not after everything that's happened.'

'Claire, you'll stick up for me if this goes to court, won't you? You'll tell them what a good dad I've been?'

'Of course I will, but I'm sure it won't come to that. Look, go to bed, try to sleep, I'm sure things will look different tomorrow.'

'Do you think I should call her folks?' Ross asked at length.

'You probably ought to, it seems the right thing to do.'

After they hung up, Ross dialled his in-laws' number. 'Stephen, it's Ross.'

'Hello.' Ross could picture Stephen checking his watch, tutting to himself.

'I'm sorry to call so late.'

'How is my grandson?'

'Stephen, I have some news. I think you should sit down. Is Mary there?'

'Mary's in bed.'

'Well, I think you should call her down.'

'For goodness' sake, Ross, what's this about? We don't hear from you in months and then you call in the middle of the night.'

'Nicola came to the house today.' The line was silent but for Stephen's breathing as he absorbed the news. Ross then heard a rustle as Stephen shouted for his wife to come downstairs.

A minute later, there were muffled voices before Mary let out a scream and began to cry. Stephen said, 'Tell me exactly what happened, Ross.'

Chapter 3

Stephen Johnston slowly put down the receiver onto the cradle. He stood in the hallway, shocked by what Ross had told him. He couldn't believe Nicola had been alive and well all these years, and had never once thought to let anyone know. How could he have produced such a selfish child? Mary was sitting on the stairs, crying and sniffing, which irritated him. She was the reason Nicola had turned out the way she had. Stephen went into the living room and poured himself a large whisky.

He'd just been about to go up to bed when Ross called, but he couldn't sleep now. It irked him that Nicola had contacted Ross and not him. Yes, they'd had their differences over the years, but he was still her father. He'd given so much of himself to Nicola. It was Stephen who had sat with her to do her homework, using a strict hand when necessary. He was the one who'd taken her to school activities and waited patiently in the car for them to finish. He had given thought and energy to her clothes and how best to wear her hair, just as he had done for Mary.

They had been a strong family, Stephen told himself, until Ross came on the scene and turned Nicola against them. 'She should have come to us,' he said to himself.

He could hear Mary still crying on the stairs. 'Stop snivelling, woman,' he snapped. 'Go back to bed.' He poured another whisky, enjoying the sound of the glug, glug, glug, as the liquid filled the glass.

Stephen had never accepted Ross as good enough for his daughter and had even asked the police if they thought he might have had something to do with her disappearance. It was a line of enquiry, they said, but they didn't believe Ross was involved.

He sat in the living room for a long time, reminiscing over Nicola's childhood and how loved she had been. A contrast to his own upbringing. Taken into care at three years old, he'd never seen his parents again. Instead, he'd spent his childhood in first one care home, then a second. The second home taught him how hard life could be and that you could rely on nobody but yourself. All the children there got a beating, but not everybody was beaten as often as him, and not everyone was called to the care worker's room in the middle of the night.

Stephen's mind sank into memories of one of the senior carers who had taken a dislike to him from day one. He seemed to make it his mission to reprimand Stephen for every misdemeanour, ridicule his lack of schooling, and taunt him about how skinny and gangly he was. How Stephen hated that man and his petty bullying. He resented the power that carer held and how he abused it. At seventy-five, Stephen felt the same shame now as he did at fourteen. He poured another whisky, having a taste for it now.

At sixteen years old, Stephen started an apprenticeship at the shipyards, and his adult life began. He had thanked God for this change in circumstance and vowed if he ever had a family, he would love those children and give them all the guidance he never got.

The shipyards had been the making of Stephen. His boss, Brian, had recognised talent in his young apprentice, had taken Stephen under his wing and helped him flourish. Brian showed

Stephen that if he worked hard and did a good job, he would earn respect.

'I've seen boys like you before,' he said to Stephen. 'Life has already shat on you from a grand height and you've survived. That part of your life is over. The next part is in your control. You can take what you want from life. Work hard, earn respect and the world will be yours.'

Stephen had listened, had worked hard and, while not everyone like him, he was respected. For Stephen, this was more important than the money. Treated as worthless all his life, Stephen finally felt like he fitted in. Never again was he made to feel as helpless as he had in that children's home. Until now.

By not contacting him directly, Stephen felt Nicola had taken his affection and effort and cast it aside. Cast him aside for that idiot Ross. Stephen imagined Ross at home, laughing at his inability to keep control of his daughter after he'd stolen her away from under his very nose.

'Screw her,' he mumbled to himself. 'She's no longer my daughter. I disown her.'

Drunk now, and satisfied he'd rid himself of a thorn, Stephen took himself to bed. He undressed clumsily and got into bed next to Mary. He rolled onto her in the darkness and made himself feel temporarily better.

• • • ● • ● ● • • •

Mary had been in bed for about forty-five minutes when she heard the phone ring. Nobody ever rang that late, and she was immediately anxious. Mary usually went to bed before Stephen, as she liked to read and he did not, and he didn't like the lamp being on when he came up. So Mary went to bed early, after ensuring her day's jobs were finished, so she could complete her bedtime routine and read a little before lights out. On the occasions that Stephen came to bed early, it threw her out of sync and she'd lie awake for hours, her brain unable to switch itself off. She needed the illusion of being taken out of her own life and into the worlds created by Barbara Taylor Bradford or Danielle Steel, where good endings were obligatory.

Not many people phoned the house, usually just a sales call, or perhaps an old colleague of Stephen's, so for it to ring this late at night was startling. Mary lay motionless in bed, trying, through the closed bedroom door, to decipher who had called. As soon as she realised it was Ross, Mary knew it must relate to Nicola. She held her breath, terrified it would be bad news. As soon as Stephen called upstairs, Mary dashed out of bed and down to the phone.

'Nicola's turned up at Ross's house,' Stephen told her. Mary let out an involuntary wail. 'Hush, woman, let me hear what he's got to say.'

While Stephen listened to Ross, Mary listened to Stephen and could make out enough to know Nicola was alive and in Glasgow. The relief was immense. For four years, she had asked that, if there be a God out there, He keep her daughter safe. The knowledge her daughter was alive left Mary feeling as though she had been holding her breath all this time and could finally take a gulp of air. She couldn't stop herself from crying and, when Stephen shouted at her from the living room, she went silently back to bed.

She didn't need to know any more right now, as it was enough that Nicola was safe. Mary knew also that Stephen would be angry because Ross was the one to tell him. For whatever reason, Stephen had taken an instant dislike to Ross, as he would have done with any man Nicola married. On the few occasions he talked about their marriage, Stephen complained that Ross had taken Nicola from him. He forgot Nicola had left them several years prior to her marriage. He omitted the fact that Nicola rarely visited. In fact, she had wanted nothing to do with them, even with Mary, who couldn't see that she had done anything wrong. Mary had always felt Nicola was punishing her for something, and her disappearance was no different. Of course, Nicola wouldn't think to give her mother, the woman who had carried her in her womb, who had given birth to and nurtured her, the courtesy of a phone call to say, 'Don't worry, Mum, I'm fine.'

The hurt Mary felt turned to anger, and she made herself stop crying. She went to the bathroom to dry her eyes and, without looking in the mirror, splashed her face with cold water, patted it dry and rubbed in moisturiser. In bed, she switched her lamp off, but left Stephen's on so he didn't have to change in the dark. Mary hoped she would fall asleep before he came up. She didn't want to listen to his ramblings about Ross; she wanted to assimilate the news for herself, quietly and in her own time.

As she lay in the dark, Mary thought about Nicola as a little girl, and the fun things they did together. In between her domestic duties, Mary would, from time to time, take Nicola on a spontaneous trip to the park or walk to the high street before she needed to be home to make Stephen's dinner. She remembered when Nicola had fallen over and got mud all over her coat. They'd had to sprint home so that Mary could wash and dry the coat before Stephen realised they'd been out. The hairdryer was on so long Mary worried it would overheat, and her heart raced again at the memory.

What a beautiful child Nicola had been, a mass of thick blonde curls surrounding her like a halo. Her hair was poker straight now. 'Our little angel,' Stephen used to call her. Nicola had been one of those children who couldn't be pushed down the street in her buggy without being stopped every three paces by someone commenting on what a beautiful child she was. Stephen always looked so proud in those moments, and those were the times when Mary briefly felt like they were a happy family.

Mary heard the clink of another glass being poured downstairs, so she knew she had a little more time before he came up. She thought about where Nicola might have been all these years. Perhaps she'd gone to Spain. That's where Mary would go, if she could. It looked so lovely on the telly. Blue skies, golden beaches, and nobody was in a hurry. She imagined long, lazy days by the pool, reading a book or a magazine, while sipping an ice-cold lemonade. She could imagine the sun on her skin, warming her flesh, her blood, her very bones. Little by little, she would shed the cold she'd absorbed through a lifetime of Scottish rain and cloud. Her entire body would relax, the biscuit weight she carried around her middle would melt away, and she'd feel younger and more alive than she had in decades. She could even picture herself dancing the night away, alone and happy.

Stephen's heavy footsteps coming up the stairs interrupted her reverie. He got into bed and rolled on top of her. When he spoke, his slurred was surprisingly gentle, almost reminding Mary why she had fallen for him in the very beginning. For such a big man, he could be so gentle.

When he'd finished, she watched Stephen roll over and waited until he was asleep before letting her mind return to her life in Spain.

Chapter 4

Contrary to Claire's counsel, Ross's feelings towards Nicola and her disappearance did not change. The very fact Nicola was alive and well meant Ross could let go of what had been. As long as Nicola's disappearance remained a mystery, he'd felt stuck in a time warp and couldn't move forward with his life. Now she was here, he could mourn his marriage and start again. To do that, he needed to draw a line under his marriage. To that end, he made an appointment with his solicitor, Simon Clarke.

'Nicola has turned up,' Ross told him.

'Wow. Is she alright?'

'Yes, she's fine. She's been fine all this time.'

'And you?'

'I want a divorce and full custody of Sam.'

'It sounds like you had better come in and see me.'

Through all the sadness of Nicola's disappearance, Sam had been his father's lifeline. For the sake of that small child, Ross had woken in the morning and gone to work. When all he'd wanted to do was turn away from the world and focus solely on finding his wife, he had taken Sam to the park and even, eventually, laughed at the little things in life again. He felt a connection to his son that was stronger than it would otherwise have been because it was Ross who had held Sam the nights he was inconsolable and calling for his mother. It was Ross who had nursed him when ill, who had put thought and energy into which nursery Sam should attend, what clothes he needed, what food he should eat, arranged play-dates, football clubs and other activities. Ross had worried and fretted about his son when he'd had a fall out at school and needed a shoulder to cry on. Ross had done his best to be both parents, and he wasn't about to let Nicola walk back into their lives and turn them upside down.

Simon Clarke's offices were in a large, modern block, and Ross stopped at the main reception to pick up his visitor's pass. They buzzed him through the barrier and took the lift to Grant McAlister LLP on the fifth floor.

While he waited for Simon to come and get him, Ross paced back and forth, too hyped up to take a seat. He resented being back here. When the police were first investigating Nicola's disappearance, he'd engaged Grant McAlister because he'd needed representation when questioned. Stephen had been very persuasive in suggesting the police look at him and his alibi. For whatever reason, Stephen had never approved of him and had done his best to persuade Nicola to leave him. Ross hadn't put it past Stephen to try to have him arrested. Anyway, he'd seen the movies. When the police falsely accuse someone, it destroys their life. He didn't want that to happen to him.

Ross looked out of the office window across the 'Dear Green Place' that was Glasgow and wondered where Nicola was and what she was doing now. A receptionist interrupted his thoughts and took him to Simon's office.

'Come in,' said Simon. 'Sit down, tell me what's been happening.'

'Four days ago I came home, after dropping Sam off at school, to find Nicola snooping around upstairs. She still had her key, and I'd never had the locks changed, so she could let herself in.'

'Where has she been?'

'Shetland. She took a ferry up there and stayed. She says she did some odd jobs in a hotel before getting a job back in Glasgow a few months ago and is working over in the Merchant City.' Simon's face couldn't hide his amazement.

'She's been back as long as that?'

'So she says, but, to be honest, I don't know if I believe her.'

'Did she say why she left in the first place?'

'She said she had a breakdown, that she couldn't cope being a mother anymore.'

'And you believe her?'

'I guess so.'

'Has she been living alone? Was another man involved?'

'I don't think so, I didn't ask.' That Nicola had run away with someone else had never occurred to Ross. When the police suggested it, he'd been one hundred percent certain she didn't have a lover.

'She would have told me if she'd met someone else.'

'Would she?' Simon challenged. 'Perhaps she'd run away with this man. Things had gone well for a time, but now the relationship has ended and she's back to rekindle her old life. Does she want to be with you or only Sam?'

'She says she wants a second chance with me, but I think it's too late for that. I want a divorce and I want sole custody of my son. She doesn't deserve him. I can't risk her breaking both our hearts for a second time.'

'Did she say what caused the breakdown?'

'Only that she wasn't coping with Sam. She says she had depression.'

'Did she get any help, professional help, I mean?'

'I don't think so, she didn't mention it.'

'Then there's no way to know if she's fit to be a mother again?'

'Exactly,' said Ross. 'I can't put Sam in danger again. You've got to help me.'

'I will,' said Simon. 'Does she know you want a divorce?'

'No, I haven't seen or talked to her since she was at the house.'

'Well, she soon will. I'll start digging into her life in Shetland, find out if another man is involved.'

'Thank you,' said Ross, standing up to leave.

'Don't look so worried, we've got this.'

When he got outside, Ross dialled the phone number Nicola had posted through his letterbox, only briefly wondering if he should have given it to Simon.

'Nicola, it's Ross, we need to talk.'

For reasons he didn't understand himself, he felt he ought to let Nicola know in person he was filing for divorce. The thought of her being served notice, completely unprepared, seemed too harsh. He wanted to tell her in person first and he also wanted to see her again, to look in her eyes and be sure this was what he wanted because once the wheels were in motion, he wouldn't be able to stop them.

• • • ● • ● • • • •

As I hoped he would, Ross called, and we agreed to meet at the Gallery of Modern Art in the heart of the city. The day was clear and sunny, and I couldn't help but see the warm sunshine as a good omen. I was certain he was going to let me see Sam, just as I'd been certain he'd phone me once he'd calmed down. I arrived early and waited outside the main entrance, rejuvenated by the feel of the sun on my face and bare arms.

Ross arrived exactly on time, which I also saw as a sign he was keen to meet and which buoyed me further. After a few awkward pleasantries, we made our way into the gallery, which was chilly after the warm outside air, and I put my jacket on.

Ross was silent and his face was serious, all too quickly taking the gilt off my mood. I got twitchy, desperate for one of us to start talking.

'I'm glad you called,' I began. Ross nodded. 'I know the other day was a real shock for you. For me, too. I wasn't expecting you.' My joke fell flat. 'What I mean is, I didn't know what to say to you, how best to explain myself. Of course, you were angry, who wouldn't be?' I knew I was rambling. 'But now you've had a chance to think about things, take it all in, we can—'

'I want a divorce.'

'... talk more and not make any rash decisions, such as get a divorce.' I wanted so much to pretend he hadn't said that.

'I have thought about it,' he said in a thin voice, 'and I want a divorce.'

'You can't have thought about it, not properly. You're still angry, you're not thinking straight.' My panic was building.

'Keep your voice down,' Ross said, looking around. 'I am thinking straight.'

'But I still love you, Ross. I know we can work through this, find a way to be a family again.'

'I've thought about you every day for four years, wondering where you were and if you were safe. Now I know and I can't tell you how relieved I am to see you alive and well, but too much time has passed for us to get back together.'

'What do you mean?'

'I mean, I've wanted to get on with my life, but I couldn't because I couldn't put closure on us. I couldn't say goodbye to you. Now I can.'

My brain searched desperately for something to change his mind.

'There's no need for a divorce, not yet.'

'I need to move on with my life.'

'I promise I'm not here to make trouble, but to make amends and prove to you I'm better now and able to be a good wife and mother.'

'You caused trouble the day you took off.'

'That's not true, our troubles started long before that, only neither of us would admit it.'

'That's as may be, but Sam and I are happy and I don't want you ruining it all.'

'I don't want to ruin it either. I want to contribute and be part of our family. Ross, I still love you.' I put my hand in his.

'It's too late,' he said, shaking me off. 'Maybe if you'd come back after a year, or even let me know you were alive, we might have been able to work things out, but now it's too late to go back. Too much damage has been done, and how do I know you weren't with another man all this time?'

'I wasn't,' I said. 'I promise you. There has been nobody else.' I pulled him round to look in his eyes. 'Ross, there has been nobody else, no other man in my life.' I searched his face to determine if he believed me or not. He said nothing, and we walked on in silence for a while, me racking my brains for something to make him reconsider. I looked at Ross again and saw he was as upset as me, but his lips were thin and rigid. He would not be swayed.

'Maybe we can move away and start again,' I tried. 'A clean slate for both of us?'

'That wouldn't work,' he said. 'Too much has happened.' Ross brought me to a halt again and we faced each other. 'I'm divorcing you and I'm keeping full custody of Sam.'

'You can't do that,' I said loudly. 'I'm his mother.' The look of contempt Ross shot at me before he walked away is something I'll never forget. 'You can't do this to me,' I said, running beside him, trying to hold on to his arm, 'You can't, I'm his mother, I love him.'

'He's not your son anymore. You gave up that right four years ago,' he said, pushing me away.

I stood, grief-stricken, and watched him leave. Whispers echoed around me and all too soon I was aware of being stared at and talked about. The threat of divorce and the public humiliation crushed the very inside of me, and I stumbled to a nearby seat.

'Are you alright?' someone asked me. I looked at the person but couldn't answer because I was trying not to cry. If I talked, the tears would come and not stop. I ran, looking for a place to hide. I saw a disabled toilet and slammed the door behind me. Before it had even locked, tears were spilling down my face.

I chastised myself for being so stupid and naïve to think Ross would forgive me so quickly. I'd needed him to so much that I'd seen in Ross's` behaviour what I wanted to see. He'd phoned not because he wanted to see me, but because he wanted a divorce. He was on time, not because he was excited to see me, but because he wanted it over and done with. Ross's look of contempt kept flashing through my mind, setting off fresh tears. In my desperation, I couldn't accept that he really wanted to make such a momentous decision before he'd got over the shock or fully understand why I left.

'He's still angry,' I told myself. 'I'll give him some more time and try again. I've got to make him understand.' Someone tried the toilet door, prompting me to wipe my eyes and pull myself together. I heard whoever it was chatting outside then cackle at her own joke before a cough took over. I splashed my face with water and took some deep breaths before leaving the safety of the toilet.

'Oi,' the woman shouted after me, 'this is a disabled toilet, you shouldn't be using it.'

I walked back to work, thinking of ways I could try again to reconcile with Ross. A letter? Flowers? Go to his office? My blurred brain couldn't think properly. There wasn't even anyone I could ask to talk to him on my behalf. I'd alienated everybody with my disappearance. The only person who might welcome me was my mother.

As much as I didn't want to see my parents, my desperation not to lose my husband and son was stronger. It was so strong I momentarily felt Sam's weight in my arms, his infant head against my cheek, and the milky smell of the crook of his neck. I wanted to recapture the very first weeks after Sam was born, when we cocooned ourselves at home, just the three of us, Ross and I full of hope for our future. I don't think we could have been more in love. It's amazing the effect that tiny baby had on us, magnifying our feelings of invincibility.

I avoided thinking about the time soon after that, when the reality of sleepless nights kicked in and the euphoria we felt melted into exhaustion and irritability and, in my case, depression. Then when I looked at Sam, my heart no longer skipped a beat, nor were my veins filled with the desire to protect him. Instead, I wanted to push him away. I wanted someone to come and tell me it had all been a mistake, that they would take Sam away and I could go back to normality. I shivered with fear at what I might have done if I hadn't left.

Only another mother would understand this primal need to reclaim their child. I looked at my watch. It was late afternoon, so there was a chance Dad would be home, but I decided to risk it. I ducked down a quiet side street and pulled out my phone.

Chapter 5

'Mum,' I said, relieved it was her, 'it's me, Nicola.'

'Oh, Nicola, is that really you? I've been waiting for you to call.' Her voice was as timid and self-doubting as ever, always conscious not to upset Dad. Bizarrely, it was comforting and linked me back to my younger self.

'Yes, it's really me,' I said.

'I've been so worried about you. I've missed you.'

'I've missed you too.'

'Why did you leave? Why did you not tell us where you were?'

'Fear.' I leaned against the wall, as if to camouflage myself within its brickwork. 'I'm sorry I didn't call and let you know where I was. I wasn't thinking straight and wanted to hide away.'

'Well, you're back now, that's the main thing.' I heard static on the other end of the phone and I guessed she'd put the receiver to her body while she checked Dad remained occupied elsewhere. 'Are you coming to see us?'

'Yes,' I said, taking a deep breath, 'I need your help.'

'Of course, Nicola, anything. I'm just so happy you're back and, of course, you must come home.'

'I have a home, I need your help with something else.'

'You name it. Will you come for your tea?'

'I can't.' The thought of seeing Dad made me shrink a little lower against the wall.

THE DAY SHE CAME HOME

'Tomorrow night?'

'Okay, tomorrow.' I hesitated before asking, 'Will Dad be home?'

'No, that's the night he goes to the Legion.'

'Of course, how could I forget.'

The following evening I made my way to my childhood home in Clarkston. It felt a lifetime ago I'd made this journey, but it was second nature. Muscle memory took me to Glasgow Central and Platform 11. Right on time, the 5.48 train pulled out and, fifteen minutes later, I stepped out of the carriage and into my old neighbourhood.

Deeply rooted feelings of unease shuffled their way to the surface, as did my old friend. Shame. Shame and I are best friends, we've lived together for so long I can't remember life without him. Throughout my childhood shame was my constant wingman, and, even now, as a grown woman, he is by my side, only now he's here at my invitation. I made the choice to leave my husband and son. I had failed in my marriage and now here I was, cap in hand, begging for mum to bail me out.

I stood on the pavement, looking at the house and, from the outside, it looked like any other suburban semi-detached home. The neatly painted front door, the net curtains and plain, but perfectly manicured front garden, gave nothing away of what had gone on behind the closed doors and drawn curtains.

When Mum answered the door, she looked older and smaller than I remembered, but her eyes were the same; anxious eyes, eyes that could never hold my gaze. They flitted from place to place, darting around like hummingbirds. That was enough to confirm nothing had changed in my absence.

We stood formally in the hallway as if meeting for the first time until she reached out and we held each other tightly. I breathed in her smell and tumbled back to lunches of fried bread dipped in egg with tomato ketchup, of bedtime cuddles and Tweed, the only perfume I'd known her to wear.

'Let me take your coat,' she said, finally letting go of me, 'then go on through.' The living room, just like my old home with Ross, had changed little. I had been through so much physical upheaval in the last four years that I forgot it wasn't the norm. I sat awkwardly on the edge of the sofa.

'Would you like a sherry?' asked Mum.

'Yes, please,' I nodded. She handed me a glass and sat down next to me.

Again, stifling nostalgia came over me as I remembered the oh-so-many evenings Mum, Dad and I had sat silently sipping our drinks before dinner, them with their sherry, me with my lemonade, giving ourselves a false air of respectability.

I hadn't yet worked out how best to ask Mum for help. I first needed to know what sort of relationship my parents had with Ross. It had only ever been cordial at best, but surely Sam gave them a reason to stay in contact? To my surprise, it was mum that broke the silence.

'Why didn't you phone to let us know you were back?'

'Oh, you know.' I looked at my glass.

'Yes.' She took a sip. 'You can't imagine how surprised I was when Ross called to tell us.'

'What did he say exactly?'

'Only that you were alive and well.'

'I am.' I took a sip with one hand and Mum put a hand on the other, squeezing it. 'How are things here?' I asked.

'I can't complain,' she said, removing her hand. 'You know. A few more aches and pains. What did you do on Shetland? Was it very cold?'

'I worked in a wee hotel up there. Yes, it was freezing in winter. Very windy.'

'Not the place for me, then, I get enough of that here.'

'Where would you go?'

'Spain. I've always thought Spain sounds lovely.'

We both took a sip of sherry before I asked, 'Have you seen much of Ross and Sam while I was away?'

'No.' Mum's voice was quiet. 'Ross and your father never got on and, without you here, the visits fizzled out. We haven't seen Sam in over a year.' Her face brightened. 'Maybe you could arrange something? We'd love to see him.'

'I can't help there unfortunately, Ross won't let me see him either.' A dead weight suddenly found itself in my chest cavity, and I slumped back on the sofa. 'That's one of the reasons I wanted to see you. I hoped you could talk to Ross for me. He wants a divorce.'

'Oh.' Mum's face fell. 'I'm so sorry, Nicola. I wish I could help, but I don't think it would do any good. He had an argument with Dad and we've not seen Sam since.'

'What happened?'

'Oh, something and nothing.' Mum looked away, unsure whether to tell me, but in the end she said, 'Ross didn't like the way Dad reprimanded Sam and it led to an argument and neither of them will back down.' I could imagine exactly how Dad would have reprimanded Sam, his voice booming and his enormous frame terrifying the small child.

'Shall we go through and eat?' Mum had set the dining room table with her best china, which told me she was nervous about tonight and trying to make a good impression. The dining room was the least used room in the house and had always felt dark and cold to me. Tonight Mum had warmed it by putting the radiator on. She washed and dried the two sherry glasses before putting them back in the living room cabinet and joining me at the table.

'Did you tell Dad I was coming?' I asked.

'No,' she said, colouring. 'You know how he doesn't like his routine disrupted.' We each had a glass of wine with dinner.

It helped us to relax a little, and our conversation picked up, overlaying the clink of our cutlery.

'Did you make any friends in Shetland?'

'A few. My best friend there was Shona. She's the one who gave me the job. Turns out she'd been through something similar and wanted to give me a chance.' I thought of my old boss, who had given me a new start in life and to whom I'd be eternally grateful. Not only had she been my lifesaver, she'd become my best friend. 'She also helped me get my transfer to Glasgow. She put in a good word for me with the hotel I'm working in now.'

'She sounds like a kind woman.'

'Mum, I know things aren't great with you two and Ross, but please, would you talk to him? I don't have anyone else to ask. He might listen to you even if he won't speak to Dad.'

'Why would he listen to me? What reason can I give him?'

'Remind him of how in love we were, how happy we had been. Tell him I'm still his wife, I'm Sam's mother, tell him I love him.'

'Do you?'

'Of course I do.'

'Even after everything that's happened? Are you sure you love him and not the idea of him and what you once had?' Mum's question surprised me. It was unlike her to be so confronting, but I was unwilling to accept she could be right.

'Of course I love him. Look, I wasn't well and now I am.'

'What was wrong with you?'

'How can you ask that?' I was incredulous. 'I was depressed. Mum, you know this.' I leaned in to make her look at me. 'We talked about it.'

'I don't remember now. It was such a long time ago. Are you better now?'

'That's what I'm trying to tell you. I'm better now and can be a good mother to Sam.'

'You were always an excellent mother.'

'No, I wasn't.' I stood up and walked to the mantlepiece. On it were framed photographs, including one of Sam. I put my finger to the glass and stroked his little face. 'I wasn't able to protect him like I should have done.'

'What's that supposed to mean?' Mum said, her voice sharp.

'Nothing.' I looked at her through the mirror above the mantle. 'Will you talk to Ross?'

'It won't do any good,' said Mum, shaking her head. 'I've told you, he's not speaking to us. Your Dad would be cross if I got involved.' I knelt down next to her and put my hand on her arm.

'You don't need to tell him. You can phone Ross when Dad's out.' Mum shrugged off my hand, stood up and collected the plates, distancing herself.

'No Nicola, it wouldn't do any good.' I followed her to the kitchen.

'There's nobody else I can ask, nobody else who knows me as well as you do. You can remind Ross I'm not a bad person, that I'm still Sam's mum and have a right to be with him.'

'Why don't you give Ross a bit more time to get used to you being back?' Mum turned on the tap and washed the dishes.

'Because he's already spoken to his lawyer, I don't have time. I've missed enough of Sam's childhood as it is.' I picked up a towel and dried the plates.

'You've only yourself to blame there, Nicola.' The truth of her words hurt.

'I know and I'm so, so sorry. I thought I was doing the right thing. Please, will you talk to him for me?'

'Stephen wouldn't like it.'

'To hell with Dad.'

'Don't say that Nicola.'

'Please Mum, please do this for me.' She picked up the dry dishes and put them in the cupboard, putting the door between us. I felt the same helplessness I had done as a teenager. 'I really hoped you'd help this time.'

'Anything else, Nicola. If there's anything else I can do –'

'Leave him.'

'... but your father wouldn't approve if I got involved.'

'Leave him,' I said again.

'Don't start, Nicola, you know I can't.' She went back to the dining room and gathered the remaining dishes.

'You can,' I urged, hot on her heels.

'No, I can't.' She turned to look at me. 'It's too late. I should have done it when you were little but I didn't and now it's too late.'

'Come and live with me, I'll protect you.'

'I can't ask you to do that.'

'You're not asking. I'm offering. I want you to leave him, you deserve some happiness too.' Mum wouldn't answer me. She busied herself with tidying up. Then she put the kettle on, a form of defence I recognised only too well. I put my hands on hers to stop them. 'Mum, look at me. I want to help you.'

'You can't help me. You have enough on your plate. Anyway, who says I want to leave? And even if I did, I have no idea how I would go about it. Your father would know I was up to something, he'd be furious and then -'

'I'll help you. We'll do it together when he's out. By the time he realises, you'll be gone. Safe. You can build a new life for yourself, you're still young.'

Mum's pale face and trembling hands told me I'd gone a step too far. The idea of being alone was so frightening to her, she'd rather live with the life she knew. I shook my head. I was both disappointed in her lack of courage, and sad at the life she'd chosen.

'Mum,' I said, resigned, 'I won't ask you to leave him again, but if you ever decide you want to, I will be here for you and

I will support you. We'll do it together.' She didn't look at me, but reached a hand out and I gripped it firmly.

Exhausted by the turn of events, I looked at my watch. 'Dad'll be home soon. Lets finish clearing up.'

Chapter 6

At home in Bearsden, Ross couldn't keep his mind away from Nicola and their conversation in the gallery. He'd felt so angry with her for thinking she could come back and pick up where she'd left off, as if he and Sam had sat at home twiddling their thumbs, waiting for her return even though that is, essentially, what he'd done. How could they return to being a family after four years apart, after the betrayal and the worry?

In his mind's eye, he visualised his wife's familiar face and worried eyes as she explained how Shetland had helped her. He softened at the remembrance of her familiar expressions and gestures, her tone of voice, the way her fingers fidgeted when she was nervous.

All too quickly he checked himself, reminded himself that she had deserted him for what appeared to Ross, nothing better or preferable to the life they'd had together. It hurt him to think she'd rather live and work in a cheap hotel in the middle of the Atlantic than be at home with their son.

After dinner, Sam went to play in his room while Ross finished clearing up. The dishwasher on, he opened a second beer and took it into the living room. His eye glanced over the mantlepiece, and a wedding photograph made him stop mid-motion. After a moment, he looked around the room. Framed photos of their wedding hung on the wall, as did ones of Nicola with Sam at different ages. He looked at them one by

THE DAY SHE CAME HOME 39

one. He used to think Nicola was smiling down at him. Now he felt she was laughing at him.

He walked from room to room, and in every one there were photographs of his wife. The atmosphere thickened around him, the air clung to his lungs and he struggled a little for breath. He panicked, certain his throat was contracting, and he wasn't taking in enough oxygen. Rushing into the hallway, he opened the front door and let the cool evening air sweep over him. It chilled the sweat on his skin and helped him calm down. He took several deep breaths, allowing his throat to open and his lungs to breathe properly, before he closed the door.

Shaken, he sat at the bottom of the stairs, where yet another photo of Nicola taunted him from the wall. These photographs had kept her memory alive and were something he could point at and say to Sam, 'There's your mum.'. But now she was here and he could move on. The photographs felt like a relic from the past. 'This place is a morgue,' he said out loud.

In the kitchen, he pulled out a large black bin bag and, one by one, he took the photographs off the wall and threw them in. He moved to the living room and afterwards, the hallway. He grabbed another bin bag and headed upstairs.

In his bedroom, he felt as if he were seeing for the first time all of Nicola's things on the dresser and bedside table, just where she'd left them. He threw them in the bag.

He did the same with the wardrobe where her clothes were still hanging and the chest of drawers, working his way from the bottom up, spilling the contents into one bin bag after another. When he reached the top drawer, he averted his eyes. He didn't want to look at her underwear and be reminded of any intimacy they had once shared. Another bin bag, another room cleared.

He stormed round the bathroom, dumping her cosmetics and other toiletries, before moving into Sam's room, where Sam was still playing contentedly by himself.

'Hey, Sam,' he said, 'we're having a clear out. A spring clean. Do you want to help?'

'No, thanks.' Buzz Lightyear was just about to destroy Thomas the Tank Engine who, it turned out, was from another world and was evil.

'Okay, well, you just tell me what you don't play with anymore and we can give it to someone else.' Ross didn't see the look of horror on his son's face.

'What about this?' Ross held up a soft toy Sam was too old for now.

'Okay,' said Sam, a wobble in his voice.

'And this?' Sam nodded reluctantly as he watched his father sweep through his room, picking up toys. 'What about this?' Ross didn't wait for an answer before tossing it into the bin bag while Sam watched on in stunned silence.

Ross was in a frenzy, tearing through Sam's belongings and casting out anything that suggested Nicola's involvement. He saw the bookshelves and went through them. Nicola loved children's stories and had bought far too many, indulging herself more than her son.

Skimming through the shelves, he pulled out and binned anything he thought looked too young or too battered. Books he knew just by looking at that Nicola had bought. In his speed and recklessness, he knocked some of them down the back of the shelves. This was too much for Sam, and he rushed to pick them up and place them back on the shelf.

'Be careful, Dad,' he said, trying to regain some order in his world. 'That's enough. I want to keep these.'

Ross heaved the bag in his hand over his shoulder, picked up another and took them to the bins outside. He kept going until he had removed every single one from the house.

Feeling spent by his whirlwind spring clean, Ross slumped onto the sofa, feeling slightly ashamed to have behaved like this in front of Sam, but so much lighter to have rid himself of

Nicola's presence. The walls had gaping patches, like missing teeth, where her pictures had once hung. He'd have to fill those spaces at some stage, but he didn't have the energy to think about it now. He heard Sam moving about upstairs, shuffling through his things, and went to check on him.

'I'm sorry, Sam,' he said, helping to put the remaining books back on the shelves. 'It was a job I needed to get done.'

'Well, don't do it again. I like my toys.'

'Fair enough.' Ross's hands fumbled down the back of the bookshelf to check he'd recaptured all the missing stories. Two more. He pulled them out and stared at them. They weren't storybooks, they were journals. They had nothing written on the front, but flicking through them, Ross recognised Nicola's handwriting immediately. His mouth went dry and his blood rushed to his face as if he'd been looking somewhere he shouldn't.

'I'm going to bed now,' said Sam. Ross didn't hear him, he was too focused on the journals. 'Dad, I'm going to bed.'

'Good idea,' said Ross, coming out of his reverie. 'Goodnight.' Clearly relieved to have his room to himself again, Sam returned to the battle between Buzz and Thomas.

Downstairs, Ross poured himself a large whisky and sat at the kitchen table, staring at the two journals. He wasn't sure he wanted to open them. But why were they here? Why hadn't the police found them at the time she disappeared? Ross was nervous and felt ridiculous for feeling so.

Although the journals were four years old and although he was angry with her, it felt wrong to look at these diaries, to invade her privacy. But, at the same time, he thought, they may explain so much. Pushing his conscience aside, he opened one journal and started reading.

An hour later he was still at the kitchen table, his only respite being to replenish his glass. With each diary entry he saw how, little by little, Nicola had fallen apart. Her minor concerns about marriage and family became larger worries until they were all-consuming. It upset Ross to read how her feelings changed from a woman who'd gladly swapped her career for motherhood, to a frustrated mum who blamed her husband for the situation she was in, believing he had forced her into the role, a role she never wanted. In the beginning, she wrote words of such tenderness and devotion about Sam, but, by the end, she referred to him only as the baby or the boy. Any description of her time with him was perfunctory only.

The diaries covered a period of about eighteen months. Over those months, Nicola's writing became less fluid and floral and increasingly stilted, some parts written in block capitals. It was as if her hand moved too fast for her brain and she had to slow it down somehow.

Ross was distraught to see this change in his wife so visibly displayed. He felt guilty and neglectful that he hadn't seen this change in her. When the police questioned him, it was clear their marriage was suffering, but, only with hindsight, did he piece together that they'd spent little time with each other, had stopped talking in any meaningful way, and had sex only occasionally, at his instigation.

Ross admitted to himself that he hadn't given these issues his full attention, and had instead blamed his workload, or the demands of motherhood on Nicola, and believed they were both adjusting to being a family of three. Never did he think his wife was sinking into a depression deeper than he could have fathomed. Had she hidden it so well, or had he just not wanted to see? Even now, looking at the words before him, he found it difficult to believe this of Nicola, his wife, the person he thought he knew so intimately.

The second journal was only half-full and started immediately where the first left off. About a quarter of the way through, the emphasis changed. Now her parents were at the receiving end, her mother in particular. Her criticism of Mary was ferocious, but Nicola never said why or where the rage came from. Her father seemed to hang around in the background of her writing. She seldom mentioned him by name, but he was everywhere, particularly in the things she wasn't allowed to do and in her criticisms of herself. It was with relief that Ross closed the diary, gulping down the rest of his whisky. He took the diaries to his bedroom and put them in the top drawer of Nicola's dresser. Out of sight, out of mind.

On his way downstairs, he checked on Sam, who was snoring softly. The duvet kicked to one side, his legs splayed and his head surrounded by toys. Quietly, Ross pulled up the duvet before closing the door and heading back to his whiskey and television. A re-run of Friends was playing, but it wasn't funny enough to take his mind off the diaries. He switched the telly off and sat in silence.

A black hole formed in his chest and, much as he tried to ignore it, it continued to grow. It was a black hole of guilt.

When the silence and the guilt got too much, Ross got up and pulled the diaries back out from the drawer. He knew he ought to do something with them, he just didn't know what. He didn't want to sit by and do nothing for a second time, equally he didn't know what the right thing to do was. Stuck in a mental quagmire, he put the journals back in the drawer and closed it.

Chapter 7

Things were going from bad to worse. Not only had Mum made it clear she wouldn't be able to talk to Ross for me, but the divorce letter from his solicitor had arrived and taunted me from the back of the drawer into which I'd shoved it.

On Shetland, I had learnt the wind works wonders on my emotional wellbeing and, although Glasgow couldn't offer me the biting air of Lerwick, it allowed me to continue my routine of getting out at least once a day and walking. It didn't matter where to; the fresh air and exercise were the elixir I needed. It was August now, and the city was warm with the summer sun. The heat didn't clear my head like the cold did, but it felt good on my skin and helped relax me when the ravings in my head threatened to take over.

I enjoy the sounds of the city. Glasgow's streets have a speed and urgency about them, and I welcomed the change of pace. I walked into town via Argyle Street and down into St Enoch's Square, where I could get a coffee from the Old Tolbooth. My vision honed straight in on my parents, as if I'd turned into the square for no other reason than to see them.

They saw me and momentarily stopped before my father composed himself and led them over. His large frame loomed towards me, dressed, as he always was, in a three-piece suit that made him look as if he'd stepped out of the past. For as long as I could remember, he'd bought his suits from a gentleman's outfitters at the Trongate. The shop itself was a relic, and I fleetingly wondered if it was still there.

As he neared me, I saw his hair was greyer and thinner than it had been, and his eyes were lined with the deep crevices of age. I noticed also that his nose was red and his face speckled with broken blood vessels, a telltale sign his drinking had continued.

'Nicola,' he said, his height and eyes bearing down on me, 'we heard you were back.' I didn't reply. 'Nothing to say for yourself?' I glanced at Mum, who said nothing but was looking at me in such a way I knew not to mention our dinner together.

'You've got a nerve,' he said, his voice gruff and barking, 'turning up out of the blue like this and not one word about where you've been.'

'I...'

'You've the bloody cheek to phone Ross but not us,' Dad continued, so close to me to me I could smell whisky on his breath. 'Instead, we bump into you on the street. Is that what you think we, your mother and father, deserve?' His voice had risen until he was now shouting at me there in the middle of the square. People turned to look. 'You disappear for four years and don't think to let us know you're back?'

In my panic, my mind went blank. I regressed to my twelve-year-old self and couldn't answer. Instead, I turned and hurried away.

'Selfish,' I heard him shout. 'You're a selfish girl and always were.'

When I was safely out of sight, I leaned against a shop front. My legs were weak and I couldn't catch my breath. His voice still had the power to frighten me, to shut me up and make me feel like a child again. Here I was, a grown woman despite that, I couldn't get out from under his shadow.

As my shock subsided, incredulity took its place. How could he shout at me like that when he knew he was at the root of all our problems? God, how I hated him. His face flashed before my eyes as stern as it always had been, his mouth mean and angry, his voice loud, repeating over and over again, 'You're selfish, you're a selfish girl.'

It made me wonder whether I was wasting my time here in Glasgow. Ross hated me and wouldn't let me see Sam. Mum couldn't help, and Dad was still the bully he'd always been. I didn't know what I could do to convince them my leaving had not been an act of selfishness. I knew it felt that way to them and could think of no way to prove otherwise.

I phoned Ross many times, but he never picked up, so I left message after message, each more desperate than the last. I wrote a letter, hoping to better explain myself, but never found out if he opened it. That morning a second envelope from Ross's lawyer dropped through the letterbox with language much more threatening than last time. After everything that had happened, I decided I had nothing to lose, so went to his office to plead for mercy.

He worked for the City Council and his office was situated in St George's Square in the city's centre. I went to the security desk and asked to see him. 'Is he expecting you?' the woman asked. She was young and had a pretty, open face. I envied her youth and carefree smile.

'No, he's not.'

'Can I take your name, please?' she said, picking up the phone to dial his extension. When I told her, she imperceptibly gave me a second glance – it was a tiny movement, but I noticed it and it told me enough. 'I have Mrs Ramsey here to see you.' Her smile remained professionally in place as she nodded her head at his instructions. 'I'm afraid he's tied up at the moment. He asks if you can call to make an appointment.' She looked almost as embarrassed asking me as I did at being asked.

'Thank you,' I said, but I wasn't going to do that. Things were too desperate.

THE DAY SHE CAME HOME 47

I waited in the reception area for three hours. Eventually, he came out with a couple of colleagues. I didn't want to embarrass him, but nor could I sit back.

'Ross.'

His face fell as soon as he saw me.

'What the hell are you doing here?'

'I need to talk to you about this.' I held up the lawyer's letter. 'Please.'

'I'll catch you up,' he said to the others before he took me by the elbow and hustled me to one side.

'You're not answering my calls,' I began. 'You didn't respond to my letter, I don't know what else to do.'

'Nicola, there's nothing else to do. Just follow the instructions in the letter and we can get things done quickly and painlessly as possible.'

'But you're asking for sole custody.'

'Of course. Did you think I'd give you, the woman who abandoned him-'

'I keep telling you, I didn't abandon him. I left him with Claire.'

'-the chance to hurt him all over again?'

'When are you going to stop being so angry and understand I didn't do it to hurt you?'

'Nicola, I...' Ross stopped and rethought what he wanted to say. 'Look, I know something happened to you when you were younger. I found some diaries.' At first I didn't know what he was talking about, but then I had a flashback of being curled up on the sofa, writing in a blue hard-backed notebook. I couldn't remember exactly what I'd written, but I knew it wasn't good. 'I know you've had stuff to work through,' Ross continued, 'and I really hope you found the answers you were looking for. But now it's time to leave that chapter of our lives behind us and move on. Both of us. Please don't make this any harder than it already is.'

'But it's not fair. I did it to protect you both. I wasn't coping, I wasn't thinking. It took me a long time to get my head straight, but I did it.'

'Well, it's a shame you didn't share any of this with me at the time.'

'And it's a shame you didn't take the time to notice,' I hissed. I shouldn't have said it. As soon as it came out my mouth, I wanted to stuff it back in.

'Get a lawyer, Nicola.' He left me standing with my head in my hands. I couldn't believe my stupidity. Rather than placate him, I'd angered him even more.

I couldn't have felt any lower and on my way home stopped in a bar Ross and I used to go to regularly. It had changed hands and name since I'd been away, but it still felt familiar, throwing up lots of wonderful memories and nights out with friends in more carefree days. I sat at a table for some time, watching people come and go. The lunch crowd left, and the place felt empty. I was suddenly conscious of being on my own and, after two glasses of wine, quite drunk. I went to the bar and ordered another glass. I had nowhere to be and nobody to see and was free to wallow in self-pity.

'Let me get that for you,' said the barman. 'You look like you need someone to be nice to you.' He smiled at me and, without really thinking about it, I accepted. I took a seat on one of the bar stools, watching as he poured the wine. He looked young, in his mid-twenties, and had a swagger as he moved behind the bar. He was comfortable there, he belonged, and that confidence was attractive.

He placed the coaster and glass in front of me, still smiling. Another customer called him over and I watched him at work. Had I ever been that confident, that easy in my own skin? He made small talk with another customer, glancing a couple of times in my direction. When the other person had paid, he moved back over to my end of the bar. We looked at each other for a few moments until I blushed and had to look away. This seemed to give him the permission he needed.

'Why the sad face?' he asked.

'My husband is divorcing me and there's nothing I can do about it.' The wine made me bold, daring him to still be interested in a woman so messed up.

'Ouch, that's tough,' he said, leaning on the bar opposite me.

'Yes, it is.' I sipped my wine.

'You look like you need cheering up.'

'I do.' Stupid, it was stupid of me to say this, but I wanted to be stupid. I wanted to be reckless and not care. 'Thank you for the drink,' I said, finishing my glass. 'Where are the ladies' toilets?' He pointed me in the right direction.

When I entered the toilets, I avoided looking in the mirror. I didn't want to see myself or acknowledge it was me flirting with this stranger. This was not something I did. When I came out, he was waiting. Neither of us spoke as he took my hand and led me to a storage cupboard. I let him hold my head in his hands as he kissed me. I didn't protest as he lifted my top and felt my breasts.

'You're gorgeous,' he muttered. My skin tingled under his fingers. It felt so good to be desired, to be thought beautiful and sexy. He pulled up my skirt and lifted me onto some boxes. I put my legs around him, encouraging him. As soon as he finished, the wine and excitement disappeared. Now I my body burned with embarrassment, not passion. I watched him button his trousers, still grinning.

'That was great,' he said, taking my face in his hands and kissing me one last time before he disappeared. As soon as the door closed my stomach lurched and nausea swirled. I needed to get out of here. To avoid walking through the bar, I left via the emergency exit.

As soon as I got home, I drank a glass of water and made a strong cup of coffee, replaying again and again what had just happened. In the safety of my flat, some of the shame gave way to the buzz of doing something so out of character. Amazed at my own daring, I wished I had a friend to share this, or anything else, with.

I thought about Claire, my best friend. Originally Ross's friend, we clicked as soon as we met. She was funny and sharp, and I appreciated that she immediately accepted me as part of Ross's life. Claire was the person I had entrusted Sam to. When I couldn't look after him, I knew she would. It was time for me to call her. Before I dialled her number, I drank another glass of water. It rang so long I thought it was going to go to voicemail, but eventually she picked up.

Chapter 8

'Hello?'

'Claire, it's Nicola.' There was silence. I prayed she wouldn't hang up.

'Ross said you were back.'

'Yes,' I said, trying to gauge what she was feeling.

'I wondered if you'd call.'

'I'm sorry I didn't call sooner, it's just, I didn't know what to say.' Claire didn't respond. 'I hoped I could come and see you.'

'How are you? Ross said you had a breakdown?'

'I'm alright. Yes, I had breakdown.' Now I had her on the phone, I wasn't sure what to say. It was as difficult as I'd imagined. 'How are you?'

'Good. Great, in fact. Never better. I have a daughter.'

'That's wonderful. What's her name?'

'Eilidh.'

'That's a beautiful name. How old is she?'

'She's four, and Alisdair is six.'

'It's so good to hear your voice.' Claire didn't speak and so I said, 'Can we meet?'

'I've got to pick the kids up from school soon. I'll meet you there just before three.'

Claire had arrived before me and as I walked towards the school gates, I watched her chat to the other mums. She looked just the same, and I was overcome with fondness for my friend. Somebody said something and, flinging her head back, she opened her mouth wide to let out her infectious laugh. I couldn't help mimic her with a smile and I realised in that moment just how much I'd missed her.

I smiled and waved, but stopped abruptly when I saw her face harden. She looked down to the ground as if unable to look at me. If I'd been nervous before, I was quaking now.

'Hello, Claire,' I said when I reached her. 'It's good to see you.'

'Look who's back from the dead,' was her curt reply. I blanched at her ferocity. 'Sorry,' she said.

We walked in silence, away from the others, following the perimeter of the school grounds.

'How are you?' I asked, unsure how else to break the ice.

'I told you, I'm fine, great, you know, life goes on.' She wouldn't look at me, so I stopped and pulled her to face me.

'I'm sorry I didn't contact you.'

'Why didn't you?' She looked at me properly for the first time and I could see that she wasn't really angry, she was hurt.

'I was too scared.'

'Scared of what?'

'Of how you'd react. I know what I did was terrible, more than terrible.'

'Yes, it was.'

'And I didn't know what people would say if I suddenly re-appeared.'

'What have people said?'

'How angry they are with me, how disappointed, and that I'm not welcome.'

Claire kicked the ground with her heel. 'I'm not sure I have much else to say. I'm also angry and disappointed.'

'Am I also unwelcome?'

'I haven't decided yet,' she said. 'Do you know what you did to Ross? To Sam?' I nodded. 'Ross was devastated. I've never seen a grown man cry like that. To just take off like that, Nicola, why did you do it?'

'It felt the best thing to do at the time, the only thing. I was struggling so much. Everything felt so hard and I couldn't cope with what was going on around me. I believed in my heart of hearts that Ross and Sam were better off without me. I know that seems crazy to you, but I couldn't see it any other way. For any of us.'

'Couldn't you have let one of us know you were safe?'

'I should have done, I know that, but the longer it went on, the harder it became. I couldn't think what I would say to people about why I'd run away, when I didn't know myself.'

'Ross says you've been back in Glasgow for a few months, is that right?' I nodded again, again blushing. It was my turn to look away. 'Working in a hotel? For Christ's sake, Nicola, that's even worse. You were right here. I come into the city centre all the time. How come I've never seen you?'

'I saw you once,' I confessed, 'I was walking to the bus and saw you on the other side of the road. I nearly called over.'

'Why didn't you?'

'I swithered for so long that by the time I made a decision, you'd gone. You were all dressed up, you looked amazing.'

'When was this?'

'A couple of months ago.'

'I rarely dress up these days unless it's for work. I must have had an interview that day.'

'Did you get the job?'

'If you'd been around, I could have told you about it.' She moved away from me before saying, 'We were best friends. I thought my best friend had maybe killed herself or been kidnapped or anything. I mourned for you. I was lost without you.'

'Corny as it sounds, I was already lost. I looked around me and everyone in my life was so together, with their great jobs and their happy families. When I looked at my life, I thought it was all fake, make-believe. How could Ross love a mess like me? How could I be any good for Sam?' I started to cry and a few other mums looked round at us.

'You want me to feel sorry for you, say that what you did was okay, is that it?'

'No, of course I don't want your pity and, of course, what I did was not okay. But it wasn't done to hurt anyone either. I'm trying to explain that I wasn't in my right mind. You know me, Claire, I might have done a bad thing, but I'm not a bad person. I deserve a second chance, I deserve the opportunity to prove myself a better mother than I had been before. I believe Sam has the right to get to know me and, in time, decide for himself if he thinks I'm good enough.' My cheeks were wet and my nose was dripping. I didn't have a tissue and had to use the back of my sleeve.

I watched my friend's face intently, hoping to see some softening. She rooted in her bag and handed me a tissue.

'I can't believe you didn't trust me,' she said, 'or come to me for help.'

'I'm sorry, Claire, I'm so, so, sorry. For everything, the mess I've made of everything.'

'Me too.'

The school bell rang, and Claire moved back to the gate. I followed her and all too quickly the children came running out, shouting noisily at each other. 'I can't do this right now,' she said over her shoulder. 'It's too hard.'

I was heartbroken and felt right back at square one. Just then Claire's son came crashing into her, arms wrapping protectively round her legs, wondering who this snotty woman was next to his mum. Seeing Alisdair hit home all too hard, Sam's absence and the possibility he may never throw his arms around me in that way.

'Wow, Alisdair, you have grown,' I said, 'you were only a baby when I saw you last.'

'Well, it was four years ago,' said Claire, hammering the point home as she hustled him into the car.

'I've missed you, Claire, I really have.' Her face relaxed.

'I've missed you too, but I don't know how I feel about it all, Nicola. It was such a shock hearing you were back and now, seeing you in the flesh, it's a lot to take in.' Alisdair scrambled into his car seat, arranged his bag and shouted out questions about nothing in particular, the way children do. 'Look, I've got your number, I'll give you a call.'

I watched them drive away, my fingers crossed she would. On the bus back to the city centre, I wondered what my next step was. I'd made contact with those closest to me, I'd tried my best to explain why I left, it felt like everything was out of my hands now. My phone beeped, and a reminder popped up:

Find a lawyer.

Chapter 9

I made an appointment with the Glasgow Law Practice, which was tucked inside tiny Virginia Court, hidden behind the chaos of the city's busy heartland. The offices were small and rather shabby, but they had been recommended by someone on an online forum for single parents and the fees were as much as I could afford. To my surprise, the reception area was crowded, which made me hopeful I hadn't made as bad a choice as I first thought. I let reception know I had arrived and sat with those already waiting. In between flicking through tatty magazines, I read the notices on the walls and ran through what I would say to my new solicitor. After what felt like an age, my name was called and I was sent to the office of Mr Kwame Martins. The yellowed signage led me out of reception and up a narrow and creaky staircase. The carpet was worn with overuse. I knocked tentatively on the door.

'Come in,' said a voice. I smiled my broadest smile before entering, hoping to make a good impression. 'Come sit, sit,' he beckoned, without looking up, scribbling some notes on another case. 'There, finished,' he pronounced with a flourish of his pen, before dropping the file on the top of an already large stack of paperwork on the right-hand side of his desk. On the left-hand side, he picked up another file that contained nothing but a single sheet of paper, on which were written the details I'd given over the phone, or so I guessed.

THE DAY SHE CAME HOME 57

'Mrs Ramsey, what can I do for you today?' He was suddenly attentive, so present to what I was going to tell him that he threw me off balance. 'Come now, don't be shy,' he urged, 'this is a busy practice, you are a busy woman, we don't have time for shyness.' He said this not unkindly, but his manner was brusque and efficient.

Pull yourself together, Nicola, I told myself, make your case. And so I told him my story and gave him both letters from Ross's lawyer. All the time I was talking, he jotted down notes, sometimes interrupting to clarify a point or probe further, before indicating I could carry on.

When he'd heard enough, he indicated for me to stop. 'From what you've told me today, I would suggest that you have a good chance of access to your son. However, I do want to prepare you that these cases can often be difficult and painful for you and your husband, particularly you. It will be your behaviour and mental health that are called into question. Many of your actions will not be seen in a favourable light.' Kwame let what he'd said sink in. He clearly knew from experience that what he said was not always heard the first time around. 'But,' he carried on, 'you are the boy's mother and that counts for a lot.' This statement lifted my spirits. I am Sam's mother, I said to myself, that counts for a lot.

'What happens now?' I asked.

'I will write to Mr Ramsey's solicitor explaining you won't agree to giving him full custody. But tell me, Mrs Ramsey, what do you want? Do you want full custody?' My immediate reaction was 'Yes,' but I knew that was unfair on Ross, and Sam would be devastated at being hauled away from his father. Also, I knew it would never be granted.

'No,' I finally answered, 'I want shared custody.'

'That is very sensible.' Kwame smiled. 'Fair for everyone, including your son. I cannot emphasise enough to you how many times a parent tells me they don't want their child to see their ex-husband or ex-wife, only to spite that person. It is so sad to see, and I am glad you are thinking about your son's welfare. I will let Mr Ramsey's solicitor know this and await a response.'

'Mr Martins, what do you think my chances are of getting joint custody?'

'From what you've told me today, I think you have a fifty-fifty chance. What I am confident of is that you will have a future with your son, that you will at least have visitation rights and, from there, your relationship can grow.'

This wasn't exactly what I wanted to hear, but I accepted it was probably the most honest answer he could give me. I pictured Sam at home with me, the two of us having dinner together, playing with his trains, or him coming to me for a cuddle after a fall, needing my love and reassurance. I knew I had to try as hard as possible to win at least joint custody. 'What can I do to improve my case?'

'If this goes to court,' he said, 'which is always a possibility, you will need to be able to demonstrate that you are in a position to look after Sam as well as your husband has done. For example, does your home have a bedroom for him? What are your working hours, are you able to pick him up after school? Can you have weekends free to spend time with him? Do you have friends and family around you, a support network? These are the sorts of things you need to think about if you want joint custody, not only visitations.

'I've dealt with many similar cases to this one and feel confident you'll at least be able to get visitations with your son.' However, it does depend on the judge appointed on the day. Some feel a mother should always have a role in a child's life, some won't be able to get past the fact you left and will rule you've forfeited your rights to him. How the law is interpreted depends on how the judge views the situation.

'In your favour is the fact there are no drugs or alcohol involved, nor a third party. The fact you've been depressed could also be seen in your favour, as diminished responsibility. However, that you chose to wait four years before getting in touch will not be viewed well.

'I want to warn you again, Mrs Ramsey, before you make any decisions, that going to court should be your last recourse. I urge you to try to work something out with your husband, for all your sakes. That includes your son.'

'Mr Martins, I have tried. I've been patient and taken into consideration how shocked and hurt Ross must be. But now he is angry and wants to punish me. I don't believe there to be any other way and, if you can't help me, I don't know what I can do next.' I covered my face with my hands, trying to hide my embarrassment and fears.

'Okay, Mrs Ramsey,' Kwame said, giving me a moment to compose myself. 'If you are sure there's no other way, then, as I said, I will write to your husband's lawyer and inform him you have instructed me to begin proceedings against him. I will urge him, as I have you, to find another way. His lawyer will, in turn, write to me with a response.

'Until then, do not contact your husband or attempt to contact your son. That will only jeopardise your situation. If your husband gets in touch with you, explain calmly and rationally that you have been advised not to speak to him unless through me. Then hang up and write down the date, time and exact conversation. Do you understand what I've told you?' he asked, noticing I had blanched and how overwhelmed by it all I must have looked. 'It's important that you understand what I've told you.'

'Yes,' I nodded. 'I understand.'

'Is there anything you want to ask me?'

'What happens after you've written to Ross?'

'So, I will tell him that you want custody of your son. His lawyer will write to me saying there's no way. After that, we'll all get together and try to find some sort of compromise. If that doesn't work, then we will need to take your case to the courts and let the judge decide. But I hope it won't come to that. What I want is for you, me, your husband and his lawyer to work out a scenario that we're all happy with. In the meantime, do as I say; no contacting your husband and, if he contacts you, write down the details. Okay?' Kwame smiled broadly. 'Mrs Ramsey, don't look so worried, I'm here to help you and help you I will.'

I couldn't help but smile back at him. His confidence was reassuring and made me feel as if all this was a mere formality. He made a few more notes before closing the file, indicating the meeting was at an end.

As I stood up to leave, I realised I had none of the things he wanted to see in place and, from where I stood, there seemed enormous obstacles to overcome. Kwame Martins seemed to read my mind. 'All things are fixable, Mrs Ramsey. I am confident you will find a way to build a home for you and your son.' He nodded at me encouragingly.

I tried not to feel despondent when I left, but the task of reshaping my life again seemed monumental. My whole future with Sam depended upon me making the right decisions now. If I made a wrong move, I could jeopardise having any future with him at all. I slowly made my way up Hanover Street to Sauchiehall Street. I then cut down Hope Street and found myself standing outside Glasgow Central Train Station, looking up at its majestic Victorian splendour, reminding me of the city's past wealth. I went inside and sat on a bench, staring at the departure board. London. Penzance, Newcastle, Manchester. I watched as the destinations filtered from one side of the board to the other before dropping off completely.

Four years ago, I hadn't hesitated in escaping my life and its difficulties. I had no option. My depression was so deep, being on the verge of psychosis, that I didn't like to think what damage I might have done if I'd stayed. My pulse raced again at the thought I might have been capable of hurting Sam. I took a deep breath and reminded myself that I hadn't hurt him, that he was safe. It served as a reminder that no matter what others thought, I had, given my mental state, made the best decision I could.

Today I didn't have that compulsion to escape. My life had taken a step forward, and I had progressed from being debilitated by my past to being ready to fight for my future. But I was scared; scared of the judge looking at my history and thinking me too unstable to look after my son; scared at the prospect of another round of changes I was going to have to make in order to demonstrate my love for Sam and that I was a good mother. Scared too of my life without Ross.

As I sat on the bench, the world rotated around me. I watched people go about their business with strident movements, walking with purpose towards their waiting train. Others were flustered, running for a train about to leave, but hindered by their luggage, unable to move quickly enough.

There were the drunks and the homeless that seemed to frequent all major train stations, offering as they did some sort of shelter from Scotland's unpredictable weather, although the wind that funnelled through the station could be biting. Sparrows darted in and out, trying to grab a morsel to eat before the larger pigeons, who had made their homes in the rafters, chased them out.

As I watched this cacophony take place around me, I began to formulate a plan of changes I would make and, with each decision, I felt stronger and I breathed a little deeper. I can do this, I told myself, one change at a time. I hauled myself up and stretched. My bottom was numb from having sat so long.

I looked at my watch and saw I had a few hours before my shift at the hotel started. The next train to Bearsden was in eight minutes, I had just long enough to buy a ticket and board. Twenty minutes later I was on Bearsden High Street and popped into the nearest letting agents.

Chapter 10

Ross was on his way to Greggs to grab some lunch when Simon phoned to say Nicola had rejected his custody demands. 'To be expected,' he said, although he was furious, 'but surely she has no rights to Sam, she forfeited them four years ago.'

Ross hadn't really expected Nicola to fight him on this. He felt certain she would, amid the pleading and the tears, capitulate because, how could she think she'd win?

'Her solicitor will have told her she's unlikely to get full custody, but she'll be seeking joint or, at the very least, visitations.'

'Will she get that?'

'Very possibly. Regardless of what has happened between the two of you, she's Sam's mother and that's given top consideration.'

'I'm surprised, I have to admit,' said Ross. 'I didn't really think she'd fight me on this. Normally she likes to avoid conflict.'

'It's probably a good indication she has recovered from whatever it was she was going through. Mama Bear is back, and she wants her cub.'

Nicola had always been the peacemaker, the first one to offer an olive branch. She had a skill for diffusing awkward situations and finding a way through conflict. She was particularly good at placating her father, something nobody else seemed to be able to do. A controlling man, he could easily fly off the handle when things didn't go his way. He had no qualms about making a scene, either by losing his temper or sulking like a toddler. It could cast a shadow over any occasion, leaving everyone unsettled.

He remembered the time Stephen had taken them all to see pantomime at Christmas. It was an unusual act of generosity on his part, and Ross always felt it had been a show of false benevolence. Right from the start it was strained, the show was busy, and there was a mix-up with tickets. Stephen made such a song and dance about it they were bumped up to house seats. After that the interval ice cream he wanted was sold out and he went into such a sulk that Nicola went to the local shop and bought one for him.

Ross once tried to reason with his father-in-law, but it escalated into such a huge argument that he never did again. The memory of Stephen's fury was still vivid. It felt like his body enlarged the angrier he became. Nobody would say anything until the situation got so awkward that Nicola was forced to intervene and calm him down. Many was the time Ross had marvelled at her forbearance.

Mary, on the other hand, always remained mute. Her eyes would dart from place to place, as if distracted by something more pleasant happening elsewhere; Stephen's behaviour was nothing to do with her. Or perhaps, having never been a strong woman in the first place, it was all she could do to retain what sanity she had. While Nicola dealt with her father, Mary would sit quietly and let the tide roll out of its own accord.

Within their own marriage there had never been too many disagreements, but when there were, Nicola was the one who made the first move to resolve things before bedtime. She was a great believer in the adage of never going to sleep on a fight, even if it meant staying up until the wee hours. Stephen had taught her this. She recalled occasions where, as a teenager, he had kept her awake until midnight or even one o'clock in the morning, asking her to explain again and again why she had treated him with such disrespect. She'd said that sometimes she fell into bed, having lost track of what had caused the argument in the first place. This was why Nicola could never sleep properly knowing Ross was cross with her. She would lie awake until exhaustion got the better of her and, even then, sleep was so fitful that neither of them felt rested. This was the reason he was so bewildered by her fighting back.

'Maybe you're right,' Ross said to Simon. 'Maybe I've underestimated her. Either that or someone has put her up to it.'

'Who is she still in touch with?'

'Apart from Claire, I don't know. It could be her parents, I suppose, but I don't know if she's on speaking terms with them.'

'Anyone at work?'

It was only then that Ross realised he knew nothing about Nicola's new life, only where she lived and worked. He didn't know what friends she had or what she did when she wasn't working. He'd been so caught up in his own hurt and needs, he hadn't taken the time to ask.

Nicola had begun a whole new career in a field he never would have pictured for her, she had secretly visited the house and now she was fighting him for custody of Sam. All of a sudden it was obvious that the Nicola of today was not the same one as four years ago.

'I've underestimated her,' he said, a shiver going down his spine.

'What do you mean?'

'It's only just hit me that I have no real sense of what has happened on Shetland, nor what her life is like now.' A cold sweat erupted. 'She might just win this.'

'We're going to have a bit of a fight on our hands,' said Simon, nodding. 'That said, we have this covered. I've asked Keeley to dig out the files from when Nicola went missing and to see what she can find out about this Kwame Martins.'

Family law was not where Simon had envisioned himself when he started at law school, but he found it to be steady, well-paid work. And, of course, there were some juicy divorces involving adultery, paternity disputes and lots of assets.

With those expensive divorces, he rarely felt sorry for either side as, generally, they all behaved as badly as each other. In this instance, however, a husband and vulnerable child had been left confused and desperately, desperately sad.

Like many, Simon had, at first, wondered if Ross had been involved in Nicola's disappearance, but it soon became clear he was no murderer and that until Nicola's depression reared its ugly head, the Ramseys had seemed a healthy, happy family. As the investigation dragged on, Ross's emotions ranged from blaming himself for her running away, to blaming the police for not finding her, and then to anger with Nicola herself for causing so much hurt in the first place. After the anger subsided came depression before things evened out, allowing Ross to carry on as best he could.

After six months of searching and questioning and never finding an answer, the case was not closed, but silently became a low priority. There seemed to be nothing more to do but hold tight and wait. She would eventually turn up, dead or alive.

'What's our next step?' Ross asked, bringing Simon back to the here and now.

'I'll arrange a mediation session for us with her lawyer and see where we go from there. Ideally, we want a resolution so it doesn't go to court, but, of course, if it does, we have a great chance.'

After the phone call, Ross needed some reassurance that everything was going to be alright, so he dialled Claire's number. 'Nicola is fighting me on the custody of Sam,' he told her, 'can you believe that?'

'Oh, I'm sorry, Ross,' said Claire, 'I suppose it was inevitable.'

'I honestly didn't think she would. I didn't think she'd want to hold herself up for scrutiny like that. She must know she can't win. I don't want to share Sam with her.'

'Listen, Ross, there's something I need to tell you.'

'What?' Ross said, immediately alert.

'I saw Nicola the other day. She called out of the blue and we met up.'

'What did she say?'

'She told me a bit about why she'd gone in the first place. I think she's lonely.'

'Uh-huh.'

'I've not forgiven her for running away and not telling us, but, at the same time, I do believe her when she says she thought she was doing the right thing.'

'Right, I see.' Ross's tone was rigid. 'Are you best friends again, all is forgiven and I'm the baddie for not welcoming her home with open arms?'

'Don't be like that,' Claire said, 'I'm not taking sides. I care about you both. Now I've seen Nicola and talked to her, I don't think she disappeared on a whim and I really don't think there's anybody else involved.'

They were both silent. Ross was hurt that Claire had forgiven Nicola so quickly, it felt like she was saying Nicola hadn't done anything wrong and shouldn't be punished. This was the exact opposite to his own feelings. He couldn't bring himself to let Nicola off the hook so easily.

'Ross, you have every right to be angry with her,' said Claire, 'Nicola broke your heart and left you in a very difficult position. Nobody would expect you to feel differently.'

'I just don't see how you can be so forgiving.'

'I want to give her a second chance.'

After they hung up, Ross thought hard about what Claire had said. Did Nicola deserve a second chance? Or would she run away again? The face of Zoe Morrison flashed through his mind, the girl he'd been infatuated with at university. She had cheated on him and begged for forgiveness, pleaded for a second chance. Of course, he said yes, he couldn't have said anything else as he was so in love with her. Not six weeks later, he caught her in the Students' Union bar, drunk and in the arms of some random guy she'd met that night. It didn't matter that they were young, that university was the place where mistakes were made and hearts were broken.

The humiliation and hurt were just as real. He simply could not allow himself to risk that level of hurt again. He knew also that if he and Nicola ever did get back together, he'd always be looking for her to make a mistake, questioning her every move. There would always be the nagging suspicion that when he got home from work, she wouldn't be there. That was no way to live with someone and it would eventually poison whatever they managed to salvage of their marriage. Claire could do what she wanted, but Ross would fight Nicola every step of the way.

Chapter 11

July had passed and August was upon them, and Mary often found herself seeking out the shelter of the garden. Stephen was like a dog with an itch he couldn't scratch. He roamed the house looking for something to take away the irritation, but found no comfort at home. He took his frustrations out on Mary simply because Nicola wasn't there. Even on wet days Mary would hide in the garden, using the branches of the cherry tree to escape the worst of the drops.

Nicola hadn't been in touch since their fateful meeting in St Enoch's Square and Stephen forbade Mary to raise the subject and Mary hadn't dared phone again. With no friends of her own, and unwillingness to talk about her home life with outsiders, Mary had nobody to talk with about what had been happening. Maureen lived a few doors down, and she seemed like a nice woman, but Mary couldn't imagine herself knocking on the door, inviting herself in and confessing all that had happened in the last four years.

Pleasant as Maureen was, they weren't friends, and Mary was all too aware of the gossip that had done the rounds when Nicola first went missing. She'd heard the awful things that were whispered about her and Stephen, and had no desire to reignite them. It had been mortifying then and would be no different now.

She considered calling Ross but knew Stephen wouldn't approve. There was always Father Leonard, but even though he was sworn to confidentiality, he may ask awkward questions, all of which would be too complicated to answer. Families are complex creatures, she reminded herself.

Mary's own parents had moved from a tiny settlement on the Isle of Lewis to the big city of Glasgow in search of work. Her father had found labouring work and was away from home most of the time, eventually abandoning them altogether. Her mother had struggled on, trying to keep a roof over her six children on almost no wages. Eventually, three of the children were taken into care and one died in a hit-and-run accident. Only Mary and Callum remained at home. Mary's mother never recovered from the loss of her children. She switched off and began drinking. A habit she never managed to quit.

When Callum was sixteen, he joined the Merchant Navy and never came back. He did write to Mary a couple of times, telling her he'd settled in Australia and asked her to join him. He told her how different the life there was to that of the slums of Glasgow, how the sun shone and how good the wages were, but, by then, Mary had met Stephen and she didn't want to risk what she saw as her one chance at love. Stephen pointed out that, given she'd never see him again, there was little point staying in touch and, eventually, she lost contact with her brother.

No, thought Mary, bringing her thoughts back to the present, families are complex and she didn't want to have to explain it to near strangers. With nobody to confide in, Mary was left to brood by herself, withdrawing, when she had the opportunity, into her imagination to wonder what might have happened in Nicola's life these past four years and why she'd suddenly returned. She wondered too about her grandson – it was such a shame there'd been that falling out. It was very selfish of Ross,

Mary always thought. We are his grandparents, after all, we have a right to know how he is.

She wished her husband would at least try to break the ice with Ross, but he point-blank refused, not even for Sam's sake. 'Sam knows where we are,' he stated resolutely. 'When he's old enough, he'll come and see us.'

Mary wasn't so sure. Children grow up, forget and move on with their lives; he might not be interested in two old people he hardly knew. Mary always admired Stephen's strength of mind, his ability to make a decision and stick with it, but, on this issue, she wished he would bend a little. Of course, so much time had passed that it was harder and harder to take the first step, until now it felt impossible.

Perhaps with Nicola's return, there was a new chance, because although she wasn't allowed to see Sam at the moment, it was more than likely things would change. Yes, Ross was angry and wanted to rid himself of Nicola, but Mary was sure, even in this day and age, a court wouldn't exclude a mother from her child's life, even with her disappearance. Nicola would be sure to get joint custody which, in turn, would open the door to them. It was imperative Stephen mend some of the discord so that, in time, they would be able to spend time with their grandchild, their only grandchild, who was growing so fast. Hadn't they missed enough already?

'That would be wonderful,' she said as she gathered herself up from under the tree and went inside to start the ironing. Despite being retired for over ten years, Stephen still wore a suit every day and wanted his shirts sharp and crisp. Making her way through the pile of laundry, she ran through possible scenarios in which she could persuade her husband to swallow his pride just this once, but it wasn't until a few days later that Mary had a chance to raise the subject with Stephen.

The day was sunny, and they were both in the garden, enjoying the warm air. Stephen had been in an usually jovial mood and so Mary had suggested they have an alfresco lunch, all the more enjoyable because of its infrequency. The novelty of sitting outside, admiring their clipped lawn and prim flowerbeds always changed them in a small way, a way that made them feel free and easy. Stephen talked wistfully of one day owning a house in the South of France where they could eat outside all summer long.

'I was thinking,' said Mary as breezily as she could, 'Sam is just the right age to enjoy this big garden of ours.' Stephen smiled at the thought of it. 'It's a marvellous space,' she carried on, 'he could run around here all day.'

'Yes, you're right. I had hoped to see that myself someday, but, well, there we are.'

'Do you think Nicola sees him?'

'I should think so. I imagine that's the reason she's returned. It certainly isn't to see us.'

'I'll bet she doesn't have a garden wherever she's staying.'

'No, probably not.'

Mary let a silence settle before adding, as if it had only just occurred to her, 'We could hang a swing from that tree at the back.'

'What would be the point in that?'

'Well,' Mary hesitated, she didn't want to upset Stephen's mood as she knew from experience that it could alter how the rest of the day would pan out. She tried to keep her voice light. 'I'm still hopeful Nicola will come to her senses.' Stephen didn't say anything.

'In what way?'

'By apologising for the way she's treated us. But I don't suppose she will. She's always been stubborn and headstrong. I'd speak to her if I thought it would do any good, but you know she's never listened to me like she does to you.' Stephen nodded his head sagely. 'It's very selfish of her to keep us away from Sam.' Mary could see her husband's face soften a little.

'Would you like some ice cream?' she asked him as she began clearing their plates.

'I'll have chocolate.'

Mary brought them each a bowl of chocolate ice cream with chocolate sauce generously poured on top. The sun whipped out from behind a cloud and bathed them in light. 'Perhaps you could have a chat with Nicola?' Mary ventured.

'I don't think that's a good idea.'

'Why not?'

'Too much has happened. And anyway, who says I want her back in our lives. Things have been much more peaceful since she left.'

'That's true,' replied Mary, not wanting to remind Stephen of the seemingly endless nights he'd drunk too much whisky and lamented on just how badly he'd been treated by his daughter. Nor did she raise the subject of the blame he'd shot in her direction, berating her for being such a pathetic excuse for a woman, a useless mother, and how much he wished he'd chosen someone else to be his wife. Instead, she said, 'But it wouldn't be for Nicola's sake, it would be for ours, so we can see Sam.'

'No, Mary, I won't do it. That's an end to it.' After a minute or two, his legs getting jumpy, he said, 'Why would you want me to go begging cap in hand to her? Hasn't she put us through enough? Do you think I have no pride?'

'Not at all darling, it's just that-'

'What?'

'I'd love to see my grandson.'

'For Christ's sake, give it up, Mary. Why are you ruining my lunch? Don't I give you enough?' He indicated the house and garden. 'It seems not. It seems everything I worked hard to give you is never enough.' His voice deepened. He slowed down. 'Still, you want more. Well, I can't give you any more. This is what you're stuck with.' He reached over the table and struck her cheek with the back of his hand. 'Clear up the mess.' He dropped his bowl onto the table and went inside.

Dismayed, Mary rubbed her cheek hard to lessen the sting of the slap. No matter how often this happened and how used to it she got, every slap, punch or kick from Stephen ushered in a fresh bout of tears. This time she pushed them back. She looked up to the sky for a moment, to find some resolve in the warm sun. As she moved her eyes back down to the table, she noticed a neighbour watching from her upstairs room. Mary placed a smile on her face and waved. The neighbour moved away from the window.

Later, Stephen headed out to the Legion, and Mary took the opportunity to have a nap. Slowly she climbed the stairs to her bedroom, one step at a time, and using her hands to hold on to the banister and wall. 'When did you get so old, Mary?' She asked herself.

She lay on her back on the bed and enjoyed the feeling of succumbing to the softness of the mattress. She felt her joints lengthen and the general aches and pains of age ease. She put her hand to her cheek, where Stephen's slap still stung slightly. She knew she'd been testing her luck in pushing the subject of Nicola, but she'd had to try. Nicola was their only daughter after all and surely, after all this time and worry, it was right to bury the hatchet and let bygones be bygones.

'That's not Stephen's way, and you know it,' she said out loud. 'He can bear a grudge like nobody else you know.' She put her hands in front of her and watched them as they shook. She placed them by her sides and lay motionless, eyes closed, and fell into a light doze in which she pictured her life in Spain. She envisioned balmy evenings on the terrace of her small flat, overlooking the sea. The floor would be tiled, like she'd seen on television, to keep the apartment cool underfoot. She'd cook fresh squid for herself and wash it down with a fancy Spanish wine. Afterwards, she'd go back to the bar and dance the night away. This time though, she thought she saw a familiar figure standing at the other end of the bar, a slim and sad looking figure and without seeing their face she knew it was Nicola. Disappointed reality was infiltrating her dreams, Mary forced herself to wake up with a sigh.

'How do you solve a problem like Nicola?' Mary sang softly to herself. She could continue down the path of trying to persuade Stephen to go and talk to her, but that would most likely include a few more slaps across the face, or worse. Mary didn't think she had the strength for that.

Or, she could cut out the middle man and go straight to Nicola herself. That too had its dangers, but it would at least mean she'd speak to or see her daughter once in a while, and who knows, in the future it may lead to seeing Sam. Mary smiled at the thought of Sam's little face gazing up at her, and it made her heart melt and her resolve firm.

With renewed energy Mary got out of bed and headed downstairs to her bag where she kept a note of Nicola's number. She sat down next to the phone in the hallway and was just about to lift the receiver when it rang, making her jump.

'Hello?'

Chapter 12

Stephen couldn't quite forgive Mary for irritating him so much at lunchtime. 'Why she has to nag me like that,' he muttered, 'she brings it on herself.' After he left the table he'd gone upstairs to change into a shirt and tie before heading out. He slammed the front door to make his exit known and feel momentarily better about himself.

On the way to the Legion, his temper began to lessen, and he was able to concede that Mary did have a point. It would be wonderful to see Sam again, to hear his voice as he ran around the garden. There was no way in hell he was going to make the first move with Ross, not after all that had been said. But Nicola, well, Nicola was another matter altogether. 'She's still my daughter,' he told himself, 'even if she is behaving like a fool.'

When Sam was born, Stephen had been surprised by his own depth of feeling for the tiny infant. He'd heard it said the emotions a grandchild brought out in a person were hugely different to those of a child. It's a different kind of intensity, someone had told him, and it was true. The tenderness Stephen felt towards Sam was unlike anything he'd experienced before, even when Nicola was born.

'You're an old man now,' he justified to himself, 'too sentimental.'

Perhaps it was because Stephen was nearing the end of his life that Sam's newness to the world made him seem so vulnerable and in need of protection. Whatever it was, the emotions felt good, but they also made him wary of spoiling the child. The result was he could be too gruff, which he knew frightened the child. It had been over a year since he and Mary had seen Sam and perhaps Mary was right, perhaps Nicola was the best way or renewing that relationship.

Seeing her in St Enoch's Square that day had been a shock, and it was only now he could admit that he had not behaved as he would have liked. At first, his pride had been hurt, so he'd lashed out in anger, but as the anger subsided, regret and nostalgia seeped in.

'What's done is done.'

He remembered Nicola as a child and how close they'd been, his little princess. He remembered the weekend he'd taken her away to Troon for an overnight stay by the sea. They'd had a wonderful time in the small hotel where they'd had fish and chips and played in the penny arcade. Stephen wanted that daughter back, the one who listened to him, trusted him, did as she was asked and loved him for it.

Part of him wanted to sort things out with Nicola, but another part was uneasy about making the first move. He couldn't put his finger on exactly what it was that made him unsure, but recent events assured him he was correct to trust his instinct. His stomach felt jittery, giving him a nervous energy he wasn't used to feeling, and he picked up speed as he walked down the street with his long, firm strides.

At the British Legion Club, where a number of his acquaintances had already set up camp, Stephen ordered himself half a lager and a whisky chaser. He was not a services man himself, he'd been a draftsman at Mowat Smith Shipbuilders for forty years, but he had somehow found himself a regular patron of the place. He enjoyed the camaraderie of the men. There was always someone to run a problem by, whether it was as simple as the missus or one of the many ailments they seemed to suffer from these days. When he didn't want to talk, but be left alone to mull, the men seemed instinctively to know and backed off, something Stephen appreciated.

Today was one of those days and, after making a few pleasantries at the bar while ordering his drinks, he sat himself at a table away from the others. From there, he could listen without involvement and take his mind off his own worries. This afternoon he listened to a discussion on the merits, or otherwise, of the new packaging on Marks and Spencer's sandwiches. It was inane stuff that usually would have amused Stephen, but today it irritated the hell out of him. He supped his beer while thoughts tumbled around his brain – namely, that inviting Nicola back into their lives might not be as good an idea as he first thought.

'She's made it clear she doesn't want anything to do with us,' he reminded himself, 'maybe we should respect that.' Unspoken went the acknowledgment that the Nicola now was not the same one who'd left.

If they'd met in the street like that four years ago Nicola would never have run away but would have stayed and answered her father's questions. By walking away she'd shown a courage she'd never previously possessed, and he wondered uneasily where it came from and what else she might be courageous about.

'She's growing up,' Mary had said to him once, 'she needs to be handled sensitively.' That was Mary's department, not his. The remit of provider did not encompass sensitivity.

Since his marriage to Mary, Stephen had taken great care to ensure he always knew what his wife was thinking and to guide her direction. When Nicola was born, he did the same thing, believing it was his right and responsibility to manage the women in his family.

Although Nicola hadn't said anything, her very avoidance of him told Stephen all he needed to recognise that he no longer held the same authority over her and he didn't like it.

He finished his drinks and threw a cursory wave as he left the club. Outside, the air was warm, but with enough of a breeze to keep things fresh. He walked towards Clarkston town centre, not heading anywhere in particular.

As he walked, Stephen passed a few people he knew. Having lived all his married life there, it was not surprising and these brief interludes of conversation were welcome distractions, but still he marched on, walking until he found himself outside the Giffnock Parish Church. He looked up at the windows and felt beckoned inside. It was dark and quiet and, as churches often are, soothing.

The walk had taken it out of him and, feeling a little unbalanced, Stephen sat down on the back pew where he took a few deep breaths and felt a little better.

This was not his usual church, and he looked around. There were one or two vergers going about their business and a noticeboard with church activities advertised. All around it were pictures drawn by the Sunday school pupils, depicting varying scenes from the Bible. There was a small attempt at a gift shop for the few tourists who passed through the church.

Straight ahead of him was the altar with its paraphernalia. The ceremony, the tradition, the same ritual performed week in, week out. He considered how comforting it was to know that, regardless of all the other changes in the world, the ritual of the kirk remained constant. Constancy. Stephen considered himself a consistent man, a man of his word, not the sort to avoid his duty or responsibility.

What was it about Nicola that made him want to shirk this duty, to duck away from his responsibility as a father when, of all the people who had ever been in his life, she was the one he'd loved the most? Nicola had been his reason for being, had kept him going, plodding on when the daily grind had ground its hardest, when Mary and their suburban life together had driven him near to distraction.

Images of Nicola toddling around the garden, still uncertain on her feet and trying to run after him, but not knowing how, played out in front of him. As did her sweet four-year-old face, looking up at him with nothing but trust. She had an innocence Stephen didn't think he'd ever possessed. He saw plain as day how she had adored him. His words had been gospel to her, and it had made him proud of for doing such a good job. She was as respectful and obedient, as loving and affectionate as she should be.

Then he remembered the eight-year-old Nicola, changed beyond recognition. Sullen and moody, she was no longer his little angel. Her tenderness had transformed into hostility and avoidance. Her eyes were no longer filled with adoration, but mistrust. He never understood why, as all he had ever done was love her.

Once, in a fit of teenage fury, she'd lashed out at him. He was so stunned by the sight of her clenched fist that he hadn't reacted, and she punched him right on the side of the eye. In retaliation, he'd pushed her hard in the sternum and she'd flown back onto her bed. He thundered to the bathroom and saw a bruise had already begun to form. Later, when Mary asked how he got the black eye, he made up an excuse, but it embarrassed him to be lying like some battered wife. Just thinking about it embarrassed him all over again, and he concluded that Nicola's lack of contact was a clear extension of the punch. If that's how she wanted to playthings, so be it. She had betrayed him, not the other way around.

'No good will come from any reconciliation,' he told himself, 'it will only open old wounds.' He wasn't going to leave himself vulnerable again.

He stood up to leave. He was going to go home and tell Mary he didn't want Nicola back in their lives. Once up, however, the unsteady feeling he'd previously felt returned with a vengeance, pins and needles coursing through his right arm. Next, a pain tore through his chest. Knowing immediately what was happening, he glanced up at the altar's image of Christ on the cross.

'Thanks a lot,' he said.

As if in response, the pain intensified and Stephen slumped back into the pew.

One of the vergers phoned for an ambulance.

Confusion and chaos surrounded Stephen when he woke up. At first he didn't know what had happened or where he was. As he regained consciousness, he became aware of the pain in his body. He groaned and tried to move, but couldn't because he was strapped down. He was aware of lights flashing around him. Was it a torch? He became aware of somebody moving around him, doing things to him. He thought it was his old care worker, Barry, and he tried to fight but was unable. He started to panic before all of a sudden the world went blank.

The next time he woke up he was blinded by white lights, interspersed with shadows criss-crossing around him. 'This is it,' he thought, 'your time has come, you're about to meet your maker.' At first he was relieved, he felt calm and happy to go. He felt old and tired and ready to move on to the next world. But then the same unease he'd been experiencing all day returned, and he was no longer so sure he was ready to move on. He wasn't certain he'd be allowed in because he hadn't resolved things here. He didn't want to end this life knowing he hadn't put his affairs in order.

'Mr Johnston, can you hear me?' A woman's voice pierced his consciousness. 'Can you hear me? You're in hospital. You've had a heart attack and we're going to do everything we can.

Okay?' A light flashed in one eye, then the other, making him wince. The woman said something, but he didn't hear it.

'You can't go,' he told himself, 'you can't go yet. You've got to sort things out with Nicola. You need to tell Mary you love her. As soon as you're out of here, you're going to phone Nicola, you're going to tell her all is forgiven and that all you want is to make peace.'

Suddenly it all seemed so clear to him. No matter what had happened in the past, none of it mattered now. Being so close to death, so close he could see the light, had opened his eyes to what was important. He would forgive Nicola and gather his family around him once more.

As if confirming he'd made the right decision, all the pain in his body eased and he fell into unconsciousness.

Chapter 13

I was shopping in Sainsbury's when Kwame Martins called. 'As we expected, your husband is not willing to give you any custody of Sam. He will still apply for full custody citing abandonment.'

My heart sank. While I'd known Ross wouldn't agree, it was still upsetting to hear it said out loud. 'What can I do now?' I asked.

'We will all get together with a mediator and with their help come to an agreement.'

'And if we don't?'

'Then we will have to fight it out in court and that will be nasty. In the meantime, we need to build your case for the family mediator. We need to demonstrate that you've dealt with all of your problems and put them behind you. You need to prove that your time away from your family and the space Shetland provided you with was what you needed to sort your head out and get back on track. We need to demonstrate you can offer your child a safe, loving and normal home life. Can you offer Sam that right now?'

'Yes, I can, and I'm working on the changes necessary to show the mediator I can.'

'Great, try to get as many of those in place before we meet. Let Ross see that you're serious in your efforts to provide the best for Sam.'

'When will we meet with the mediator?'

'It will take another few weeks to get an appointment and the mediation can also take a few weeks depending on how much progress you make.'

'Why so long?'

'It's a busy department. But for us, that's a good thing. It gives you more time to sort yourself out, make what changes you need to make. Do you have a bedroom for Sam to sleep in, for example? Is your home near his school? What support network do you have in place? Can you afford to have Sam even part time?'

'This is so hard,' I said. 'It feels like everything is taking so long that my life is slipping away from me.'

'You're right, it is hard, and it won't get any easier for a while. You have to keep reminding yourself that patience now will be rewarded later. What are a few months in comparison to the years you may spend with your son?'

Kwame's words hit home, and I knew he was right. 'I want you to get out there and be active. Join a club, make some friends, see if you can't make up with your parents to show you have some support. That would look especially good with the judge, if we have to go down that route.'

The next day I headed into work early to speak to my boss, Dawn McEvoy. It was nearly the end of September and we'd had a few days of strong, cold winds. I enjoyed them whipping around my head, waking me up and injecting me with renewed energy. The leaves had well and truly turned and the colours of the city's trees were vibrant, lifting my spirits against the cooling weather and the impasse Ross and I had reached.

'How can I help?' Dawn asked as we sat down in her office. My coffee cup rattled in its saucer so much that I was forced to put it down.

THE DAY SHE CAME HOME 85

'As you know,' I began, 'I'm separated from my husband and we're divorcing. Our son currently lives with him and I'm applying for joint custody.'

'I see,' she said, nodding her head.

'As part of my case, I need to be able to show the judge that I'm in a position to offer Sam a stable home life.'

'Go on.'

'One of the ways I can do this is to demonstrate I can work around Sam. If he's with me during the week, I need to show I can pick him up after school, or if he's with me at the weekend, I must show I won't be working those days. I know it's a big ask, but I hoped it would be possible to arrange my shifts around Sam's visits when they happen. I know I've not been here very long, but being able to demonstrate my availability to the judge really could make all the difference.' I wanted to say more, but stopped myself before I started to ramble or, even worse, burst into tears.

Dawn didn't say anything immediately, I could see her thinking it through. I held my breath in case it disturbed her train of thought and swayed her decision in some way.

'Let me think about,' she said at last. 'I'm not promising anything, but I'll see what I can do. As you say, you've not been here long, so I don't have a lot of work history to back up your request with management, but I'll do what I can. Leave it with me.'

'That's great, I appreciate it. Thank you.'

'I remember what it's like to have young children and how demanding they can be.' Dawn leaned back in her chair and took a sip of coffee before saying, 'Sam's six, isn't he? It's a great age, they've started school and are discovering a whole new world that doesn't involve Mum and Dad. I also know how difficult divorce can be.' She sat forward again and said, 'My best friend went through it and, even though it was the best thing to do, it was tough. You have a lot on your plate at the moment. How are you coping with the job?'

'I love it,' I told her truthfully. 'We have a wonderful team here, most of our guests are pleasant and enjoying their time in Glasgow, and that makes for a great working environment. I can't tell you how glad I am you gave me this opportunity and for trusting Shona's judgment.' Shona had been my boss at The Harbour Hotel in Shetland and put the good word in for me here at the Strathclyde City Hotel.

'I've known Shona for years,' said Dawn, 'she's great and would never have recommended you if she didn't think you were up to it. I'm glad to hear you're enjoying things here.' Dawn hesitated, and I felt there was something more she wanted to say, but, instead. She stood up and our meeting was finished.

Later, when I took my break, I checked my phone. Mum had called but hadn't left a message. I opted not to call back, but, as I was putting my phone into my bag, it rang and Mum's name flashed on the screen.

'Nicola, I have terrible news,' she said. 'Dad has had a heart attack. He's in hospital.' She paused, waiting for a response, but I didn't say anything. 'I've spoken to the nurse who says he's stable, but he needs to stay in for observation.' Again, she paused and again I didn't say anything. 'Oh, Nicola, isn't it terrible? Aren't you going to say something? He could've died.'

'Are you at the hospital?'

'Not yet, they've just called, and I straightaway phoned you. Will you come with me? You're so good in these situations.'

'Are you sure that's a good idea?' I wasn't sure I wanted to go. 'Dad and I aren't exactly on good terms. My being there might cause more trouble.'

'Please, Nicola.'

'Alright, I'll meet you there.'

After we'd hung up, I tried to figure out how I felt. For so long, I'd hated this man and wanted him out of our lives. I'd left home as soon as I could, seeing less and less of my parents as time went on, especially after I met Ross. Ross became my family, my support, my rock, and I was happy to distance myself from my parents. And now here we were, Dad on the point of death, and I didn't feel happy. Despite everything, he was still my father, the man who had raised me, albeit badly. I needed a bit of time, so decided to finish my shift before heading to the hospital.

When I walked out of the hotel, a heavy drizzle was falling. I didn't have an umbrella and, by the time I reached the hospital, I was soaked through. Reception told me Dad was in Intensive Care and I followed an orange-coloured line on the floor. Strip lighting bounced brilliantly off the linoleum. Around me, I heard the muffled echoes of trolleys being wheeled, doors opening and closing, doctors in discussion and porters joking with patients. I was surprised, when I reached the ward, to see Mum hadn't arrived yet, so I shook the rain off myself and waited.

Half an hour later, she came in looking a lot calmer than I expected.

'You were ages.' I told her.

'There was no rush. The doctors will look after him.' She seemed different somehow. Maybe she was in shock.

'Are you alright?' I asked.

'Yes, fine.' Mum hesitated before saying, 'I was thinking, when I was at home, what life would have been like without your dad. When the hospital called, I panicked, thought I needed to be here as quickly as I could. Then I thought, why? There's nothing I can do for him, the doctors are here. I got some tea and biscuits and sat down.' I watched my mum like she was a stranger. This was not the Mary Johnston I recognised. The one I knew would be fluttering aimlessly and batting her wings noisily in my face. The Mary Johnston in front of me was calm with a strong, clear voice. 'I enjoyed that cup of tea.' She turned to look at me. 'Have you spoken to anyone?'

'Not yet. Do you want me to ask a nurse if you can see him?'

'That's a good idea, love.' I stopped a passing nurse and explained who we were.

'I'll let the doctor know,' she said before disappearing.

A few minutes later, she returned. 'He's on his way.'

Not long afterwards, the doctor arrived looking, to me, young and flustered. He led us into a consulting room.

'Mrs Johnston?'

'Yes, and this is my daughter, Nicola. How is he? Will he be alright?'

'I'm Dr Shackley,' he said with a soft Liverpool accent I found soothing. 'Your husband is in a stable condition. He's had a severe heart attack, but a bystander acted quickly and the ambulance was with him in no time. That's made a huge difference to his recovery. He also has a lot of fighting spirit.' The doctor smiled, not realising just how apt his words were. 'It's clear he doesn't want to leave us just yet. That said, he does remain in a serious condition. He's been awake and is aware of what's going on around him, but he's very weak. I suggest you go in only for a few minutes, talk quietly to him and to each other, and leave. I don't want him tired out, he needs his strength for his recovery. He's no longer attached to a ventilator,' the doctor went on, 'but does have an oxygen mask to help him breathe.'

He led us from the family waiting area into the ward itself, which felt cramped and had only ten beds in it, each one heavily partitioned with curtains that could be pulled shut at any given moment. Beside each bed were machines that blinked and bleeped, measuring every movement of the body. Dad's bed was diagonally across from the door.

THE DAY SHE CAME HOME

He looked small lying in the large hospital bed. My normally strong, robust and ever-present father lay pale, gaunt and unshaven, wires and electrodes attached to his body and arms. The ward felt small and stuffy. There was an underlying smell of illness and bleach. It clawed at my throat and I felt nauseous. I stepped back outside the ward for a moment, resting a cheek against the cool wall of the corridor. The same nurse as before appeared by my side.

'It looks worse than it is, honest,' she said to comfort me. 'Come in when you're ready. He'll know you're here, even if he isn't awake.' Yes, I thought, I bet he will.

When I re-entered the ward, the nurse and Dr Shackley were talking in quiet voices, each writing their respective case notes. 'Nurse Rodriguez will be able to answer any questions you've got,' Dr Shackley said, 'I've another patient to check on, but I'll be by again later.'

Mum sat down in a chair and the nurse pulled a second one over for me, motioning me to sit down. Once she'd left, Mum leaned over to look at Dad more closely and, as she did so, his eyes slowly opened, blinking as he adjusted to the brightly lit room.

'Stephen,' she whispered, 'It's me, Mary.'

Dad tried to respond but didn't have the strength to make himself audible.

'Don't try to talk, the doctor said you've got to save your energy. Nicola is here and we've brought you some things from home.' He started at the mention of my name and looked around for me, but, being unable to lift his head, he couldn't see me. 'I phoned her as soon as I heard and she's come to see you.'

Mum indicated with her eyes that I should say something, but I couldn't. 'Say something,' said Mum firmly. 'Stop hiding.'

I stood up so he could see me and to my surprise he looked pleased to see me. He lifted a hand, indicating he wanted me to take it. 'Go on,' Mum urged, 'take it.'

As I looked down at his hand, unsure whether to take it or not, I reminded myself I could leave if I wanted to. But even from his sickbed, Dad's strength was overwhelming, and I was drawn to him. Again, he tried to talk and, again, he was too weak. His hand lowered to the bed, and he closed his eyes.

I looked at him, really looked at him, for what felt like the first time. I realised I'd been wrong all these years. I'd believed that if he died so would all my problems, but it was suddenly clear, like an epiphany, that they wouldn't magically disappear, they'd live on and consume me. If he escaped the punishment due him and didn't answer for his actions, I really would go mad.

He felt me leaning over him and opened his eyes. The look of tenderness in his eyes nearly derailed me, but I dug deep.

'I hate you,' I said quietly.

'Not now, Nicola,' said Mum.

'You stole any chance of normality I had. It's you who's made me like this. It's your fault I went mad and left my son.' I picked up his hand in mine. 'I'm glad you didn't die because you're going to be held accountable.' I watched a mix of emotions rampage their way through my father. His tenderness changed to confusion, then fear and finally anger. My voice remained calm and even. 'I will do everything I can to see you put away for the rest of your life.'

'Nicola, stop it,' hissed Mum, looking to see if any of the nurses were listening. 'This is not the place to air your childhood grievances.'

I leaned closer to Dad and whispered, 'I'm not disappearing again, don't worry, but I can guarantee you'll wish I'd never returned.'

I strode towards the exit, empowered and feeling as though I'd sprinted a hundred metres. My breath came short and shallow as the adrenalin made its way round my body. I was shocked by my own bravery; I'd never talked to my father in that way. It may have been his weakened body, or simply my desperation not to lose Sam, but now that I recognised him as a mortal man, not an all-powerful authority, I was able to say what I'd wanted to for so long.

I knew what I had to do if I ever wanted full control of my life. If I was ever going to truly move forward and be a strong mother to Sam, I had to make my father accountable for raping me.

Chapter 14

It was still raining the next day. There was no strong wind to clear my head, but I didn't need it. After the previous night, my mind was crystal clear, and I knew exactly what I had to do. I was confident that once Ross knew my story he'd understand, once and for all, why I'd left him all those years ago. Anticipation made me edgy, and I did my best to keep extra busy that day, keep my mind occupied.

Carmen, a colleague, asked if I was okay, 'You seem, you know, a little crazy today,' she said in her strong Spanish accent.

When my shift finally ended, I made my way to Bearsden and the home I'd shared with Ross and Sam. I hadn't been back since the day Ross had found me.

The journey seemed to take forever, but mile by mile, the bus made its way through the rainy streets. I went over and over in my mind what I would say to Ross, how best I could explain what I'd never been able to before. In a bid to burn off some nervous energy, I got off the bus a few stops early to walk the rest of the way. I still didn't have an umbrella, but I didn't care, I needed the cool rain on my skin to calm me and keep me grounded.

I didn't want to knock or ring the doorbell in case I woke Sam. By now, it was after eight o'clock and he'd be in bed. I walked round to the back of the house and stood in the garden

THE DAY SHE CAME HOME 93

looking in through the kitchen window. Ross was moving about loading the dishwasher, putting things back in the fridge, the domestic routine he must follow every night after Sam was asleep. Putting the house to rights, preparing for the next day.

He must have sensed somebody was watching him because he suddenly looked up and stared right at me. I felt myself flush as here I was again, trespassing and caught in the act. The difference was this time I wanted to be found. I moved and indicated I wanted to come in. Reluctantly, he told me to go around to the front door, grabbing a few extra moments to compose himself.

He opened the door to a bedraggled sight but didn't notice at first. His defences were up and he eyed me with suspicion before taking a quick glance up the stairs to check that Sam hadn't emerged from his bedroom. It was when he looked back at me he saw what a drowned rat I was. I think he also saw a change, something he couldn't place, but which was enough for him not to close the door in my face.

'I need to talk to you,' I said.

'Do it through your lawyer,' he replied, still not closing the door.

'It's not to do with my leaving, well that's not totally true, it does have something to do with it, but that's not why I'm here.'

'You're rambling.'

'I know, can I come in?'

Ross hesitated, knowing both our lawyers would strongly disapprove, but something compelled him to let me in.

I stood in the hallway, dripping and wiping rain from my face, unable to stop myself from glancing upstairs to where I knew Sam was sleeping.

'I'll get you a towel,' he said, 'wait here.'

I saw him watching me as he came down the stairs and guessed he was trying to figure out why I was there. I took my coat off and hung it on the banister.

'Thanks,' I said, dabbing my face and hair. He led me through to the kitchen and I looked around. He'd made a lot of changes since my last visit, and I understood the meaning.

'So,' Ross said, leaning against the kitchen units, arms folded. I stood in the middle of the room feeling very exposed. 'What is it you want to tell me?'

The enormity of what I had to say reared up and hit me square on, opening the door for shame to walk on in. This was why I hadn't told him in the first place. The nagging voice that had pestered me all my life, whispering that the abuse was my own fault, returned stronger than ever. I found myself flying back through memories, looking for a word or a look I'd given my father, that told him he could do what he did.

'I... I wanted to tell you something about my past.'

My hands were clammy, and my body was so flushed I had to take my cardigan off.

Ross waited, his expression unreadable.

'You know my dad, he's a difficult man. He makes it difficult to say no to him.'

I set my face into a stony grimace, working hard to keep the tears at bay, I wanted Ross to see my strength and not pity me.

'Even as an adult, it's hard to go against him. He has a strength, I don't know where it comes from, but it's there.' Still, Ross said nothing. 'You can imagine that as a child I found it impossible to say no to him. He was my dad, after all.'

I looked again at Ross for some sort of reaction. He was listening but giving nothing away.

'My mum is a weak woman, she's been dominated by him for what, forty-five years, and was unable to protect me.' Not knowing what words to use or how to form them in my mouth, I stumbled. 'My father raped me,' I said at length. 'Repeatedly. He raped me and my mother let him.'

I couldn't look at Ross. I was too ashamed and too scared of his reaction. It felt sickening to say the words out loud.

THE DAY SHE CAME HOME

'My God,' Ross said, eventually. 'I knew something must have happened, but I didn't think that.'

'What do you mean?' I asked, surprised.

'Over the years, I've wondered. Your relationship with Stephen and Mary has been so full of anger. On the surface of it, there didn't seem to be a real reason for that level of hatred. Then I saw the weird hold your dad has over you and guessed there was something you weren't telling me.' I was stunned. If he'd guessed, then why hadn't he said anything? 'I didn't say anything because I had nothing to base it on, it was just a feeling. And I was sure if something had happened you would have told me.'

Ross came to me and held me in an almost desperate embrace. 'I'm sorry,' he said. 'I'm sorry I didn't ask you.'

We stood like that for a long time and it felt wonderful to be in his arms, to be close to him again. I felt my resolve begin to weaken, so I pushed away.

'Don't be,' I said. 'That's why I've come tonight. I'm not going to be sorry any more. It wasn't my fault that he did those things and I'm sick of feeling guilty for it.'

We sat down at the table, Ross next to me and holding my hand. 'I don't know how old I was when it started. I have vague memories of sitting on his knee, his hand up my skirt, stroking my leg and, later, touching me. I do know that by the time I started school, he was visiting my room. I remember being so sore, I remember the bleeding, the –'

'Stop,' said Ross, getting up and moving to the sink. He breathed heavily as if he felt nauseous. 'Why did Mary not stop him? Take you away? Tell the police?'

'I don't know. We've never talked about it. She was scared, I suppose.'

'What about your teachers? Didn't they see something was wrong?'

'Every now and again someone would ask if everything was alright at home, but I couldn't say anything. I was scared nobody would believe me. Dad always said who would take my word over his?'

'When did it stop?'

'When I was fifteen.'

'He did this to you for over ten years and nobody tried to stop him?' I could hear the outrage in his voice.

'When I was a little girl, I thought it was normal, that all dads must do this because dads love their daughters, right?'

'No, it's not right, it's wrong. It's abuse. Abuse of power, abuse of responsibility, abuse of trust, you name it, he abused it. It's not love.' After a moment, he asked, 'Did he do this to anyone else?'

'I don't know, I don't think so.'

'God, Nicola, I'm so sorry.' He looked at me intensely and I could see he was trying to hide the pity he so obviously felt. But how could he not feel pity? How could anyone not feel sorry for a child this happened to? 'I don't know about you,' said Ross, 'but I need a drink.' He fetched a bottle of whisky and two glasses.

'He had a heart attack yesterday,' I said, sipping my drink. The hot spirit flowed like honey down my oesophagus and warmed my stomach.

'Is he dead?'

'No, he's not, and I'm glad he's not because I've realised that I've got to report him. I'll never properly move forward if I don't tell someone about what happened.'

'Have you told anyone else?'

'No, you're the first person. I buried it away. When I left home, I put those memories in a box, closed the lid and thought I'd never have to look at them again. But trauma, it seems, doesn't work that way.'

THE DAY SHE CAME HOME

'Why did you never tell me? The nights we sat up talking, putting the world to rights, sharing our histories.'

'Shame, it's as simple as that. Would you want to tell the person you loved, the person you wanted to spend the rest of your life with, the person you were married to, that you'd been abused?'

'Maybe I could have helped.'

'How?' Ross shrugged his shoulders, not able to give a solid answer. 'I didn't want to share this with anyone. I wanted to put it all behind me and never think about it again. The day I left home, I became a new person with a future. I did not want to look back.'

'I can't believe Mary let this happen. My God, they both make me sick.' Ross poured us both another drink. I saw his hands trembling as he poured, a mixture of shock and anger, I guessed. He came and sat down with me at the table. 'Why is it all coming out now? What made you change your mind about telling me?'

'When I became a mother, the box I'd hidden those memories in flew open and, the more I tried to stuff them back in, the harder it got. So you see, I ran away not from you and Sam, but from my parents and myself. You can see now I'm not a danger to Sam.'

Ross stood up and made a pretence of getting something from the fridge. 'I've stopped running and now I want to face up to my past. I want to get rid of all those demons living in my head. With you and Sam by my side, I can do that.'

'Is that why you told me? So that I'd let you see Sam?'

'No, not at all. I wanted to tell you what I should have done years ago. It's only now I have the courage.'

Ross took his time before saying, 'It does explain why you did what you did, but it doesn't mean it didn't happen. I still can't be sure you won't do it again.'

'How can you say that? How many more times can I say sorry? What else can I do to show you I'm not the same woman who left?' I lay my forehead on the table to stop me falling over. I watched my tears pool on the floor beneath. 'You're being so unfair. The punishment is too harsh.'

'I'm not punishing you, I'm protecting myself and my son.'

'He's my son too.' My heart was broken. 'Have you no compassion left for me at all?' He didn't answer.

'What are you going to do?' Ross asked.

'I'm going to tell the police. I'm going to report him and have him put away.'

'Do you want me to go with you to the police?' I sat up.

'You'd do that?' He nodded. I wasn't sure I wanted that. He'd just made it clear he still didn't trust me, and yet here he was offering to support me. I couldn't make head nor tail of it, but given I didn't have anyone else to ask, I said, 'Yes please.'

Later, when we were both too drained to talk any further, Ross called a taxi. 'I'll see you tomorrow,' he said as I got in.

I felt small and exhausted sitting in the back of the car. It was late now and there wasn't much traffic. The taxi sped through the streets, ramming its way through puddles and over potholes. I felt safe in the belly of the vehicle, speeding past homes and shops, landmarks and memories.

Falling into a dream state, I recounted all that had been said that night. The relief of telling Ross was immeasurable and was topped only by the disappointment in not being with Sam.

I had alternate bursts of optimism, certain that after tonight things would move forward between me and Ross, and I fantasised about a future where my father was in prison and I was home again with my husband and child. But there were also troughs of pessimism, making me certain too that tonight had changed nothing. The fact remained, after all, that I had left him and Sam, without a word, for four years.

The rain had stopped by the time I got home, but the ground was still wet and puddles lingered. The blurred lights reflected in them encapsulated the half-real fug I felt at that moment, somewhere between reality and dreamtime. Perhaps it was simply the whisky.

Once inside, I lay on my bed for a long time, jittery and unable to sleep. I imagined what might happen at the police station, scared the police would call me a liar, as Dad predicted. After all, I had no proof. It was my word against his. The memory of my father's face, bearing down on me, reignited old fears.

'Who would believe you, Nicola, eh? Do you think anyone would take your word over mine? Don't be ridiculous, girl.' He'd told me this so often I had no choice but to believe it was true.

Eventually, exhaustion took hold of me and I fell into a fitful sleep.

Chapter 15

I met Ross outside the Police Scotland station on Bothwell Street. I arrived first and loitered on the pavement, self-consciously adjusting my coat and scarf around my neck to keep the cold out and to hide my face a little because just being there made me feel like a criminal. Did I look guilty of something, I wondered, or did I look like a victim?

The rains of the past few days had been blown away by strong winds that threw leaves and debris up into the air, driving them round in circles, intermittently lifting them high above me before they hurtled back down to the ground.

'Are you ready?' Ross asked when he arrived.

'I'm not sure.' Out of the blue I felt hot and sweaty, I unwrapped myself from my scarf and coat, my breath a little short. I took a breath. 'Do you think I'm doing the right thing?'

'This isn't my decision to make, you've got to do what you feel is for the best.'

'You do believe me, don't you?' I searched his face for any sign he was simply mollifying me. He took my arms in his hands and squeezed them tightly.

'Nicola, I believe you and so will the police. But you have to be sure this is what you want.'

'I don't know anymore.' I was panicking. 'Last night I was so sure, but as today's gone on, I've been less so. I'm confused. What if they don't believe me and Dad has been right all along?'

I moved away and backed up against the wall of the building because that's how I felt. I felt I'd backed myself into a corner and didn't have the strength to get out. I thought of Dad and what I'd said to him at the hospital. I knew that if I didn't follow through on those promises, I'd forever feel complicit in the abuse. This was my chance to put right the wrong he'd done to both me and Mum. I felt Ross watching me, waiting for a decision. 'I don't know what to do,' I said limply.

'What's the right thing to do?'

'Tell the police.'

'Then you have to be strong, go into that building and tell them.'

He was right, of course he was. Without knowing it, this was what I'd been building up to my whole adult life. I couldn't back out now. 'Okay,' I said, nodding.

'Are you ready?' Ross asked again.

'Let's do this.'

We walked up the steps to the entrance, but just before we went through the revolving door, Ross awkwardly drew me to him and hugged me. He'll never know how much that meant to me and the strength it gave me.

The station was just like the ones I'd seen on television, white walls with blue skirting, brightly coloured public information posters pinned up to encourage people to take care of their belongings, to report anything suspicious and to be vigilant to terrorist activity. Glasgow had a long history of violence, terrorism seemed just another chapter in its story. Plastic chairs were fixed to the floor, so they couldn't be thrown in a temper.

At the reception desk, behind a glass partition, was a young male officer. He was plump, verging on the fat side, and the thought flickered through my mind that he didn't do much chasing of criminals. He had a pleasant face, and his seemingly innocent smile made me feel guilty for bringing him my sordid story. I looked at the badge on his breast pocket. Police Constable Peter Gunn.

'How can I help?' he asked.

I faltered. Do I just come out with it, I wondered? Tell them I'd like to report my father for child abuse? It felt vulgar to say it in the harsh light of day in a public place like this.

'I need to speak to someone, please. I've something I want to report.'

'What would you like to report?'

I again hesitated, embarrassed now that I was going to have to say it out loud. Moving closer to the glass partition, I said quietly, 'I'd like to report my father.'

'Your father?'

'Yes.'

'Has something happened to him?'

'Just tell him,' said Ross gently, moving next to me.

'My father abused me when I was a child. I want to report him.'

Saying it out loud to someone in authority and who was there to protect me was oddly liberating. It made this whole scenario less dreamlike. Mixed in with the shame of admitting it had happened was a feeling of achievement. I had taken the first small step of many needed to hold Dad accountable for what he'd done to me.

'Can I take your name?' asked the officer.

'Nicola Ramsey.'

'Take a seat, Mrs Ramsey,' he said, his jovial expression of only a moment ago replaced with earnestness and perhaps a little panic, as if, like me, he wasn't sure what his next steps were. He disappeared for a few minutes, during which time Ross sat down and I paced the floor.

The revolving entrance door spun, and a man came in. I found myself instinctively turning away from him. I didn't want anyone, even a stranger, knowing I was here. He waited at the reception window for a few moments before PC Gunn came back.

'Someone will be with you in a moment,' he said to me before turning to the man.

Not long afterwards, a woman buzzed herself through from a door I hadn't noticed. She was smartly dressed in a navy-blue trouser suit. She had thick, dark blonde hair that fell just past her shoulders, with a long fringe that covered her eyes. She unconsciously flicked her head slightly to move it out of the way. She looked at me intently, and I could tell she was making an initial assessment about whether I was the genuine article or not.

'Nicola Ramsey?' I nodded as she held out her hand and shook mine. She looked at Ross. 'Are you Mr Ramsey?'

'Yes,' he said, 'Ross Ramsey.'

'Can Ross be with me?' I asked.

'Of course.' She used a key card to open another door, beyond which was a small interview room. She indicated for us to sit down on one side of a small desk while she sat on the other. 'My name is Inspector Gail Brown and I'm part of the Sexual Offences Unit in Scotland.' She showed us her ID. 'I'd like to take down a few preliminary bits of information and then I'd like you to tell me what happened.'

Her tone was light and informal, and the interview lasted about half an hour. It was amazing how liberated I felt. Not only had she listened to me, but taken me seriously. There had been no suspicious glances in my direction, or sarcastic comments, or even suggestions I brought it on myself. I turned and smiled at Ross. This had been far easier than I'd anticipated.

'Thank you, Mrs Ramsey,' said Inspector Brown, 'I've got enough information for now but will need to take a fuller, more in-depth statement from you in the future. Will that be alright?'

'You mean I have to do this again?' My smile immediately disappeared. 'Why? I've just told you everything?'

'What we've done today is take a brief statement, so I can gather the basic facts. The next step is to spend more time together so I can take a more detailed statement.'

'What else do you need to know?'

'Names, dates, your family circumstances at that time, anything you can tell us.'

'We've just done that.'

'No, I'm afraid we haven't.' She looked at Ross, then back at me. Ross took my hand; she smiled sympathetically at me. I felt like a child being comforted before being told there would be no ice cream for pudding. 'It's only fair to warn you that this can be a very difficult journey. Confronting an abuser and bringing them to justice is very important, but it will have a profound effect on you. It will be one of the toughest things you'll have to do. You'll be asked to talk, in detail, about very personal and often painful experiences. That's not easy.'

I must have looked awful because Ross put his arm around me and it felt like he was literally holding me up. 'Nicola?' he asked, 'Are you okay?'

'I don't know if I can say it all out loud again.'

'You don't have to make a decision now. I appreciate how hard this is. Here's my card, in case you want to ask me anything.' She pushed it over the table towards me. I picked it up but didn't really see it. 'I'll also pass on your details to our liaison officer, who will be in touch with you to offer ongoing support and information, as and when you need it.'

'Thank you.'

'If she decides to go ahead, what happens next?' asked Ross.

'After we've taken the full statement from your wife, we'll carry out an investigation, gathering as much information as we can about what happened to put together a comprehensive case. If we find enough evidence and we're satisfied there is a case to be brought, we'll put it to the Procurator Fiscal who will make the final decision on whether we can prosecute your father.'

'What sort of evidence do they need?' I asked.

'Because there is unlikely to be any physical evidence, we'll need to talk to both your parents, any friends or family who might remember something. We'll investigate your father's background and find out if there's anyone who can corroborate your statement. Sexual abuse is a serious crime and we will treat it as such.'

'How long does it usually take for a case to go the Procurator Fiscal?'

'How long is a piece of string?' she said, apologetically shrugging her shoulders. 'It depends on what we discover. All I can say at this stage is that because the abuse happened historically, it will take longer to piece things together. It will be difficult and you'll need to be patient.' DI Brown looked at me. 'No matter what you decide, you've done a very brave thing coming here today.'

I didn't feel brave, but her words gave me reassurance that I had, indeed, done the right thing and must carry on.

'Let's go on,' I said. 'I can't come this far and not see it through. Yes, I'll make the full statement.'

'Are you sure?' DI Brown asked.

'I've gone through so much to get to this point, I can't give up now.'

'You're doing the right thing,' she said, showing us out. 'Stay strong and be patient. We'll be here to help you as much as we can.'

It was jolting to be out in the cold night air, and I shivered.

'How do you feel?' Ross asked.

'It's easy to say be patient, but now I've started this thing, I want it to get moving. What if he dies before he's punished?'

'Come on, I'll take you for a drink. The babysitter will be alright for a little while longer.'

We went to a nearby pub, and Ross ordered us a couple of drinks. The adrenaline of going to the police station had worn off, and I felt shaky. I took a deep gulp of my wine.

'Tell me about Sam,' I said. I knew this was dangerous ground, but it was the first time I'd seen Ross without him being angry at me, and I really did want to know about my son.

'He's great,' said Ross defensively.

'I mean tell me about him, what he likes and doesn't like. What are his favourite toys? Who are his friends?'

'Oh, I see.' Ross visibly relaxed when he realised there was no hidden agenda to my question. 'He loves his trains, those are his favourite toy. And his bike. We just took the stabilisers off a few weeks ago, you should see him bomb along in the park. He's had a few falls though, he doesn't seem to have any sense of self-preservation.' Ross laughed as he recalled Sam's attempted stunts, his face alight with pride. 'We were in the park and he thought he could jump over a log. He couldn't, of course, and went flying. I nearly had a heart attack and went running over, but he bounced up none the worse for it.' Ross faltered, evidently suddenly conscious that he was gushing about a son we were battling over.

'What does he like to eat?' I asked, not wanting Ross to stop.

'He loves sausages and, believe it or not, broccoli. He hates mushrooms, but I can't blame him for that. He'll do anything for Nutella, so I always keep some in the cupboard for bribery reasons. His best friend is Javad, they're in the same class, and he loves books. We read every bedtime. We're reading about dinosaurs at the moment and he loves learning their names and about how strong they are.'

Hearing about Sam's life, rather than living it with him, made my heart ache, and I burst into tears.

'I know you don't want to share custody with me,' I said, 'but I miss him so much. Please, can I at least visit? I've been so patient, trying so hard to do the right thing, but he's my son and I miss him.' My tears were in freefall.

'Nicola, let's not talk about that now. I'm here to support you about your dad, but that doesn't change the fact I want a divorce or that I won't share custody.'

'Please let me see him, Ross.'

'I'm sorry, Nicola, but no. I can't guarantee you won't desert him again. What if all this stuff with the police gets too much and you decide to run away a second time? I can't do that to him.'

We finished our drinks in silence.

Chapter 16

Stephen had been moved out of the Critical Care unit onto the High Dependency ward. Although the atmosphere was still sombre, it wasn't as deathly silent as in Critical Care. Stephen had taken this as a good sign he wasn't about to die, but he still lay on his bed morose and silent. How dare Nicola threaten him when he was on his possible deathbed, especially after he'd decided to put all their differences behind them.

'She's as gutless as her mother's always been,' he said to himself. 'She waits until now, until I'm weak and defenceless in this bed, before she comes to me with her accusations.'

He watched his wife as she dozed in her chair. When Nicola had left the hospital, after making her vile accusations, he'd been glad of Mary's company and support.

'It was terrible of Nicola to say those things,' she'd said, 'to do this to you when you're so ill. The doctor said you nearly died, that we're lucky to have you, and this is the way she behaves. I wish I'd never phoned her. There was me thinking she'd see this as her chance to make amends, and what does she do? She makes threats. But, there, don't you worry yourself, you concentrate on getting better.'

Mary had a tendency to ramble on, and this was no exception. Before long, he was regretting her presence and, because he didn't have the energy to tell her to be quiet, he closed his eyes and shut out her voice.

He concentrated, instead, on remembering exactly what it was that Nicola had said. The cocktail of drugs in his body had left him woozy, so he couldn't recall her precise words, but he was sure she talked about going to the police. He couldn't think what she'd have to tell them. He hadn't done anything except protect Nicola, look after her, be a father. He hadn't raped her, he'd loved her.

But beneath his drugged stupor, there was another, darker, apprehension. Something niggled in his stomach, making him feel unsteady, even from his bed. He couldn't be sure that it wasn't the drugs, but it left him so agitated he'd rather listen to Mary witter on than be in his own thoughts. Stephen opened his eyes again to give his full attention to her, but she'd fallen asleep. Mary's eyes were closed and her face had slumped forward onto her ample bosom. He watched her for a long time – the first time in many years that he'd taken the opportunity to really look at his wife. He remembered how beautiful she'd been when they married.

Over the course of their relationship, he'd helped Mary, little-by-little to dress better, wear her hair in a style that suited her better than the plain bob she'd always worn. By the time they were husband and wife, she always looked immaculate and well put together, but not in a showy way. The gaudy make-up and big hair of the other girls he'd courted made him think of black crows dressed up as parrots; their plumes were fake. Mary's plumage was natural and there'd been nothing pretend about her.

She was still an attractive woman, he conceded. Her skin had wrinkled and fallen, her body had formed a ring of fat he found distasteful, but, even with that, he saw she retained her natural beauty. If only she wouldn't talk so bloody much, he thought.

Nurse Maxwell came to administer Stephen's next dose of medication. After she'd syringed various liquids into the catheter on Stephen's hand, she busied herself plumping up pillows, checking the machinery and making perfunctory conversation.

'Your daughter was very upset yesterday,' she said, 'but she must be pleased you're going to pull through. Still, it's always a shock to see a loved one so poorly.'

'Yes,' said Mary vaguely, startled awake by the nurse.

'Well, you can tell her that she mustn't worry too much, Dad'll be up and about in no time.' Mary smiled half-heartedly. 'Right, Mr Johnston may be on the mend, but he still needs lots of rest. I dare say you could do with some as well,' she said to Mary in a tone that made it clear she was to leave the room. 'It's been a long day for you both.'

Stephen could only admire the efficiency with which Nurse Maxwell hustled his wife out of the ward.

In the days that followed, Stephen was as alert as he could be in case Nicola was true to her word and did go to the police with her lies. But as the outrage of Nicola's threats waned and there was no sign of any police contact, Stephen began to wonder if he'd imagined it.

As always, Stephen was woken early to be given his first round of medications. Afterward, he dozed off and on for a few hours, losing track of time until he was roused by unfamiliar voices. He thought a new patient must have come on to the ward and these were their relatives.

Opening his eyes, he saw a man and a woman standing beside the ward door, not far from his bed, talking to Dr Shackley. Stephen instinctively knew they were the police and his pulse quickened. What had Nicola said? Dr Shackley listened to the officers before his face registered surprise. Stephen watched him frown and think about what his best course of action would be, mentally running through his class notes on unusual procedures. After some more discussion, and still uncertain, Dr Shackley came towards him, followed by the couple.

The man was tall and broad, much as Stephen had been in his youth. He didn't look fit, but he did look strong, and, in his tailor-made suit, looked as intimidating as he intended to. The woman officer was tall and skinny, which Stephen found unattractive.

'Mr Johnston, how are you today?' Dr Shackley asked. Stephen could tell the police presence was making him jumpy. 'Feeling any better?'

He was feeling better, but nowhere near being able to manage a questioning by police. He didn't move, only stared at the couple.

'These two inspectors would like to have a chat with you. Do you mind if they ask you a couple of questions?'

Stephen shook his head. It would give him the opportunity to find out what Nicola had said to them.

The man moved to the bed and showed his ID. 'I'm Detective Inspector Brian Morton. This is Detective Inspector Gail Brown. Are you Mr Stephen Johnston of 42 Calderbeck Street?' Stephen nodded. 'Are you the father or Mrs Nicola Ramsey?' Stephen nodded again. 'Mr Johnston, are you able to speak?'

Stephen shook his head. The inspectors looked at each other and then Morton said, 'We'll need to talk to you when you're feeling better.' He looked around the cubicle, for what Stephen didn't know, before nodding in acquiescence to the doctor and leaving the ward, followed by DI Brown.

The knowledge that Nicola had gone to the police and made her vile accusations made Stephen feel vulnerable in a way he hadn't done since living in the children's care home.

As soon as his voice returned, Stephen demanded to be sent home, discharging himself against all advice. Despite having lost some movement in his arm, which may or may not return, and needing a lot of bed rest, Stephen was not dependent on any machines, so Dr Shackley reluctantly agreed. Before Stephen was discharged, however, Dr Shackley was obliged to call DIs Brown and Morton and let them know Stephen was fit enough for questioning. They came straight over.

This time it was DI Brown who led the conversation. 'How are you feeling, Mr Johnston? Dr Shackley tells me you've regained your voice and are about to be discharged. That's good news.' She smiled as she spoke, her manner friendly and expectant. Stephen didn't say anything, so she carried on. 'To remind you, I'm DI Gail Brown and this is DI Brian Morton.' They flashed their IDs a second time and pulled out their notebooks. 'For the record,' she continued, 'can you confirm you are the father of Nicola Ramsey, formerly of 86 Dalderse Road?'

'Yes,' he said.

'She has made an allegation against you. Do you have any idea what the allegation could be about?' Both inspectors watched him closely as they waited for a response.

Stephen shook his head.

It was Morton's turn to speak. 'She has accused you of sexually abusing her between the ages of four and fifteen years old.'

Stephen reeled. What was Nicola doing? After a moment, Brown asked, 'Do you deny the accusation?'

'Of course he does,' said Mary from behind them.

'Are you Mrs Johnston?' Brown asked, turning around.

'Yes, I'm Stephen's wife.'

'I need to ask you wait outside,' she said, moving towards Mary, 'while we ask your husband a few questions. It won't take long.'

'I think I should be with my husband,' said Mary, using all the courage she had.

'Mrs Johnston, please, I really must ask that you wait outside. But we would like to talk to you next, so don't leave the building.'

'It's alright, Mary,' Stephen said, not giving her a chance to refuse again.

'Only if you're sure,' she complied.

'Let me ask you again, Mr Johnston?' DI Morton resumed. 'Do you deny the accusation?' Stephen didn't say anything. 'Mr Johnston? Do you deny it?'

'Yes.' There was a hush as both inspectors made notes.

'Is there any reason you can think of why she would make the allegation?' DI Brown asked.

'Only that things have been...' Stephen searched for the right word, '... strained in our family over the past few years.'

'Strained? In what way?' Morton asked.

'I'm sure you know why, Inspector.'

'Humour me.'

'Nicola disappeared a few years ago,' said Stephen with a sigh of irritation.

'Disappeared?' Morton asked. Stephen nodded his head.

'Nobody knew where she'd gone. We thought she was dead. A few months ago, she returned, but she hasn't come to us. She refuses to see us, or even speak to us. And now this. So, as you can see, things have been strained.'

He'd said too much and was left a little breathless. The inspectors gave him a few moments to recover.

'How did you know she'd returned?' Brown asked.

'Ross.'

'Her husband?'

'Yes. Apparently, she just turned up at the house one day. He thought we'd want to know.'

'Apparently?'

'That's what he told us.'

'Have you any reason to doubt him?'

'No.' Again, notes were written.

'Do you know where Nicola was for those four years?' Brown asked.

'Ross said Shetland. I told you, she won't speak to us.'

'Can you think of anything that would have caused her to run away?'

'No. Except maybe that husband of hers.'

'You don't like him?' Morton asked.

'It's not that I don't like him, I just never understood what she saw in him. He's a bit, well, a bit namby-pamby. Never struck me as having much backbone. Still, she liked him.'

'Would you say that, growing up, Nicola had a good relationship with you and your wife?'

'As good as any other family. Why? What has she said?' Stephen's face had paled. He was still out of breath.

'Alright, Inspectors,' interjected Dr Shackley, 'that's enough for today. You can see he's tiring.'

'We'll leave it at that for now, Mr Johnston,' said Morton, 'but within the next couple of days, we'll need you to come down to the station and give a full statement.'

'A full statement about what?' Stephen was annoyed at being summoned like this.

'Mr Johnston,' said DI Brown, trying to hide her incredulity, 'your daughter has accused you of sexually abusing her over the course of eleven years. This is a very serious allegation, and one we shall investigate thoroughly. As part of that investigation, we will interview you. That interview will culminate in your statement. You do want the opportunity to defend yourself, don't you?'

Still breathing hard, Stephen stayed silent, but with a nod of his head he dismissed them.

After they'd gone, Stephen went through in his mind all the things Nicola might have said to make the police visit a man ill in hospital. The niggling feeling he'd felt in his stomach only a few days ago returned with a vengeance. He again felt unsteady and lay back down on the hospital bed. As the inspectors walked away, Dr Shackley said, 'Mr Johnston, I really don't think you're ready to go home. I advise you to wait another few days.'

'No,' said Stephen, watching Brown and Morton leave the ward. 'I want out of here.'

Next, Inspectors Morton and Brown were shown into a consulting room where they could talk to Mary in private.

'Mrs Johnston,' Brown said, 'your husband has been accused of sexually abusing your daughter, Nicola Ramsey, between the ages of four and fifteen years of age. She says that you knew about it. Is that true?'

'It's nonsense,' said Mary, her eyes darting this way and that, but never at the inspectors. 'Stephen would never do such a thing.'

'You're never felt Mr Johnston's behaviour towards your daughter to be inappropriate?'

'No, of course not. Stephen has always been a devoted father. He's taken more care than most fathers in Nicola's upbringing. I remember so many times when he helped her with homework, took her shopping or for ice cream. A couple of times he even took her away for the weekend. He's been devoted.'

Brown and Morton took down notes, and the scratching of their pens made Mary uncomfortable.

'How would you describe your relationship with Nicola?'

'Non-existent at the moment. You know she's been away? In Shetland? She came back to Glasgow just a few months ago but didn't come to see us.'

'That must have hurt?' Brown said.

'Yes, yes, it did.' Mary lowered her eyes.

'But you've seen her since?'

'Yes, we bumped into her in town one day. And, of course, she came to the hospital.'

'How do you feel about your son-in-law?' Morton asked.

'Ross? He's nice enough.'

'Did you approve of him?'

'Yes, I suppose so. He and Nicola got on, they were very much in love in the beginning.'

'Your husband isn't as keen on him as you are.'

'No, well, you'd have to ask him about that.'

'Why do you think they never got on?'

'I suppose Stephen never felt Ross was quite good enough. As I told you, Stephen adored Nicola. Perhaps nobody would have been good enough.'

'Thank you for speaking to us, Mrs Johnston,' Brown said. 'We'll need you to come down to the station at some point, to make a formal statement.'

'Must I?' she asked, obviously horrified at the thought.

Brown repeated the question she'd asked Stephen. 'You do want the opportunity to defend yourself, don't you?'

Chapter 17

True to her word, Claire did call, and we arranged to meet outside Byres Road underground station. I hugged her and wouldn't let go until she softened and returned my embrace. When we stood back to look at each other, it was clear we were both a bit weepy.

'I'm still angry with you,' she said, 'that hasn't changed.'

'I know.' I put my arm through hers, and we walked slowly towards Great Western Road.

When Ross and I were dating, and I was working at the university, my life revolved around the West End of Glasgow. It was a great place to be at that time, with lots of students and young graduates about to make their mark on the world. The shops were plentiful and cheap, just like the beer. These days the pubs had turned into bars, cafés into trendy coffee shops, and the secondhand stores had upgraded to vintage boutiques.

'Why did you do it, Nicola, why did you run away? I still don't fully understand and I want to.'

'I had a breakdown. I wasn't coping with anything and the only solution, as far as I could see, was for me to get out of all your lives. I felt Ross and Sam would be better off without me. I wasn't suicidal, I just needed everything to stop.'

'Ross was devastated. I've never seen a grown man cry like that.' My face flushed, and I looked at the ground. 'Couldn't you at least have let one of us know you were safe?'

'I should have, I know, but at the time I was struggling just to get through the day and then the longer I left it, the harder it became.' We walked in silence for a while. 'I understand more about my breakdown now, why it happened.'

'Tell me.'

'I developed post-natal depression after Sam was born but didn't realise it and so didn't get help. But what made it worse was that it brought to the surface memories from my past.' I took a deep breath. It was still a struggle to find the right words and say them out loud.

'What memories?' Claire prompted.

'Memories of abuse.'

'Abuse?' Confusion was etched on her face. 'You were abused?' I nodded.

'By Ross?' she asked.

'No, not by Ross,' I said quickly, 'by my dad. He sexually abused me when I was a child.'

'Oh God, Nicola, that's awful.' She hugged me tightly, and I didn't feel so isolated.

'When I left Ross, I'd hit rock bottom, I didn't know why and I didn't know what to do about it. I was carrying around so much hurt that eventually my body and my brain couldn't take any more and collapsed under the weight of it all. With time, I got myself together and came back to Glasgow. It was only when I saw Dad in hospital and could see that he was as mortal as you or me, and not some indestructible force, that I found the courage I needed.'

Talking about it still made me cry, and I wiped away my tears. 'When I told Ross he was amazing. He came with me to the police station when I filed a complaint against Dad. It was just about the most scary thing I've ever had to do, but I want him to pay for what he's done to me.'

We walked in silence for a while.

'I owe you an apology,' said Claire. I turned to her with surprise. 'I could see you were struggling, but I didn't do enough. I didn't realise things were as bad as they were. I should have tried harder. One of the reasons I was so angry with you was because I felt guilty.'

'Claire, stop.' I pulled her round to look at me. 'You have nothing to feel guilty about, absolutely nothing. I should have asked for help, Ross should have seen I needed help. We are the ones to blame for this mess, not you or anybody else.'

Now we were both crying. 'Look at us,' I said, smiling, 'both in tears and getting in everyone's way. Come on.' I put my arm through hers and pulled her onwards.

We reached the beautiful Kelvinside Parish Church on the corner of Byres Road and Great Western Road. No longer a place of worship, it was a theatre and bar. We crossed the road and headed into the Botanic Gardens. Eventually, Claire asked, 'Do you want to tell me about your dad?'

'It's not a nice story, but the gist of it is he abused me for a long time. I'd buried it away and thought I'd moved on with my life, that I was in control. What I've learnt is that until I face up to my past, Dad is in control. When I went to see him in the hospital, after the heart attack, it hit me that if he died, I'd never be able to put this to rest. I need to confront him and hold him accountable if I'm ever going to move forward with my life and be the best mum I can be to Sam.'

The sun had come out, and we sat down on one of the many benches lining the grassy lawns, watching passers-by. 'Now you've told the police,' said Claire, 'what happens next?'

'I have to go in and make a full statement.'

'When are you doing that?'

'Next week. I'm nervous about it. It's going to be more detailed and the thought of talking about it all makes me feel horrible inside.'

'Do you want me to go with you?'

'Thank you, Claire, but I have to do this by myself. I don't want anyone to hear what he did.'

'You're amazing,' said Claire out of the blue.

'What do you mean?'

'You've been holding in all that stuff about your dad, keeping it to yourself and being so strong. I don't know how you did it for so long. Whatever you need, Nicola, I'm here. I won't let you down again, I promise.'

'Thank you.' I felt weighed down by it all and needed something to lighten the mood. 'Let me buy you an ice cream.' For as long as I could remember, rain or shine, there had been a Mr Whippy ice-cream van parked in the Botanic Gardens. Mum used to bring me here during the school summer holidays and we often rounded the visit off with an ice cream and raspberry sauce.

'Does Sam know you're back?' Claire asked as we waited in the queue. 'Have you seen him?' I shook my head. 'Why not?'

'Ross won't allow it. He still doesn't trust me and is scared I'll disappear again.' Claire nodded and made a quiet sound of agreement. 'You think he's right to keep me away?'

Claire turned to look at me. 'Will you?'

'No. I'm in control now, not my dad.' I could see Claire trying to work out the right thing to do.

'I can understand his concern,' she said.

'I used to, but not anymore. He's been around me enough recently to know I'm not going anywhere. He knows I'm facing up to Dad and making things right there. I don't think it's fair of him to ex-communicate me like this.'

'He's being cautious, he's right to be. You must be able to see that?'

'I miss my son.'

We were at the front of the queue, and I ordered us two cones. After I'd paid, we wandered back to the bench.

'Ross says you're working in a hotel?' said Claire.

'The Strathclyde City Hotel, it's nice, I really like working there.'

'Quite a change from the library. Do you miss the university?'

'Sometimes, but, in all honesty, that feels like a different life. I don't think I could go back to it now. Things have changed in so many ways over the past four years. Instead of hiding away in the library stacks, or even in Shetland, I'm enjoying being in a busy hotel with all the comings and goings that are part of it. I'm ready to face the world.'

Claire laughed, 'Listen to you, you always did have a bit of the dramatic in you. Do you feel settled there?'

'On the whole, yes, but of course the divorce and being apart from Sam means I don't feel I can totally be at rest. And, if I'm honest, I'm a bit lonely. The people I work with are lovely, but they're colleagues, not really friends. A lot of them are young and go out a lot, others are older and have families of their own. Sometimes I feel in a bit of limbo, not one thing or the other.'

'You've got me.'

'I've missed you so very much, I'm so happy we're friends again.'

'Come over for dinner next week, Jamie would love to see you.'

'Are you sure, about Jamie, I mean?'

'Don't worry about him, he'll get over it.'

'I'd love that.'

'I'm freezing after that ice cream. Come on, show me this hotel of yours and I'll buy you a cup of coffee before you start work.'

We took a bus into the city centre and I gave her the grand tour before we headed into the lobby café for coffee and cake.

'Where are you living?' Claire asked once we'd sat down.

'I found a nice studio flat down by the river. I need to find a bigger place though, I need a bedroom for Sam.' I blushed, knowing that Sam may never use that room.

Eager to change the subject, I told Claire what Kwame Martins had said about getting out more, making more friends and building a stronger support network.

'Divorce or no divorce,' said Claire, 'that is bloody good advice. It'll be good for you to have something else to think about. What do you fancy trying? Most people join book clubs these days, but maybe you need something outwith your normal interests. Plus, I think book club is code for wine club. At least, mine is,' she smiled. 'What about a cookery class? Or a dance class?'

'Dance class, me?' I said, 'I don't think so, I've two left feet.'

'That's what everyone says about themselves,' Claire said, dismissing my excuses. 'Nope, dance class it is, but what sort of dancing is the question? I don't see you as a belly dancer and given this isn't for a hen night, we'll say no to pole dancing.'

I laughed and thought what a ridiculous conversation this was while Claire pondered my options.

'Hip hop!' She announced. 'Only joking,' she added before I could reply. 'Line dancing is what I really think would be perfect. Yeehaw and all that.' I looked at her doubtfully. 'It will be fun – good exercise, no tricky dance steps or fancy gear needed, it's perfect. In fact,' she said, 'I know of a class on Thursday nights. You know St Anthony's Church on Tiree Road? It's there.'

'Claire, I don't think it's a good idea.'

'Why?' she asked, suddenly serious. 'Because you've never done it before? Because it sounds silly? Because you won't know anyone?' I didn't respond. 'Aren't they the reasons to do it? You might enjoy it and you'd soon get to know people.'

'I'll think about it.'

'Right,' said Claire, looking at her watch, 'I've got to pick the kids up from school. I've been unable to get them into After School Club this term, which is a pain because I'm trying to get back to work.' Claire had worked in the HR department of an accountancy firm before having children.

'How is it going?'

'Badly. I've been out of the loop for so long I'm not even getting interviews for jobs I know I could do blindfolded. I might have to do some refresher courses to get my skills up to date.'

'It might be fun?' I suggested.

'I'm sure it would be, but they don't come cheap and we're not exactly flush at the moment.'

'If I can do anything to help, let me know. Maybe I could pick up the kids some days?'

'That's sweet of you, but I think you have enough on your plate right now, don't you?'

'How does Jamie feel about you going back to work?'

'I think he'd like me to stay home. His mum was a single parent, and he feels he didn't see enough of her because she was always working. He doesn't want that for Alisdair and Eilidh.'

'What do you want?'

'An easy life,' she laughed.

After Claire had disappeared down the street, I went back into the hotel to get ready for my shift. As I changed, I thought about what Claire had said about the line dancing class. It seemed a preposterous idea, something I would never have come up with myself. But was Claire right, was that the reason to do it?

I could hear my Shetland friend Shona telling me to do it.

'It's what you need,' she'd say, 'you need to get out of your comfort zone. That's when good things happen.'

Maybe she was right.

Chapter 18

All too soon, my appointment with the Sexual Offences Unit came around. Its very name made me feel sordid. I self-consciously adjusted my coat and bag before going in, feeling paranoid people were looking at me and that they knew why I was there.

Brown appeared from the same doorway she had done before, only this time she was with a colleague. They led me through to an interview room and arranged for me to be brought a cup of tea and a glass of water. We settled into our seats and I watched them both open expensive-looking leather-bound notebooks. These notebooks were the polar opposite to the small spiral bound one DI Brown used last time and looked like they meant business. For some reason they intimidated me and made me feel more nervous than before.

'Nicola, this is DI Bruce Morton. He works with me here at the Sexual Offences Unit and will be with us when you make your statement.'

DI Brown pressed a button on the video camera and I saw a small red light.

'Nicola,' she said, 'as you know my name is Detective Inspector Gail Brown and this is my colleague Detective Inspector Bruce Morton. We're going to take your statement today.'

'Okay,' I said, trying my best to listen to everything she said.

'It's important that you know you're in a safe place where everything you say is listened to and will be treated with respect. We may ask you questions about some of your statement, but that's only so we fully understand what you're telling us.' Both Brown and Morton smiled at me encouragingly in a bid to put me at my ease, but the longer their preamble went on, the tighter my stomach became.

'Okay,' I said again.

'Shall we begin?' Brown asked. I nodded. 'You stated in your last meeting with me that your father sexually abused you.'

'Yes.'

'How old were you when the abuse started?'

'I was about four years old. I don't think I'd started school. At first, he would just touch me, but in a way that didn't feel right. If he was getting me changed for bed, he'd tell me that he needed to look at my body to check everything was alright.'

'Do you mean that he'd look at your torso, your arms and legs?' asked Morton, speaking for the first time.

'No, he'd ask me to lie on the bed and open my legs. I remember if felt strange because Mum never did that and she put me to bed most nights.'

'At this stage, was he touching you or only looking?'

'I think he just looked. I wonder now if he was testing me out, seeing how biddable I was. Grooming, I think, is the word used now.'

'When did it progress from looking to touching?' Brown asked.

'I'm hazy about that, but I remember he would ask me to sit on his knee for a cuddle. He'd put his hand on my thigh, but that was okay, he was my daddy, but when...' I faltered, feeling my old shame raise up.

'You're doing really well,' said Brown. 'Remember, you've done nothing wrong.'

'He'd sort of cup my crotch with his hand, which I didn't like. And when he rubbed it, it felt wrong. I didn't like it, and I told him that. "No, Daddy, don't do that." He laughed and told me not to be so silly, that's how daddies show their love.' I felt foolish now, as it sounded like such an old trick. 'Why would I not believe him?' I asked, 'He was my father, he knew everything.'

'Don't be embarrassed, Nicola,' said Morton. 'This is a common ploy used by abusers. Always keep in mind that you were a child. Your father did this, not you. It wasn't your fault.'

Their understanding, the very fact they seemed to believe me, was like a floodgate opening. The relief that I wasn't alone in my gullibility, that other children had also believed the lies their fathers told them, was immense.

'I can't tell you what it means to be believed. For so many years, I was sure people would think I was making it up. That's what he always told me. Who would believe a child with a fanciful imagination over a grown-up who tells the truth?' I took a few moments to gather myself before we continued.

'In your last interview,' Brown went on, 'you said that your father had penetrative intercourse with you.'

I nodded, a vision of my father's face close to mine flashed across my eyes. I could still feel his stubble when he kissed my cheek and my neck, his suffocating weight on top of me. The memory forced me to take in an extra breath of air. 'How old were you when he first raped you?'

'Seven, maybe eight years old. I was still in primary school. Mum had gone away for the night, I can't remember why. He took me to the cinema and then for dinner somewhere. I had sausages and beans and chips, and ice cream for pudding. I didn't normally spend much time with Dad and to do stuff like that with him was special. I wished it could be like that with him all the time. Somehow, though, in the back of my mind, I knew that, when we got home, he'd want something in return.'

THE DAY SHE CAME HOME

That day, in the small interview room, was the first time I'd told anyone the full horror of what happened that night. I'd told Ross bits of it, but had missed out the details, for my sake, as well as his. Reliving the details of my abuse was terrifying and humiliating.

'How long did the abuse carry on for?' asked Brown.

'I was fifteen when it stopped. He came to my room and I just couldn't face it again. I'd reached my limit and started fighting him off. The first time it happened, I punched him and he got such a fright, he just left the room. The next time it happened, I came off worse. After a few of these fights, he stopped coming to my room. Instead, he called me names, ridiculed me. He wanted to punish me for saying no to him. Not long after that, I left home. I'd managed to save some money, and I stole some more from him. It was enough for a deposit on a crappy flat share. I signed on until I got a job and started to build my own life away from them.'

'Throughout this time, do you think your mother was aware of what was going on?'

'I didn't used to, but now I think she must have done. Even if she didn't know exactly what was happening, she must have had some idea things weren't right. But she's always been so terrified of Dad that, even if she did suspect something, I don't think she'd have said.'

'You say she's scared of your father?' asked Morton. 'Has he ever been violent with you or your mother?'

'When I was younger, he was. I used to hear him shouting at her, her being thrown across a room, things being thrown. I used to hide under my duvet and sing to myself, you know, to get rid of the noise. As I got older though, he only used to hit her when he needed to.'

'What do you mean, when he needed to?' I thought how best to describe my father and the dark, almost unquantifiable power he has.

'He's a big man. He's not just tall, he's strong and solid. But it's more than that. He has a presence, an inner confidence, I think it is, and people just seem to do what he says. Nowadays, he rarely raises his voice or threatens when he gets angry, he just looks at you and you find yourself doing whatever he's asked you to do. He can be so charming when he wants to be, a real smooth-talker. I remember other adults, strangers even, found it difficult to contradict him.'

'Can you give us an example?' asked Morton.

'When I was fourteen, I started selling cigarettes to classmates. Needless to say, the school didn't approve. My parents were called in to see the headmaster. I remember feeling, for a short time, smug because I knew Dad wouldn't be made to feel apologetic for his daughter. I could feel the tension in the office as he and the Head vied to be in control of the situation. Dad smiled and stared him right in the eye with a look that said, "Don't you dare contradict me," and, in the end, Mr McLeish backed down, apologised for bringing my parents into school and didn't suspend me. I think that was the first time I was properly aware of Dad's power. Mum didn't stand a chance.

'I remember how he used to talk to her, always calling her stupid, or useless, or a hindrance to him. He liked everything to be done just so, and he had trained her to do things the way he wanted. Meals were always the same, at the same time. He chose Mum's clothes. Mine, too. I used to leave clothes in my school locker and change there. I couldn't bring anything new home because he always checked my bag. Nothing got by him.'

I thought of my mum and what her life must have been like all these years, living with a man who controlled her every movement, made every decision for her and had sucked the very life out of her. For possibly the first time, I felt pity for her.

'Did you confide any of what was going on with a teacher or a friend?'

'No. I was a weird kid, I suppose. I didn't have many friends and I certainly never had anyone over to play or for sleepovers.'

'Why not?' asked Brown.

'How could I? I didn't want anyone knowing what sort of family I came from. Anyway, Dad would never allow it. He was always wary of my friendships, didn't like me getting too close to anyone.'

'What sort of social life did your parents have?'

'None, really. Dad would go to the Legion on a Tuesday night. Sometimes, if there was a function on, Mum would go too.'

'Does your mum have any friends of her own?'

'I'm not sure. When I was little, she used to invite some of the other mums over, but that seemed to stop. Actually, when I was a bit older, she did start going out to play at the whist drive. Maybe she made friends there, but, again, I'm not sure. I certainly don't remember anyone ever coming over to the house.'

'Were there any family members you could talk to?' asked Morton. I shook my head.

'Dad never knew his parents and Mum's are both dead.'

'Aunts and uncles?'

'Mum has one brother, but he's in Australia.'

'What we're trying to find out,' said Brown gently, 'is if there's anyone who can corroborate your story. A friend, a teacher, anyone, who you might have confided in at the time?'

I wracked my brains, desperate to dredge up someone or some incident that would be helpful.

'No,' I said at length, 'I can't think of anyone.' I had a sudden panic. 'Does that mean there is nothing you can do? Has this been a waste of time?'

'It's true that historical child abuse can be harder to prove, especially if there were no witnesses, or the victim didn't tell anyone at the time,' said Brown. 'But, no, this is absolutely not a waste of time.'

'What will happen now,' said Morton, 'is that we'll talk to the people you've mentioned, as well as any other friends and family who arise. Your statement is the foundation upon which we will build our case. Once we've gathered as much information as we can, we'll take it to the Crown Office and Procurator Fiscal. They will then decide if there's enough evidence to prosecute your father.' He let the information sink in before he cautioned me. 'If the Procurator Fiscal does decide to go ahead with the case, you may be called in as a witness. This would mean telling the court what you've told us, very possibly in the presence of your father.'

'That can be scary,' said Brown. 'It can be enough to stop a witness from taking the case forward.'

'Not for me,' I told them. 'I'm ready for this. I need to do this if I'm to move forward with my life. I need to do this for the sake of my son.'

Chapter 19

The next day, Ross surprised me at work. 'I wanted to know how you got on making your statement with the police yesterday,' he said.

'Actually, it was fine. Can you meet me when I finish at six?'

'I can't, I have to collect Sam from after-school club before then.'

'Give me five minutes while I get someone to cover the front desk.'

Outside, the weather was miserable. A thick rain was falling, and the clouds were low and heavy. Ross had an umbrella, and we huddled underneath it. In our pursuit of shelter, we ended up in the Old Fruitmarket and loitered in the foyer.

'Well?' prompted Ross, 'How did it go?'

'It was bizarrely cathartic. Telling them things and saying out loud what I've never said before was scary, but it felt like a step in the right direction. I feel like I've taken action.' I looked up at Ross, genuinely touched by his concern. 'Thank you for coming to check on me.'

'It's alright.' I noticed for the first time how anxious he seemed to be, as if he had something to tell me.

'What's wrong?' I asked.

'I had a tidy up and found these.' From a bag, he pulled out two notebooks. I recognised them immediately as the diaries I'd written when I was unwell. It had been an attempt to self-heal. I'd read it could help to put one's thoughts in order. I took them from Ross.

'Have you read them?' I asked.

He nodded. I was embarrassed and, while I couldn't remember exactly what I'd written, I was pretty sure it wasn't good.

'I didn't know what they were at first, but when I started reading, I couldn't put them down. Some of it is rambling, but, in other parts, you talk about your dad.'

'You shouldn't have read them, they're private.'

'Then you shouldn't have left them where I could find them.'

'I didn't, I hid them.'

'Yes, in Sam's room. How stupid was that? He could have read them.'

'He can't read.'

'He can now. He's six, remember, not two years old.' We'd both raised our voices and were suddenly aware of people watching us. 'Look,' said Ross in a calmer voice, 'the point is that the police might find them helpful.'

'You're right, I'm sorry. I need to get back to work,' I said, 'thank you for bringing these over.'

'There's nothing in the diaries to be embarrassed about,' said Ross, as if reading my mind. 'I'm actually glad I read them because it's helped me understand a little more about what you were going through.'

The rain was still falling as Ross walked me back to the hotel. 'I spoke to Cherry,' he said. Cherry was Ross's sister, and we had always got on, but she had a sharp tongue and I dreaded to think what she'd said about me over the past four years.

'Is she still in Byreburn?'

'Yes, but she and Wayne divorced.' We walked on in silence for a few moments.

'How's Sam?' I asked.

'Fine.'

'Have you told him about me yet?'

'Not yet.'

'You can't keep me a secret forever.'

'I know, I'm just not ready to tell him yet.' By now, we'd reached the hotel, and we said our goodbyes.

I locked the diaries away in my locker but couldn't keep my mind away from them for the rest of my shift. Not only in quiet moments did my mind drift back to what I might have written, but even in the middle of a conversation with a customer or checking bookings for the upcoming week. I should have been concentrating on the job at hand, but instead images of me lying on my bed writing jumped to the forefront. Sentence fragments appeared as if from nowhere, infiltrating where they weren't wanted.

At the same time as not being able to think of anything but those diaries, I wasn't one hundred percent convinced I wanted to read them. I knew they contained my darkest thoughts, at a time when I was already ground down in a quagmire. Would they reveal anything of use or would they simply be self-indulgent ramblings which I'd be ashamed of now?

As soon as I'd convinced myself I didn't want to read them, the ghost of a paragraph would loom and I'd be certain I must read the diaries. And as soon as I'd made that decision, I feared that perhaps they would contain something that would incriminate me. I didn't know what, but there might be something.

When I got home that night, I poured myself a large glass of Shiraz and sat down with my diaries. I stared at them for a long time but in the end I couldn't not read them.

20th March

Ross got home late tonight. No surprises where he's been. Whisky on his breath. Made me think of Dad. I always hated the smell of stale whisky, Dad stank of it. Stale. Like him.

28th March

I didn't get dressed today. It was too hard to decide what to wear. What was the point anyway? Not going anywhere. Sam will just puke on me or spill something on me. Someone once told me that if you don't wash your hair for long enough, it starts to clean itself. I wonder how long you have to wait.

30th April

I hate Ross. He's a lying, cheating, son-of-a-bitch. It makes me so sad. Why doesn't he love me anymore? Sex isn't everything. Why is it so important to him?? Why can't he take no for an answer? Just like Dad, making me feel guilty about everything. I'm not selfish, I just don't want to. Why does he need it so badly he'll risk our marriage? Marriage is more than just sex.

2nd May

Poor Ross. I'm such a horrible woman. He does so much for me, he's given me a beautiful home, a beautiful son and a good life. Why am I so unhappy? Why is it not enough? He deserves better than me. I've always been ungrateful. Dad always said that, and he's right. I'm just like Mum. Ross needs better. A better wife and a better mother for Sam. Sam. Sam. My baby, Sam. Today I forgot to make him lunch. I fell asleep and when I woke up, he was crying. I don't know how long he'd been crying for, but his face was red and blotchy. I gave him cereal. Not good enough. Must try harder. I looked at him when he was sleeping in his cot. I love him so much, but his crying is like a laser drilling through my brain. I just want him to go away.

22nd May

Bla bla bla. That's all I hear coming out of Ross's mouth. I look at him, but don't hear a single word he says. All he does is shout at me, all the time, and when he's not shouting at me, he's ignoring me. Dad, Dad, the staring man. When he's angry with me, he stares at me with his cold eyes sending rays of hatred until I can't take any more and will do anything to make him stop. He makes me feel so guilty for saying no, but I hate what he does, what he makes me do. I am so sure it's not right, but I don't want to ask anyone in case it is normal and it's me that's weird. I so don't want to be weird. It will just be something else I've failed at. I see Sam watching me, judging me, wishing he had another mum. A mum who's nicer, more fun. Better. Why can't I be better? I let Dad down, Ross down, and now Sam. Maybe they'd be better without me? Claire would be better than me. Or maybe the woman Ross' is sleeping with. He must prefer her to me. Maybe Sam would too. I should ask Ross. Yes, I'll ask Ross.

30th July

I've realised that I can't do this anymore. It's time to go. No one will miss me. I'm doing the right thing. A note will be enough to tell Ross I love him and I love Sam and not to worry. I am leaving so they can get on with their lives. They'll be happy and I'll know I've done the right thing. It seems so obvious now. I don't know why I didn't see it before.

It was startling to read those pages. In those notebooks was the voice of a past life, the voice of a person I recognised, but whose life has now been reincarnated. The diaries gave me perspective on how far I'd come since those dark days of isolation and self-loathing.

What it didn't say was what Dad had done. It didn't say anything about the abuse. If anything, it made Ross look like the bad guy. I blanched at the thought of him reading those words and believing I actually felt that way. I prayed he realised I wrote those things because I was ill, not because they were true. I remembered now that we had indeed argued a lot. He had grown increasingly frustrated with me because he couldn't help me, and I had grown resentful of his help because I didn't think I needed it. In the end I had what I thought was the answer, and that was to leave.

For this reason, I was disappointed with the diaries. They weren't going to be the game changer I secretly hoped they would be. There was no stark evidence, nor mention of anyone I might have told about the abuse. What was also startling was the fact I hadn't mentioned Mum at all. Her voice was absent. Was it worth taking the diaries to the police? Would they add anything to the case? I suspected not, all it would do was confirm I had been depressed and not thinking straight, but not why.

Maybe I would be better off giving them to Kwame. They might help with my custody case by demonstrating to the Sheriff that I had indeed been ill. I poured another glass of wine and made myself a sandwich. I needed to eat, but the diaries had left me with little appetite.

Underneath it all, however, I recognised I was ashamed of having felt the way I had. I didn't want anyone else reading these diaries and seeing me at my very worst. I didn't want someone judging how badly I had behaved and the extent to which I'd neglected Sam.

I phoned Claire and told her about the diaries.

'It must be awful to read those things, but remember that was the old you. Remember, you've found a new inner strength.'

'Yes,' I said feebly.

'One of the things you said to me when you came back was that you're a good person who went through a bad time. And that's true.'

'You're right, I'm sure you're right, but -'

'I am right. In the past you felt weak and out of control. Is that how you still feel.'

'No.'

'No. You're here fighting for a better life, a life in which you've put the sins of your father to rest, and in which you're the best mum you can be to Sam. Isn't that worth doing everything you can, even if it's uncomfortable or difficult?'

Again the words of my Shetland friend Shona rang in my ears, encouraging me to get out of my comfort zone, because that's when good things happen.

'What do you want to do with the diaries?' Claire asked.

'I'm going to take them to the police. They can make of them what they can.'

'Nicola,' said Claire, 'I'm really proud of you. No matter what happens with Ross, or with your dad, I'm proud of you.'

'Thank you, Claire, I cannot tell you just how much your support means to me.'

Chapter 20

Ever since Claire had told me about the line dancing class, the idea had tossed back and forth in my mind. I needed to make friends and having something for myself outside of work and Sam. My confident self argued with my nervous self, but, to my own disbelief, I found myself outside St Anthony's Church on Tiree Road that Thursday evening. A part of me hoped the class would be cancelled and I could go home again, but music was being played loudly inside so I forced myself to open the door and peer round.

It was quite a large hall with a stage at the far end. In the middle of the floor were four lines of about eight people, all of them moving in unison. Stepping inside, I closed the door behind me and watched the dancing. Most of the dancers looked to be retirees, people at least fifteen years my senior, and I inwardly despaired. At the front of the group was a middle-aged man leading the charge. He wore jeans, a gingham shirt, cowboy hat and boots. He shouted out the moves, and the group followed his instructions. Watching the posse of dancers more closely, I was relieved to see a few of them get their steps wrong, move a beat or two behind the others. At least, I won't be the only beginner, I thought.

Just as I was settling into a corner of the hall to watch, a woman pulled herself out of the troupe and came over. 'Hi, I'm Mags,' she said, 'welcome to Tony's Heel Diggers.'

THE DAY SHE CAME HOME

'Hi, I'm Nicola.' Mags had flame-red hair and a lively face, I couldn't help but smile at her.

'Are you new to line dancing?' she asked.

'I'm very new, I've never done it before.'

'Well, you'll love it,' Mags announced with the confidence of a woman who had heel dug for many a year and never grown tired of it. 'It's such fun and the people who come to this class are a crazy bunch.' This was a fact Mags was clearly proud of, although looking around the room, I wondered what the retiree definition of crazy might be.

Mags invited me to take off my coat, dump my bag and watch them for a while.

'You can join in when you feel the urge.'

I did as I was told and, after twenty or so minutes, and what felt, at the time, was against my better judgment, I got up on my feet and tagged on the end of a line.

The man to my right swapped places with me so that I had someone on each side to follow. I'd been dancing for only a few minutes when the music stopped and a tea break was announced.

From nowhere, a trolley was wheeled out, upon which was a large urn of hot water, cups, milk, tea and coffee. People milled around, grabbing a mug of something in between discussing a step they just couldn't master or generally catching up on the previous week's events.

'Kit Kats!' someone shouted. There were a few Oohs and Aahs as people dashed for the biscuits before they were all gone. The man who had swapped places with me invited me to the tea trolley. 'My name is Gavin,' he said.

'Nicola. As you can tell I've never line danced before.'

'Not to worry. Most people at this class had never danced before, but they soon picked it up. Isn't that right, Roy?'

Roy was the name of the man in the cowboy hat who had led the dances. I was relieved to see most people were wearing jeans and a T-shirt, just as I was. A cowboy hat and boots were not compulsory.

'That's right,' said Roy. 'I'm sure you will too if you decide to join our merry band. I take the class each week and, when I can't, my wife does. You've met Mags?' I nodded. 'We joined a class a number of years ago now,' Roy continued, 'but we didn't like the direction that group was going in, so we absconded with a few others and set this one up.'

'Who is Tony?' I wondered.

'Our Saviour,' Roy cried with a flourish. 'We're in St Anthony's Church Hall.' Gavin gave me a look as if to say don't mind him, he's a bit dramatic, but alright really.

During the break, a few more people came over to say hello and introduce themselves. I was genuinely touched by how welcoming they were. They asked me a little about myself and, more critically, my dancing experience, to which I answered as briefly and as honestly as I could.

Tea break over and it was back to the dance floor. Gavin placed me beside him once again. 'Just follow me,' he said. I tried my best to move my feet the way he did, clap when he clapped, turn when he turned, but it was so much more difficult than it looked. I was completely out of sync; my clap reverberated around the hall long after everyone else, and I turned a beat behind the others.

I felt myself getting more and more flustered, so keen not to make a fool of myself. In a bid to catch up with everyone else on a spin, I spun myself as fast as I could. The result was that I lost my balance and fell over, which in turn nearly tripped my neighbour over.

Wordlessly I got up and went to the side of the hall, trying to look like I wasn't bothered when in fact I was mortified. After I'd dusted myself down I felt a pain in my knee. Grateful for an excuse to hide in the toilets, I dashed into a cubicle. I pulled down my jeans to inspect my knee but there was nothing there but the beginnings of a bruise, nothing serious.

'Are you alright?' It was Mags. 'It looked like a nasty fall.'

'I'm fine,' I called, forcing a cheerful tone. 'Just a bruise, but that's all.' Coming out of the stall I put on a big smile, but Mags's sympathetic face made tears spring up and I was embarrassed all over again. 'I don't think I'm cut out for this,' I told her.

'Nonsense,' she said. 'This is your first time line dancing. Of course you were going to find it hard. I know what people think when they see the dancing on television, they think the steps are really simple and I'm sure some people even think it's not proper dancing. But I can assure them it's way harder than they think.'

'I'm not sure I'm ready for it.'

'What do you mean?' She looked so earnest that I fleetingly thought about opening up and telling Mags all about Ross and Sam and my father. But rather than scare her, I said, 'I've got a few things going on in my life at the moment and I thought this would be a nice change. But maybe I'm not ready to take on any new challenges at the moment.'

'Don't let the fall put you off. Every one of us has tripped up or fallen over at some time. How can we help it with such tricky footwork and fast routines?' I was still reluctant. 'Come on,' she said, 'give it one more chance and if by the end of the night you still don't like it, well, fair enough. Come on out when you're ready.' She gave me a wink of encouragement before leaving me.

Shona's voice went through my head again and I felt I couldn't let her down. I took a deep breath and headed out. To my relief nobody said a thing except Gavin who came up beside me and asked quietly, 'Are you alright?'

'Yes, thank you.'

Very quickly after that I learned how to Heel Dig and Grapevine, and by the end of the class, I was flushed from the exercise and tired from the concentration involved. I was elated to have been part of the class and to be mastering something new.

Mags joined me as I put my coat on. 'Did you have a good time?' she asked, eager to know I had, and I was able to answer in the affirmative. 'Will you come next week?'

'Yes, I'd love to.'

'That's great news. We can sort out membership details then.'

It was with a light heart I made my way home, chuckling to myself that of all things, I never would have envisaged myself a line dancer. It was invigorating to have had some exercise and meet new people, but more than that I had enjoyed it. Despite my fall, I had genuinely had a good time. It was pleasing to know I'd be able to report back to Kwame that I was making new friends and that my manager was supportive of my workplace changes. It felt like things were coming together.

Chapter 21

It was late October now. Autumn was well and truly with us. Over the last week or so, the temperature had fallen, and the trees had dropped their leaves in response. This morning though, there was a burst of sunshine and the air felt warmer than it had for days. The walk to work was so pleasurable that I took the scenic route, if it can be called that, along the river, before turning left up The Saltmarket as far as Ingram Street. There I turned left again towards Brunswick Street and the hotel.

My thoughts dipped in and out of what Sam might be up to at this time of day and invariably wandered to the diaries and whether or not they would help my case. I'd handed them in to DI Brown and she'd been very interested in them but hadn't come back to me with any feedback as yet. Despite efforts not to, I was getting anxious to hear from her.

In fact, the waiting was an aspect of this whole business I was finding increasingly frustrating. I didn't feel like I was being told anything about the investigation. Brown and Morton had explained to me that I was now regarded as a witness. That wasn't enough for me. It was my family and life they were investigating, after all. I felt I had a right to know what was going on and that I was more than just a witness.

I'd been in to the Bothwell Street Police Station to ask for Brown a couple of times to get an update, but either she hadn't been there or had, in the nicest possible way, fobbed me off. I was pissed off, but Claire said it was probably a good thing.

'Let them get on with it,' she'd said last night.

Claire and I had finally managed to arrange for me to go round for dinner. It had taken a while because Jamie was still angry with me. On the evening itself he was a bit off with me, despite Claire's instructions to be nice. At first he found it difficult, I could tell, but as early evening turned into night, he'd relaxed and I could feel we were making progress.

Despite the initial awkwardness, I enjoyed being in a family home again, with all the energy and chaos that comes with it. I felt nostalgic for my life with Ross and Sam and for what could have been. We finished eating and Jamie took Alasdair and Eilidh upstairs to get ready for bed, while Claire and I went through to the living room.

'Let them get on with the investigation and you get on with rebuilding your life. You said your lawyer advised you to prepare in case you get joint custody of Sam, how's that going?'

'Good,' I said, sipping my coffee. 'I've nearly saved enough deposit for a two-bed flat, plus a bit more for any decorating and furniture.'

'That's brilliant. Let me know if you need anything, we might have some kids' stuff we don't use any more. What about your shifts at work?'

'Honestly, they've been amazing. I think they're happy with my work, so are being flexible. I told my boss what's happening, told her I want joint custody and would need to prove to the court I can be available when Sam is with me. She said we can work something out. And get this,' I couldn't hide my pride, 'my manager, Dawn, says she'd be happy to testify how good and reliable an employee I am. You know, a character reference.'

'Wow, Nicola, that shows just how much you've pulled yourself together.'

We sat quietly for a moment and listened to the noises upstairs as the kids got ready for bed.

'Claire, you have fantastic kids,' I said, 'really, they're lovely. Eilidh is the spitting image of you.'

'I know,' Claire blushed a little, 'she really is a mini-me. She comes out with things and I cringe because I know she's heard me say it.'

'You must have been pregnant with her when I left?'

'I was, but I hadn't told anyone yet. Actually, her birthday is coming up and we're having a small party. Ross and Sam are coming. I would have invited you too, but, given how things are at the moment...' She let the sentence hang in the air, unfinished. This was how things would be from now on, I realised, with any of our mutual friends who still wanted to know me. They'd be caught in the middle of our divorce and would have to make a choice about whether to invite me or Ross to any given event.

'Claire, I was wondering,' my hands were suddenly hot and clammy, 'if you would also consider being a character witness? It would be great to have someone who knew me before my illness and can see how well I am now.' I held my breath.

It was Claire's turn to look embarrassed.

'I'm so sorry, Nicola. Ross already asked me if I'd be a witness for him, you know, to tell the court how well he coped after you'd gone.'

I felt the floor shift underneath me and had to put my hand on the arm of the sofa to steady myself. 'It's alright, really, it was just on the off chance.' I felt so stupid, of course Ross would ask her, it was naïve of me to think he wouldn't.

'I'm really sorry, Nicola, I'm not taking sides, I promise, but he asked and I couldn't say no.'

'It's alright, really.' Embarrassed, I shook my head back and forth as if to deny I'd even asked the question. 'I understand, think no more of it. Listen, thank you so much for dinner. It's been lovely to sit down and have a family meal again. It's getting late though and you need to put the kids to bed, I'll get out of your hair.'

I stood up and gathered my things together, unable to meet Claire's eye.

'Nicola, don't be like this, you don't have to go, honestly.'

'I'm fine, honestly.'

'If you'd asked first, of course I'd have said yes.'

'I know, it's just that you're the only person I can ask. I've lost touch with everyone else from my past.'

'What about your mum? Or an old work colleague?'

'I'll figure something out, please, don't give it another thought.'

By now, I had my coat on and was at the door.

'That's right, run away.' Claire's tone stopped me dead. 'Isn't this what happened last time? You ran away?' Horrified, I turned to face Claire, unable to believe she'd said what she said. Her face was stony. 'Don't look at me like that. It's the truth, isn't it?'

'How can you say that? I thought you understood?'

'I do, or at least I thought I did. But here you are, fully recovered and you're still running away when things get hard.'

'That's not true.'

'Then why are you running away now?'

'I'm not,' I said, with no conviction.

'Yes, you are. This is just like the day you left Sam with me. You could have reached out for help, talked to me, instead you ran.'

'I have asked you for help and you've said no.'

'I've said I can't, not because I don't want to, but because I've already made a promise. If you had asked me first, I would have been a witness for you. You're choosing not to hear that.'

I was mute.

'Nicola, you are so exasperating.'

'What do you mean?' I shifted my weight to one leg, my hand on my hip.

'You're making too big a deal of this.' I was about to protest, but she beat me to it. 'It's your dramatic side, I get it, you can't help it.'

'Don't patronise me.'

'Then don't behave so childishly. I'm your friend, I love you and want to help. Right now, the only way I can see to help you is to be honest. You're under a lot of strain right now, I know, but don't push me away.'

Any anger and indignation I had originally felt disappeared, and I collapsed in another flood of tears. 'I'm so sick of crying,' I told her. 'That's all I've done since I got back to Glasgow. I felt so strong before returning, but that strength is being chipped away at every week. I feel like I'm jumping through hoop after hoop and not getting any further towards Sam.'

Claire put her arms around me and let me cry. 'Why me?' I asked her. 'Why did he have to be my dad? What did I do wrong that he'd want to do those things to me? It feels so unfair. All I've ever wanted was a normal life, and I seem to be unworthy of even that. What did I do wrong?'

To her credit, Claire didn't try to appease me by providing answers or explanations, because there weren't any. My life was what it was, and that was all there was to it. Like a child, she led me back to the kitchen and made me a mug of sweet tea. 'How do you feel?' she asked.

'Better. Thank you.'

'I know you don't feel it, but you really are making progress. You have a job, a home, a relationship, albeit tentative, with Ross. You have reported your father. You have achieved a lot and it will come together when the time is right.' She was right, I didn't feel that way. 'Even our argument,' she continued, ' is progress. We would never have said those things to each other in the past, but I'm glad we said them because it shows our friendship is strong enough to handle it.'

'I feel utterly...' I searched for the word, 'despondent. I thought I was past all this.'

'Maybe you're never truly past it.'

'Oh God, I hope that's not true. I don't want to feel like this for the rest of my life.' I half laughed, able now to see how funny and tragic this was all at the same time. I dried my eyes, finished my tea and headed to the door.

'I don't know if I can get through this,' I said. 'It's so hard.'

'It is hard, but you will get through it.'

'Will I?'

'Yes,' she said with certainty. 'I love you,' Claire said, giving me a hug. 'Take care of you.'

Chapter 22

The surprise of Mum accosting me in the street and my renewed disappointment in her stayed with me for days to come, so much so that on my next day off, I took a train out of the city and headed north to Aberdeen. I needed to feel the strong North Sea wind whipping around me, pushing me one way and then the other. I headed to the pier and sat in the cold. I liked feeling the numbness work its way through me. My brain and my body slowed down.

I closed my eyes and listened to the gulls talking to one another, squabbling over scraps of food. I listened to the boats chugging in and out of the harbour, the chatter and laughter of the fishermen. I could smell diesel mixed with the slightly rotting smell that accompanies the sea. Salt and seaweed. Aberdeen was a long way to come, but it was worth it.

'Fit like?' a voiced knocked me into the present. I must have looked bewildered, and the man said, 'Are you alright?' His Aberdonian accent was strong.

'Yes, fine, thanks.'

'If you're sure?'

'I'm sure.' I smiled to let him know it was safe to leave. Perhaps he thought I was suicidal. He wasn't to know it was this anonymity on a blustery harbour that renewed my zest for life and stopped me from heading down the wrong path.

I don't know how long I sat there, but by the time I left, my body was frozen to the marrow, however my spirit was lifted. I walked back into the town centre to warm up my limbs with a large bowl of soup and a chunk of freshly made, crusty white bread. Afterward, I pottered around the town, popping in and out of the little boutique stores. I went into one that sold beautifully made wooden toys. A hanging mobile with dinosaurs on it caught my eye, and I pictured it spinning in the bedroom Sam would have in our new flat together. I looked at the price tag and winced, but my need to feel close to him in whatever way I could outweighed my need to be frugal and I bought it. It would be my talisman for our future.

At the train station, I purchased a coffee before stepping aboard. My good spirits carried me all the way home to DIs Brown and Morton, who were waiting for me at my flat, and I was convinced it meant they had good news.

'This is a surprise,' I said, 'do you have an update for me?'

'We'd like to have another chat with you,' said Morton.

'Sure,' I said, 'come on in.'

'At the station,' Morton's tone drew me up short.

'Is something wrong?'

'Let's talk at the station,' said Brown gently.

We were silent as we drove. I wracked my brains to work out what they looked so serious about. Why they couldn't talk to me at home? What could my parents have said to provoke such a change in attitude from them?

Something told me I was being treated as a criminal now, not as a witness. 'I want a lawyer.' I said from the back of the car and Brown nodded.

'That can be arranged,' she said.

In the interview room, there was no offer of coffee, only a cup of water. The atmosphere had changed. Empathetic looks of encouragement had been replaced with formal stares of observation. Soothing tones were replaced with an abrupt, clipped interrogation.

There was no video recorder this time, as, after all, this wasn't my formal statement. Instead, Brown switched on the audio recorder and went through the preliminaries while the duty solicitor sat next to me, looking over the notes of my case. He looked young, and he looked flustered. He didn't inspire confidence, but I didn't have any other choice.

'Why didn't you tell us you were a missing person?' asked Morton as soon as Brown had finished. I was taken aback by his aggressive tone, but understood immediately that they were pissed off, thinking I had deliberately withheld this information from them.

'I wasn't hiding it from you.'

'Oh, really, that fact that you left your husband and son for four years, without one word, just slipped your mind, did it?'

'No, of course not. The interview was so focused on my childhood, it never came up.'

'Well, let's talk about it now, shall we?' I understood that Morton felt he should have known from the beginning, but his manner was unnecessarily aggressive. I hadn't left him, after all.

'Alright,' I said, 'What do you want to know?'

'When did you leave your husband?'

'The summer of 2012.'

'Where did you go?'

'Shetland.' I could tell by his response he knew all this, he just wanted to hear it from the horse's mouth.

'What did you do there?'

'I worked in a local hotel.'

'How long were you there for?'

'Four years. I came back to Glasgow in May.'

All this time, Brown said nothing. She just watched me. Finally she asked, 'Why did you leave your husband and son?'

'I had a breakdown. After Sam was born, I developed post-natal depression.' Saying the words out loud made my throat catch and had to pause for a moment. One tear escaped and, feeling foolish, I wiped it away. 'But really, I think it was my past catching up with me,' I carried on. I looked them both in the eyes, wanting them to understand. 'You hear a lot about victims of abuse turning to alcohol or drugs to forget about what happened to them. They want to sink into oblivion, they don't care about their lives. Some would be happy if they died, as it would put an end to their misery.'

Brown and Morton's expressions told me they'd encountered a few like that in their careers. 'Well, that wasn't me. I coped by staying in control of every other aspect of my life. My bedroom was immaculate, I controlled what I ate and how much, I was the best I could be at school, I never drank, I saved every penny I earned because one day I would escape and have my own life in which my parents would have no part.'

'That included selling cigarettes behind the bike shed?' Morton said.

'Yes, it did.'

'And leaving home, building your own life, that worked?' Brown asked.

'For a time. I met Ross and fell in love. We got married and had Sam. That's when it started to unravel. The compartments into which I'd placed my life blurred. The emotions that come with being a parent jumbled in my brain and I lost that control. I broke down.'

'So you ran away?' Morton said.

'It's not easy for others to understand,' I said to him. 'Depression is not simply about cheering yourself up with a bit of retail therapy. It's deep inside.' I prodded my sternum so hard it hurt. 'I didn't leave for my own benefit, I left for theirs.'

'Why do you say that?' Brown asked.

'Because I was failing at everything. I was failing at being a mother, I was failing at being a wife. I thought Ross had begun an affair-'

'You were punishing him?' Morton jumped in.

'No, not at all. I didn't blame him, as, after all, I was a useless wife. Why wouldn't he look elsewhere?'

'So are you saying you thought they'd be better off without you?'

'Yes.'

'And now you're miraculously better?' said Morton.

'Of course not,' I raised my voice, by now fed up with his dismissal of what had been one of the hardest periods of my life. 'It took four long years to rebuild myself, to come to terms with my childhood and understand that if I'm ever going to move forward with my life, if I'm ever going to be the best mum I can be, I need closure with my parents and that includes Dad taking responsibility for the abuse he inflicted on me. Can you understand that?'

'No,' said Morton. 'I can't. Instead, it sounds to me like you ran off because you thought your husband was having an affair. You wanted to punish him. And now you feel bad, so you've made up this story about your father to get yourself off the hook.' I was winded, breathless. It was too close to what my father had always said would happen, that nobody would believe me. 'Why didn't you just have it out with Ross, divorce him? Why abandon your son into the bargain?'

'How can you say this to me?' I was horrified. 'After everything I've told you, how can you be so cruel?'

I couldn't stop the tears now, my head was in my hands, the shame of being branded a liar was as powerful as I imagined it would be.

'You talk of cruelty, yet you bring this accusation when your father has only just been released from hospital. You wait until he is defenceless, at death's door, before you come to us because you know he won't be able to defend himself.'

'That's not how it happened.'

'Nicola,' said Brown, 'you have to admit the timing of your accusation is questionable.'

'It's just like he said it would be,' I wept. 'He said nobody would believe me and he was right. You've proved him right.'

They let me cry for a while, which was just as well because I couldn't stop.

'Nicola,' said Morton, this time in a condescending voice which made me hate him in that instant. 'Why don't you tell us what's really behind all this?' I looked at him and wanted to argue, but I'd run out of fight. 'Isn't this what happened?' He continued. 'You punished Ross for cheating on you by running away. And now you're punishing your parents because you never got on with them, resenting the strong stance they took in your upbringing. It seems you've never dealt well with not getting your own way.'

'You'd love to believe that, wouldn't you?' I said. 'It would make your job much easier. Case shut. No rooting around. A case that's hard to prove and might not get you anywhere. Too much work with no guarantee of a promotion.' Neither Brown nor Morton said anything, but they waited for me to carry on, no doubt hoping I'd dig myself into a hole, when from out of nowhere I realised something. 'What is it, Detective Inspector Morton? Why are you so angry with me? Is it because your own wife left you for another man and you're taking it out on me?'

Brown's response told me I was right.

'Let's stick to the case,' she said, before Morton could reply.

'Have you spoken to my father?' I demanded.

'Yes.'

'So you know what he's like. You've felt how he dominates a room. I doubt his stint in hospital has softened him any. Can you imagine being his daughter, his four- or five-year-old daughter, and saying no to him? Even if I'd had the strength of mind, I certainly didn't have the strength of body.'

'Nicola,' Brown said, 'it's clear that your childhood was not an easy one, that you didn't always get on well with your parents. The trouble we're having is finding anything in your past that supports an allegation of abuse.'

'That doesn't mean it didn't happen.'

'It does mean it's hard to prove.' Brown could see I had nothing left to offer them. 'Let's call it a day for now,' she said, 'but we'll have to speak to you again, Nicola.'

I felt light-headed as I left the station. The fresh night air hit me full force after the stuffy air-conditioning of the station. The interview with Brown and Morton left me feeling trapped, like I'd hit a new brick wall. I'd been struggling to stay positive but had just about managed to with help from Claire. Little by little I was regaining control of my life and laying the foundations for my future with Sam, but after this interview it seemed all that hard work was ebbing away. Morton clearly didn't believe a word of what I'd told him. Between the police and Mum, I felt I was being backed into a corner with no way out. I couldn't think what else to do or say to make them see the truth.

At home, I made some toast as it was all I could stomach. I also pulled a bottle of vodka out of the freezer and downed two shots in quick succession. It was enough to make me drowsy.

Before I crawled into bed, I hung up the mobile I'd bought for Sam and, watching it spin and dance, it wasn't long before I was asleep.

Chapter 23

They say trouble come in threes and the third thing to go wrong came in the shape of my father. He caught me unawares by following me in his car one morning. I was heading to the bus stop on my way to meet Claire and her kids at Pollok Country Park and he drew up parallel to where I was walking, rolled down the window and shouted for me to get into the passenger seat.

'No,' I said. 'Go away. I don't want to talk to you.'

'Don't be so bloody ridiculous, I'm your father, get in the car.'

By now, I had reached the bus stop, and people were staring at us. I did my best to ignore him, hoping he'd give up and drive away.

Instead, he stopped the car, struggled out of the driver's seat and bellowed at me.

'Do as you're told and get in the car. Do you want to make a scene?' I looked around again. People had stopped what they were doing, openly watching the drama unfold. A bus pulled up behind the car and the driver beeped his horn, shouting obscenities. Shame, my old companion, reared its head and I got in. We drove away in silence.

'What do you want?' I eventually demanded.

'For you to stop all this nonsense.'

THE DAY SHE CAME HOME

'It's not nonsense. I want you to pay for what you've done to me. Everything bad that's happened to me in my life began with you.'

'Don't be such a child. You're the one who ran away, you're the one who feels guilty and is now looking for someone to blame.'

'Is that what you told the police?'

'Of course. It's the truth.'

'No, it's not. You are the reason I had a breakdown.'

'A breakdown, what pish and nonsense. You discovered marriage and parenthood are difficult and you ran away. You're a coward.'

'Nobody could accuse you of being a coward, could they? You have bullied your way through life, first Mum and then me.'

We stopped at the traffic lights.

'Stop whining. You can say what you want about me, but I stuck by you and your mum. It wasn't always easy, believe you me, but it was my duty – my duty – to support you both.'

'I don't believe you. I think this is because you knew you'd never find another woman who would let you treat them the way you treat Mum. Let me out.'

Dad was breathing heavily and perspiring. Not long out of hospital, he shouldn't have been driving around Glasgow picking fights. I turned to look at him and realised he was panicking. He'd come to find me, to force me to take back my allegation, but I wasn't the pushover I used to be.

'Do you really want to go through with this? Do you really want all our friends and neighbours to hear your stories?'

'I've done nothing to be ashamed of.'

'Oh no?'

'No,' I said, and I believed it. None of this was my doing, I need not be ashamed.

'Won't they ask why you didn't tell anyone? A teacher or a friend? Won't they ask why you didn't run away?'

'I've done nothing wrong.'

'It's because there was nothing to run away from. You had a good home, where you were looked after and loved.'

'I've done nothing wrong,' I repeated.

'All too quickly the police will see you're an ungrateful, spoilt child and you'll be laughed out of court.'

'That's not true.'

'And for what? For nothing, that's what, because you'll still be the only person to blame for you abandoning your child.'

'Don't say that, I didn't abandon him.' Even as I said it I knew that was how he and everyone else saw it. Only I seemed to understand that wasn't the case. 'I did not abandon my son, I removed myself before I could hurt him, which is what you should have done for me. You should have removed yourself.'

'Who would have taken care of you then? Your mother? Ha! Don't make me laugh. She can barely get out of bed in the morning without being told to. How could she have raised a child by herself?'

'She'd have found a way. She's only the way she is because you've browbeaten her, told her everyday she's useless. Of course, she believes it.'

He swung the car over to the kerb and slammed the brake so forcefully that we both jolted forward in our seats. He grabbed my hair, pulling my head back. I tried to resist, but even in his weakened state, he was too strong for me.

'I want you to stop this fucking nonsense.' His face was only inches from mine. His voice was low and menacing, and memories of the past flooded my mind. I was immobile, unable to get out of the car or even push him away. For the first time, I felt genuinely scared. I closed my eyes tight. 'I've told you I don't know how many times, that nobody will believe you. And they don't.' He clamped his other hand around my jaw, forcing me to face him. I felt his breath on me, I smelt the stale whisky. Suddenly, his grip relaxed, his finger traced my cheek and jawline. 'You were such a beautiful child,' he said, 'I never could believe I had produced such a beautiful wee girl.' I opened my eyes. 'How could you do this to me?' he said.

He looked so hurt. His voice was so uncharacteristically gentle that I wondered for a second if he was having another heart attack. 'How could you treat me and your mum so badly?' His voice hardened again, as did his grip. 'I gave you everything and then you leave home, out of the blue, and we hardly ever see you again. You abandon your child and now this?' He moved his face even closer. 'Look what you've made me do.'

I don't know what possessed me, perhaps desperation, but I spat in his face. He was so surprised, he let go, and I scrambled out of the car as fast as I could. I stood there on the pavement, ready to run if I needed to. But he stayed where he was, slumped in the car. He looked pale and clammy. Coming after me had taken it out of him. He looked at me with loathing before, to my relief, he drove off.

I breathed heavily as I walked down the road. I needed to keep moving, to keep my body in action, in case it collapsed under the weight of my assault. All of a sudden, I felt nauseous, went to the kerb and was sick. I was literally sick with fear.

How did my father know where I lived? Would he come back? I looked at my hands and they were trembling. I clenched my fists to make them stop. As a child, I'd made the mistake of not telling anyone about my abuse, I couldn't do that again so pulled out my phone and called Brown.

'Hello, DI Brown,' she announced.

'It's me, Nicola Ramsey.'

'Is everything alright?'

'No, no, it's not.' I tried to keep calm, but I could feel panic rising in my voice. 'Dad was here. I don't know how, but he found me and threatened me.'

'Nicola, calm down and start from the beginning.' I took a deep breath and steadied myself against a parked car.

'Dad has found out where I live. He waited for me then followed me down the street.'

'When was this?'

'Now, just now.'

'He's had a massive heart attack, he's in no fit state to be running around the city.'

'He was in his car, he followed me in his car. He was shouting and everyone was looking. I didn't know what to do, so I got in.'

'You got in the car?' I could hear disappointment in her voice.

'I wanted him to stop shouting at me,' I said defensively, 'Everyone was staring.'

'What happened when you got in?'

'He drove away, we argued. He said nobody would believe me, and I'd still be blamed for leaving Sam. He's right, you don't believe me and Ross still blames me.'

'Nicola, where are you? Stay there, I'm coming to get you.'

By the time she arrived, I'd stopped crying, but the sight of her made me start again.

'I don't know what to do,' I told her.

'Get in,' she said, and she drove us to a nearby café where she bought me a cup of tea.

'Nicola,' she said, 'I do believe you. I believe your dad abused you and your mum did nothing to stop him. I believe you.' Her expression told me she wasn't just pacifying me, that she really did.

'I don't know what to do.'

'You'll come to the station and give us a statement. Then you'll carry on with your day. If he turns up at your door again, don't speak to him. Take a photo of him on your phone and call me.' I nodded and took a deep breath. The hot tea was kicking in, reviving some of my strength. 'In the meantime,' Brown continued, getting out her phone, 'I'll get Morton to speak to your dad.'

THE DAY SHE CAME HOME

As we left the cafe, I remembered I was supposed to have met Claire at Pollok Park. I called her straightaway.

'Claire, I'm so sorry,' I said immediately.

'What happened?' she asked, 'We hung around for a while, but eventually the kids got fed up so we've come home.'

'Dad turned up at my flat and threatened me.'

'That's awful, I'm so sorry. Are you okay?'

'I called DI Brown, and she collected me, she's with me now. I'm going down to the station to make a statement. Can we rearrange? I really do want to see you.'

'Do you want to stay with us tonight? If you're feeling unsafe, you're more than welcome.'

'It's okay, thank you. I'll be fine. I'm a bit shaken, but I'll be fine.'

After we hung up, Brown drove me to the station, where I made a formal statement. Afterwards, the motion of the walk home calmed my body, which in turn calmed my head. I was fine, I realised. Dad had scared me and I'd relived, for those few minutes, the fear I'd felt as a child. But here I was, coping, staying strong and able to deal with this. I knew now I could take on anything Dad had to throw at me because I wasn't alone. I just had to reach out and help was there.

Chapter 24

I flung myself into work over the next week, taking on any extra duties I could. I didn't want to leave any space to dwell on the case or my impending divorce. Although I wasn't afraid of Dad anymore, it wasn't so easy to rid myself of the shame I'd felt all these years. It hung around the edges of my mind, old memories inculcating themselves as I checked a guest in at reception, made a stock order, listened to a complaint or gave someone directions. It was driving me crazy, and I needed something positive to focus on.

'Why don't you start flat hunting?' suggested Claire. 'You've got the money saved, what are you waiting for?'

'I guess I don't want to jinx anything,' I said, 'I feel like as soon as I put down a deposit on a place, fate will come along and kick me in the stomach.'

'Keep thinking about what your lawyer said about getting yourself in a position that you're ready for Sam to come home with you.' It was my meal break at work and we were talking on the phone. I could hear dishes being moved around in the background and guessed Claire was clearing up after the kids' lunch, throwing into contrast my own domestic affairs, which usually involved a microwave ready meal or a hastily thrown together pasta dish.

I was never a great cook, but making a meal for a family felt much more worth the effort than for one person. Every now and again I'd plan and prepare a nice steak, or a good piece of fish, or even create a delicious stew, but it wasn't often because I found it depressing to sit down to a carefully crafted dinner for one, accompanied by a tiny bottle of wine for one. It seemed only to highlight how alone I was. I didn't know I could be envious of someone with washing up to do.

'You're right,' I said, 'I know you are. I'm scared, that's all.'

'How are things with Ross?' I heard a tentativeness in her voice. The topic was still a little sticky since she'd told me she was being a character witness for him.

'The divorce is still going ahead. A hearing date has been set for the end of December. Just in time for Christmas,' I said sarcastically. 'It feels so soon.'

'I'm sorry, Nicola, I know it's not what you want.'

After work, I headed west, walking up Great Western Road towards Byers Road. It was an area I knew so well because it's where I'd lived after I left home, and for many years after that. It was close to the town centre, and the University of Glasgow was situated there, where I would later work. What would it be like to live here again? I wondered.

It amazed me how many places had changed. There was a succession of new shops and hairdressers and bistros. I stopped at Strawberry Fields, a children's clothing store, and one of the few remaining die hards. I remembered my mum taking me here one day. I must have had a day off school because it was just her and me, no Dad. We chose a dress for my birthday. I remember it took forever to choose because Mum couldn't decide which one Dad would approve of the most. Eventually, she decided on a pink one with lacy sleeves and a wide satin ribbon around the waist. I felt like a princess in that dress. When I wore it, I felt nothing bad could happen to me.

I carried on past the opulent facades of Belhaven Terrace and thought about how grand this street must have been at one time. Today, that grandeur was camouflaged behind grubby looking bushes and litter that swirled around in the traffic fumes of a busy city. At Byers Road, I turned left and walked down to where it meets Dumbarton Road, passing by The University Café. They made the best ice cream in Glasgow, as far as I was concerned, and was where Mum and Dad used to take me now and again. I thought of the sunny afternoons Ross and I had spent there in the early days of our relationship. It was the time when we were so much in love it didn't matter what we were doing as long as we were with each other. Even a trip to Safeway was fun if we were together. I thought about how much I'd love to take Sam to the café, buy him a 99 cone with raspberry sauce.

In the distance was a skyline which had once been filled with the cranes and machinery that had built the empire's ships. Instead of shipyards, there were museums and concert halls, modern buildings with modern architecture. I couldn't believe how much Glasgow had changed, even in my lifetime. It was a timely reminder that I had to press on with my changes, and I couldn't put off flat hunting any longer. Although I was scared of jinxing things with Sam, he would never be given permission to live with me if I wasn't able to provide him with a home. This meant moving away from the City Centre and West End, and out to the suburbs to be near his school. I would start the next day.

I slept well that night and woke refreshed, ready for work and to begin my flat hunt. As I drank my morning cup of tea, I looked out the window. It was November, and the sun had lost its vibrancy. The light coming in through my living room window was now soft and milky.

I had gathered my things together, ready to head out the door when the intercom buzzed. I stopped dead in my tracks. I rarely received unexpected visitors, and I was scared it was my father. I edged to the window and peeked out, hoping not to be seen by whoever it was. DI Brown was below and, looking up for an indication I was home, waved when she saw me. I reluctantly waved back, relieved it wasn't Dad, but anxious at the same time. Why was she here so early in the morning? I didn't want to talk to her, but now she'd seen me, I had no choice.

'I've got to get to work,' I said as soon as I stepped outside. 'I can't come to the station.'

'We'll give you a lift,' said Morton, ignoring my reluctance. 'Don't worry, the car's unmarked.' I got in the back. They got in the front, Morton driving.

'We need to talk to you about the case,' began DI Brown. My heart sank. I could tell from her tone that they weren't going to pursue it.

'You're not going to charge him, are you?' I did my best not to sound angry, to be matter-of-fact and unemotional, but my bitterness seeped out all on its own.

'I'm sorry, Nicola. There just wasn't enough evidence. The Fiscal didn't think we had a case.' I was crushed. I felt violated all over again. 'Nicola,' Brown went on, 'I know it doesn't help, but I do believe you. I wish we could charge him, I really do, but we've so little evidence the result would be the same, but with the added stress of a court case.'

'You're right,' I said, 'it doesn't help. He still gets away with what he did to me.' Brown held up a business card for me to see.

'Call these guys,' she said, 'they're excellent and they'll be able to help you make sense of what's going on.' The card read Glasgow Child Abuse Support Group. 'Please take it, Nicola. This is a difficult time and you shouldn't be alone. You need support from others who understand what you've been through. Friends are great, but sometimes they're not enough. They don't get it.'

I took the card and stuffed it into my pocket.

When we arrived at the hotel, I made to get out of the car, but before I did, I said to DI Gail Brown, 'Please don't give up looking for evidence. He did this to me.'

I spent the rest of the day under a cloud. My face was set in a scowl and I couldn't shake myself out of it. I managed to swap with a colleague so that I didn't have to do the front desk, I would not have been a good ambassador for the hotel that day. Hour by hour the day dragged on, hindered by my own lack of energy and resentment at having to carry on even though life sucked.

Eventually my shift finished, but I had lost all enthusiasm for flat hunting but, tired as I was, I took myself to line dancing. The company and the movement were a welcome distraction from everything else that was happening in my life. The big space of the church hall was inviting, the sound of shoes shuffling on the wooden floor was soothing and the clapping of hands was reviving. I stood at the door, just for a moment, to take it all in, thankful for this one night of the week when I could forget my father, my mother, Ross and even Sam. This was an evening to think only about what was happening in the here and now, the direction and tempo of my feet and hands. The music itself was liberating with its simple rhythms and crooning melodies.

St Anthony's Church Hall was a cocoon that gave me safe harbour for an evening. As it should be, I thought, since he was the patron saint of lost things, after all. I remembered a holiday Ross and I had taken to Milan. We visited the church of St Anthony there, where his effigy was surrounded by letters and messages, photographs and even Post-it notes, relating to people who were lost.

I remembered feeling so melancholy as I left the cool, dimly lit church and stepped into the vibrant, blinding sunshine. The loved ones of those missing people prayed to St Anthony, hoping he'd select them to work his miracles upon.

THE DAY SHE CAME HOME

I snapped out of my reverie and joined the others, calling hellos to those already dancing or those that came in after me. The heel digs, the kicks and claps were coming to me easier now, so much so that I didn't have to concentrate as intently as I once did, I could now simply enjoy myself.

Another newcomer, Alan, and I found ourselves drawn together and often paired up for the simple reason that we had joined at the same time and were equally inadequate dancers. Over the previous weeks, we'd chatted at tea break and practiced unfamiliar steps together.

'My divorce came through today,' he told me at break.

'Congratulations?' I said, unsure how best to respond.

'Thank you, yes, it is. It's been a long process, but it's finally over.' I sensed the conversation was going in a direction I didn't want it to. 'Are you married?' Alan asked.

'Yes.'

'How long have you been married?'

'Eleven years.' It was technically true.

'Is line dancing not his thing?'

'We're separated.' I said, not wanting to lie.

'I'm sorry to hear that.' Alan said. 'It's not easy.'

'No, it's not.'

'Any children?'

'One. A son, he's six years old.'

'How's he taking it?'

'As well as can be expected.' I shuffled from one foot to the other, looking about me self-consciously. I didn't want to have this conversation.

'Sorry,' said Alan. 'I'm asking too many questions. Tell me to shut up if you want to.' My expression was enough.

'Chitchat over, everyone!' called Roy. 'Back to it. Gavin's going to lead this one.'

At the end of the class, Mags came over to me, 'A few of us are going for a quick drink. Do you fancy joining us?'

'Oh, yes, please do,' said Roy, coming over. 'We never get to chat during class and that's half the fun of coming, isn't it?' They both looked so eager that I couldn't refuse.

'Alright, just one.' They each put an arm through mine and led me to the Bruce Arms, a nearby pub. It was clear from the moment they passed through the doors that this was Tony's Heel Diggers' local haunt. Banter was exchanged between the dancers and the bar staff, beer and wine was ordered, and tables were moved to accommodate everyone.

Once settled, people fell naturally into groups, picking up on unfinished conversations and running through routines. It turned out some members danced competitively, and costumes were a big part of this.

I listened in, enjoying the lively company, and saw these retirees in a whole new light. These people were not like my parents who stayed home in the evening, only venturing to the Royal Legion on a Friday night to meet Dad's drinking friends and their wives.

These people had full lives, were involved with their grandchildren and their local community. They holidayed and went to concerts. They behaved and talked as if they were in the first half of their lives, not the second. I admired their gusto, and it only emphasised the solitary, joyless lives my parents led. Did I want to replicate my parents by playing it safe and shutting myself off the from the world? Or did I want to be like these people, busy and engaged with life and all it came with? It became clear to me that although things with the police hadn't worked out as I'd wanted, Ross, Claire and DI Brown did believe me, they hadn't ridiculed me as Dad has said they would. There wasn't enough evidence, Brown had said. That was out of my control. What I could control, was how I moved forward.

The collapse of the case was a setback, but it wasn't the end of things, and although I'd lost my gusto for finding a new home in the suburbs, it was something I could action to move a step closer to Sam. I couldn't give up now.

Chapter 25

Despite my intentions to ignore what I couldn't control and move on with what I could, Brown and Morton's news felt like the last straw and I found it hard to pull myself out of the fug into which I'd fallen. I wondered what the point of it was. For about the hundredth time since I'd stolen it, I pulled out the photo of Sam. There, right there, was the reason I was doing this. I did not want to be replaceable in his life. I am his mother, I am her. I couldn't give up this fight because he needed and deserved to have a mother in his life who loved him beyond any shadow of a doubt, who had never stopped loving him even in her absence. He deserved to know that.

A hotel guest interrupted my reverie. 'Is that your son?' she asked in an earnest and enthusiastic Deep Southern American drawl.

'Yes,' I said.

'He's gorgeous,' she replied, as she took the photograph from me and inspected it. 'What a handsome young man. How old is he?'

'He's six, he started school last year.'

'You must be so proud,' she said, handing back the photo.

'I am,' I said, putting it in my pocket. 'How can I help you?'

Once the woman was on her way, I pulled the photograph out again. I am proud of him, I thought, but I don't know him. I want to know him. I welled up with the ache of wanting to hold him in my arms, to cuddle him and kiss him until he asked me to stop. I can't give up, I told myself. I need to keep on trying.

The next morning I took the train out to Clarkston. I needed to see Mum, talk to her again. I loitered on a nearby street for quite a while, working out what I was going to say to her because in my eagerness to do the job, I hadn't given it any thought until I got off the train. I realised too that Dad would be there and I needed to talk to her alone. I thought about phoning the house, asking her to come and meet me, but he'd want to know where she was going. I considered sneaking round the back to the kitchen window and getting her attention that way, but disaster was written all over that idea.

I had just decided to go get a coffee to buy myself some more thinking time when I spotted Dad's car coming down the street. I turned my back to the road, looking over my shoulder to watch him go by. As soon as he was out of sight, I quickly made my way to the house. I was so nervous I kept turning to check he wasn't coming back.

When Mum opened the front door, it was clear she wasn't overjoyed to see me. She looked up and down the street as furtively as I had walked it. Ridiculous, I thought, we're behaving like criminals and we haven't done anything wrong.

'What are you doing here?' she asked, ushering me in. 'Your father is so angry about you going to the police.'

'I know, but he doesn't need to worry, does he? They haven't got enough evidence.'

'I'll put the kettle on,' she said, not looking at me, 'but you can't stay long.'

'Where's he gone?'

'The police called, they want to talk to him again.'

'Mum,' I began, all anger absent. I needed her and didn't want to put her on the defensive. 'I really need to understand what makes you stay with him. If I can understand that maybe I can understand everything else.'

'What a question to ask?' she said, tutting.

'But an important one. Why did you marry him?' Mum poured the tea before she answered.

'You might not be able to see it now, but he was so handsome when we met. I remember being dazzled from the very first time I saw him. I could tell he was strong, a man who would look after me. I needed that, that feeling of safety. He gave me the security I'd never known before.' A smile was on her lips as she told me. There was even a tiny flush in her cheeks, brought on by happier memories. 'I'd always been a bit of a wallflower. Pretty enough, but I didn't have the confidence my girlfriends had. Flirting didn't come naturally to me like it did with them. My friend, Sheena, had so many admirers and I always got lumped with the friend. Or rather, he got lumped with me. Stephen, your dad, was different. He singled me out right from the start and that made me feel special.' She took a packet of ginger biscuits out of the cupboard.

'It was a whirlwind,' she went on, 'within six months we were married and before I knew it you were on the way.' She looked at me when she said, 'I loved you from the moment you were conceived. We were going to be a family, a proper family.' She smiled at me lovingly as she took a bite from her biscuit. I felt so sad for her, that that proper family didn't work out as she'd dreamed. 'My childhood hadn't been great, and I wanted something better for you.'

'You've never really spoken about your family.'

'I was one of eight kids.'

'Eight? I thought there was just you and Uncle Callum?' I'd never heard mention of any other siblings.

'Jimmy died of meningitis. My mum was devastated. I don't think she ever recovered from losing him. He was seven when it happened. He'd always had poor health, but getting to age seven, they thought he was past the worst of it.'

This was a revelation to me, a whole family history that had been kept hidden. 'You said there were eight kids. What happened to the others?'

Mum shook her head and let out a sorrowful breath of air.

'They got sent away.'

'Sent away?'

'Social services. There were too many of us and they said Mum and Dad couldn't cope. Maybe that was so, but they shouldn't have taken them away. There was only me and Callum left at home because we were the oldest. I never saw the others again.'

'You said things weren't easy, but was it better with fewer kids to support?'

'Not really. Mum took to the drink and Dad left her. He couldn't take it anymore, so me and Callum more or less had to look after ourselves.' She disappeared into herself. I could tell vivid pictures were flitting around in front of her. 'Callum joined the Merchant Navy and left for Australia as soon as he could. He used to write sometimes, but eventually, we lost touch. It's not like today, when everything is sent by email and whatnot.'

'Do you miss him?'

'I miss them all. I loved being part of a big family, lots of brothers and sisters around.'

'Did you ever see any of them again?'

'No, they got sent all over the place and I hoped to have more children of my own, but it wasn't to be.' She poured herself a top-up of tea. 'Anyway, your dad came and whisked me off my feet and here we are.'

'Have you been happy with him?'

'Is any marriage happy? Were you and Ross happy? I come from a different time, Nicola. In my world, you make your bed and lie in it.' She got angry now, not so much at me it felt, but at her situation. 'Of course it's not been a happy marriage, but

I'm stuck. Stephen and I both are. What would I do without him now? I've got no pension, no savings, nothing. I've never even lived on my own. No, I'll see out my days here with your dad.'

'What if you didn't have to?' I asked tentatively.

'What do you mean?'

'If he wasn't here, you'd have the house. His pension would be your pension. You'd be alright.'

'And what would I do with myself in this big house?'

'You'd get in touch with old friends. You'd go for coffee, to the cinema, to the whist drive. Remember, you used to go there? Why did you stop?' Mum halted mid-movement and looked at me sharply before answering.

'I didn't feel comfortable leaving your dad to do bedtime. It wasn't his sort of thing, he didn't like doing it and asked me not to go.' I didn't contradict her version of things as I didn't want to upset her.

'If Dad wasn't here, you could start again. Just imagine all the things you could do. Retirement isn't what it used to be, you know, these days it's like reliving your twenties, but without young kids in tow.' She waved a hand in dismissal of my suggestion, but I could tell it resonated.

'Where would he go, anyway?' she asked, not looking at me.

'If the police knew the truth,' I said slowly, leaving the sentence unfinished.

Mum looked at me, confusion clearly visible. Just at that moment, we heard Dad try to put his key in the lock. His movements were still slow after the heart attack, which bought us a little time.

'Go out the back,' Mum hissed. She grabbed my cup and rinsed it under the tap. As quietly as I could, I opened the back door and snuck out. I hid to the side of the door, so I could hear some of what was said without being seen.

'That didn't take long,' I heard Mum say.

THE DAY SHE CAME HOME 175

'I forgot something,' he said. I peeked round the corner and saw his hand on the stairway banister, helping him slowly make his way up to retrieve something.

'Will you be back for lunch?' Mum called up to him.

'I've no idea. It depends on how long they insist on wasting my time. Prepare me a sandwich just in case.'

I stood outside for what felt an eternity, and pressed my back as tight against the wall as I could manage, in case he looked out of the window for some reason. I could sense Mum pacing around the kitchen, making a pretence of tidying and wiping surfaces. Finally, I heard the slow thump of his heavy footsteps as he made his way back down.

'Are you sure you should be doing this today?' Mum asked him, 'you seem very tired this morning.'

'I'm fine,' he said, coming into the kitchen. 'I just need a glass of water.'

'I'll get that for you,' Mum said, 'you sit down.'

'I'll do it myself, I can manage.'

I held my breath. The sink was next to the window and there was every chance he'd either see me or feel something was different. I slunk round to the side of the house and waited.

When I heard the front door slam shut, I returned to the back door and waited for Mum to give me the all clear. She opened the door and quietly ushered me in before going through to the living room to check the street.

'He's gone,' she said, coming back into the kitchen. We both breathed deep, unaware that we'd been holding our breath for the longest time.

'That was a close one,' I said, attempting a smile to lighten the mood. 'Mum, did you hear what I said, before Dad came home? That if the police knew the truth about what happened?'

'I don't know what happened. I never saw any of the things you say he did to you. I know he's not perfect, but I just can't believe he did those things.'

'Mum, he did them. Why is that so hard for you to believe?'

'Because I... he... has temper, but he's not an evil man.'

'He's not a good man either. He hasn't been good to me and he certainly hasn't been nice to you over the years.'

'Your father has been very good to me, he's looked after me, both of us. Where would we be without him?'

'We'd all be a lot happier. There's a good chance I wouldn't have had a breakdown and we wouldn't even be having this conversation.'

'Why is it I always feel you're blaming me for your unhappiness?' She was angry now, or perhaps defensive. I didn't want to alienate her, but still found it incredible that she didn't see the part she played in my abuse.

'I'm not blaming you,' I tried to appease, 'but just think, if we'd left him years ago, we'd be in such a better place. And it's not too late. You can still leave him, and it will be easier with no child in tow.'

'I've told you I don't know how many times, I can't leave. I just can't.' She walked through to the living room, trying to escape me. I followed on her heel.

'I don't agree. You can, you're just scared.'

'Wouldn't you be? If you'd lived all your life with one man, and that man had done everything for you, wouldn't you be scared?'

'Yes, but I'd do it, anyway. Don't you think I was terrified to come back to Glasgow and face the wrath of everyone I had ever loved? I was terrified, but I knew it was the right thing to do. I had to face up to my past and what I'd done. I'm asking you to face up to what Dad has done, and to help me. Help us both.'

'You're asking too much of me. You're asking me to disrupt the only life I've known, and you're asking me to believe your father capable of the things you've accused him of.'

'Because they're true. Don't you remember?' I listed one instance after another of when he'd abused me and where she'd been when it happened. 'Don't you remember the bruising I had all over my body?'

'You were a clumsy child, you were always falling over.'

'That's not true, I was a nervous wreck who was stressed all the time, and who was constantly worrying about what Dad would do next. He was the person bruising me. And if I did fall over a lot, is it surprising? I was under such a lot of stress. Mum, please, don't you remember?'

She composed herself, set her shoulders straight and looked at me. 'No,' she said.

Defeated, I left the room and the house. I'd tried and failed to persuade Mum to leave Dad, to tell the police the truth and help us both. It wasn't that she didn't love me, it was that her fear of Dad and being alone was greater and I was unable to persuade her otherwise.

Chapter 26

Not quite a week later, DI Gail Brown called me on my mobile. It was mid-morning, and I was at home. 'I have good news, Nicola.'

'Oh, yes,' I said as casually as I could manage.

'We're reopening your case.' I couldn't help myself and fist pumped the air.

'That's brilliant news, what's changed?'

'I can't say much, but a couple of new witnesses have come forward.'

'A couple of new witnesses?'

'Yes.'

'Who?'

'I can't say, I'm afraid.'

'You mean more than one?' I was incredulous. I assumed one witness to be Mum, but who could the other person be? Brown's silence told me she'd say no more. 'So what happens now?'

'Well, we now feel we have enough of a case to resubmit to the Fiscal. Nicola, are you alright?' She could hear me sniffing on the other end of the line.

'I'm fine, I'm just so relieved. I nearly gave up hope.'

'Nicola,' Brown cautioned, 'this is just the first step. There's no guarantee the case will go forward.'

'It will,' I told her, 'It has to.'

'I don't want you to celebrate just yet, this is only the first step.'

'How long will it take for them to make a decision?'

'At least a month.'

'A month?' That was ages.

'At least, so try to put it to the back of your mind for now. Easier said than done, I know. Have you called the support group I recommended?'

'I don't need a support group. I need my father behind bars. My life is on hold until he's in prison.'

'That feeling won't go away,' said Brown, 'not for a while. That's why I really recommend you get in touch with this group. Only their members can understand what you've been through. They will really be able to help you, whether the case goes to court or not.'

'I'll think about it.'

After we hung up, I dug the card out from the coat pocket into which I'd stuffed it. I turned it over and over in my hands, reading and rereading the contact details as if I might divine some mystical answer to all my problems.

I put the card in my handbag and, in a bid to take my mind off the support group, decided to spring clean the flat, especially since I would be moving out soon. I'd found a two-bed flat in Bearsden, not far from Sam's school. It was strange to be going back to the old neighbourhood. I didn't need to hide behind trees anymore, but I was still nervous about bumping into people from my past, worried it might pull me back to that time and remind me of instances I'd rather not recall. But as I searched online, the street names and flat locations felt familiar and that was comforting. I was worried I might not find anything in the area and in my budget, but I got lucky and found a clean and spacious flat that immediately felt like it could be home.

I packed my books and the vast bits of paperwork involved in custody battles and divorces. I hoovered and scrubbed and cleaned. The physical work was a great outlet for the jitters that seemed to be my new normal.

My home spotless, I headed to the library to return some books. I wandered into the Children's Section, looking at the many and varied illustrations and anticipating a time when Sam and I would visit the library together, choosing books to read at bedtime. I watched a mother and daughter debating their choice. I smiled at their easy, natural conversation and enjoyed how they laughed together. It brought back a vague memory of myself at a young age, looking through colourful books that were huge and unwieldy in my tiny hands. I'm sure Mum was there with me, but I couldn't picture her. It was a brief memory, more of a feeling than anything, but it was there and it was a happy one. I wanted to be able to build happy memories with Sam so, taking Brown's advice, I found a quiet spot in the library, pulled out the card for the Child Abuse Support Group and dialled the number.

'Hello,' said a woman's friendly voice, 'Hayley speaking.'

'Hi,' I said nervously. 'I was given your card.'

'I'm glad you called. Are you calling for yourself,' she asked gently, 'or for someone else?'

'Myself.'

'First, let me say well done, I know it's hard to make this call, I imagine you've battled with the decision of whether to or not.'

'Yes,' I said quietly, 'I have.'

'You're not alone in that, honestly, it took me a long time to make the call, but it's the best thing I ever did for myself. Would you like to know a little more about the group?'

'Yes, please.'

'We meet weekly to share our stories and offer support. Everyone's history is unique, but there are common themes and that's where we can offer a level of empathy that nobody else can. Through the group you will feel less alone, that I can promise.'

'I've never been to a group like this before.'

'It's a very safe space. Everything said in the room is confidential. You don't have to share every week, although we encourage you to let us know how you are doing. This lets others support you, and it also lets me know how you're doing more generally. Come along next week and see how you find it.'

It was cold the night I went to my first survivors' meeting. The night was dark, the street lights were on and a strong wind was blowing. It was the sort of wind that lifted debris and bits of grit blew into my eyes, making me feel more off-kilter than I already did. As I made my way to the venue, I was hyper-vigilant, scared of bumping into someone I knew, a colleague perhaps, who would ask where I was going. What would I say? I didn't want to admit I was going to a support group for victims of child abuse.

The meeting was held in a church hall on Renfield Street. I was the first there and hung around outside until another woman arrived with keys. I guessed she must by Hayley, the woman I'd spoken to on the phone.

'Hello,' she said, 'are you Nicola?'

'That's right.'

'I'm so glad you came. The first time can often be the hardest.' We went inside and I helped her set the chairs out in a circle.

'How does the evening work?' I asked. I had a horrible vision of having to stand up in front of the whole group and tell them about my past.

'We go around the room one by one and share something either of our story, or of what's going on in the here and now.'

'Do I have to say something?' I wasn't sure I was ready for that.

'Not at all, but you are encouraged to share with the group every few weeks. That's why we're here after all, to share and heal together.' She must have seen how nervous I felt and smiled reassuringly. 'Of course, you're never under any pressure to say anything, it's only if you feel comfortable.'

One by one, the others arrived, men and women of different ages. I was startled by how young a few of them were and marvelled at how brave they were to come somewhere like this. Should I have found a group like this at their age, to seek help and talk about my abuse? If I had, how different my adult life might have been. Perhaps Ross and I would still be together, happy with our lot. Maybe Sam would have a little brother or sister. But there was no point dwelling on what might have been.

'Hello, everyone,' said Hayley after we'd all taken our seats. 'I'd like you all to welcome Nicola to our group this evening. She's told me this is her first time at a support group. Nicola, thank you for being brave enough to not only pick up the phone, but to come along this evening. Everyone here has been in your shoes and knows it isn't easy.' I was embarrassed and touched by Hayley's kind words.

Not everyone spoke that evening, but it became clear that some people had been attending these sessions for a long time and that others were new members like me. Some of what I heard was horribly familiar, histories of parents or other family members who had shamed a child into silence and complicity. For some, it was only when their abuser had died that they found the strength to tell anyone. One man, Rob, was in the middle of a court case and was visibly shaken by his experience of being on the stand.

'It was horrible,' he said, 'the lawyer made me out to be a liar. Everything I said he twisted until I didn't know if I was coming or going, until I began to wonder myself if it really happened.' He stopped to gather himself and the rest of us waited to see if he wanted to continue. He had a craggy face, crisscrossed with lines and wrinkles. It was difficult to determine his age, but I suspected he was younger than he looked. Was that due solely to a lifetime of cigarettes and alcohol, or was it also living with his childhood shame? I guessed it was both, that one had led to the other. I'd been tempted down that road myself many times, but my inability to lose control of myself prevented me, bringing about its own kind of destruction.

'I just can't bring myself to do it,' said a young woman called Ruby. 'I can't bear for all my family and friends to know. I'm too embarrassed.' She blushed, suddenly scared she'd offended Rob. 'I don't mean that you shouldn't have, Rob, but I just don't think I can.'

Hayley interrupted. 'Everyone here is at a different stage of their journey. What is right for one person isn't necessarily the right route for another.' There was a general murmur of consensus and I got the impression this was something of a mantra, the belief that there's no right or wrong course of action, only what is right for that individual. Later in the session, Hayley asked if I felt up to sharing some of my story. I felt myself blush and start to say no, but, at the last moment, I changed my mind.

'My name is Nicola,' I said, 'and I was abused by my father from about the age of four until I was fifteen.' Everyone was silent, listening. 'I recently reported him to the police and they've finally said they have enough evidence to go to the Procurator Fiscal. We're waiting for their decision.'

'If the case goes to trial,' asked Hayley, 'what do you want to get out of it?'

'What do you mean?' I asked.

'Is it about punishing your father or is it about more than that?' I didn't have an answer for her. 'Sometimes we can feel that a conviction will solve all our insecurities and wash away the hurt of our past and, if it doesn't, we can be left feeling very disappointed.'

'I suppose I want him to take responsibility. I want to move on with my life, put the abuse behind me.'

Hayley didn't say any more, but I was left wondering if perhaps I was expecting too much from his prosecution, and that, in fact, nothing would actually change. I dismissed the thought. I wasn't ready to contemplate the possibility I'd feel the same then as I did now.

At the end of the session, Hayley came up to me.

'How did you find this evening?' she asked.

'Good. Interesting.'

'Well done for talking to the group, it can be daunting to speak in front of a large number of people. I don't want you to be discouraged by what I said about our expectations of court cases. If we can, it's important to bring abusers to justice. What's equally important is what survivors take from it. Mull it over and if you want, we can talk more about it next week.'

My mind was buzzing on the walk home as it was full of questions for the others in the group, running and rerunning all that they'd said. It took me a long time to get to sleep that night and, when I woke in the morning, my head was still full of the meeting, imagining what I might say next week.

It was as if a light had been switched on and I could now see that I wasn't alone in my universe of shame and guilt, of broken families and disowned parents. As sad as it sounded, I took great comfort from the stories I'd heard the previous night. Simply knowing I was not alone in my anguish and self-inflicted silence was immensely reassuring and gave me courage. There truly is strength in numbers. I began to think that, even if Dad didn't go to prison, I might still be okay with the support of the group.

Chapter 27

Since Nicola had made her accusation, Stephen had been quiet and morose, speaking only to snap at Mary when she annoyed him, which, to her, was too often. Why is he cross with me? She thought, I didn't phone the police. They think I'm as guilty as him.

They were sat at the kitchen table, eating dinner in silence. Mary glanced up at him, his face stony, deep in his own thoughts. It's natural he should lash out at me, she thought, he's hurting so badly at what Nicola is doing that he's got to take it out on someone. Her hand instinctively went to her cheek, which was still stinging from earlier. She'd put a cold cloth on it and hoped it was no longer scarlet.

I wish I knew what he wanted, Mary said to herself, I've tried to make things as easy as possible for him. When he came out of hospital, Mary had moved anything she thought might get in his way, she'd plumped the cushion on his chair before he sat down and ensured his slippers were close to hand. She'd watched him make his way slowly around the house, his arm still stiff and not yet fully functioning, quick to offer support if he needed it. Somehow, it was never enough.

'Shall I put the kettle on?' she asked when they'd finished eating. Without a word, Stephen got up and made his way to the drinks' cabinet in the living room to pour himself a whisky. 'Stephen,' protested Mary following him through, 'I don't think it's a good idea to drink spirits, you're not long out of hospital. You're still recovering.'

'Shut up, woman,' he said, taking his drink to the window and staring out at the street. Mary went back through to the kitchen and filled up the kettle. She took her time making the tea, going through the same ritual she did every time she retreated to the kitchen. That Stephen had headed straight to the whiskey bottle was not a good sign. She'd been hoping his heart attack and stay in the hospital would make him see he needed to cut down. Too often he came to bed drunk and Mary could never be sure he wouldn't turn on her in anger. He increasingly mocked her, calling her names and laughing at the things she said. He liked to remind her of how old she'd become, how she'd let herself go.

But what hurt the most was when he muttered to himself that he should never have married her, hinting that he should have married someone else. This someone else was never named and Mary didn't think there really was a particular someone else, but it hurt, nevertheless. It pained her to know he hankered after some non-existent person, rather than the wife he had and who loved him.

By the time Mary went through with the tea, Stephen was gone and his glass was sitting on the window ledge, empty. She went upstairs and found him curled up in bed, hidden under the covers.

Mary knew not to push him and closed the door as she left. In the kitchen, she poured herself a cup of tea and opened a fresh packet of biscuits. As soon as one was finished, she picked up another until they were all nearly gone and she felt a bit nauseous. She sipped her tea to help the biscuits go down, making no effort to wipe away her tears. The phone rang.

'Hello.' Mary answered, sounding as bright as she did every day. It was DI Brown.

'I need you both to come in tomorrow and make a statement,' she said.

'But why, you said there wasn't enough evidence to take things any further.'

'There have been some new developments.' Mary wracked her brain, but could think of no excuse not to go.

'Okay. I'll tell my husband.'

Mary went upstairs and stared at Stephen for a while, trying to discern why he was behaving this way, why he was angry with her. 'That was the police,' she said. 'We've to go down to the station tomorrow to make another statement. Apparently, there's some new evidence.' Stephen made no response. 'Stephen, did you hear me? I know you're awake. Did you hear me? Talk to me.'

'I heard you.'

'Then talk to me.' He made no movement. 'Why are you angry with me? Why won't you talk to me? It's not fair, I've done nothing wrong.' She was crying again, unable to stop. 'All I've ever done is love you, why are you punishing me?'

The stress of the last few months had finally hit her. The relief of Nicola's return, Stephen's heart attack and now the accusations, were all too much. Mary's stomach was constantly in knots and, no matter how much she ate, it never went away. This final insult from Stephen was the last straw. She couldn't hold in her hurt and anguish any more. She wanted her husband to acknowledge her and what she'd been through.

'I'm not the one who made allegations,' she shouted at him. He got up and went into the bathroom, shutting the door in her face. 'Everything you've ever done, I've tried my best to understand. I would never hurt you. You do know that, don't you?' Stephen opened the door.

'What do you mean by that?'

'Nothing, I don't mean anything by it. All I'm saying is that I love you and I don't want you to be angry with me.'

'Who else should I be angry with? You're her mother, it was your responsibility to raise her properly, but you messed that up, you silly, stupid, simpering woman. And now we're being hauled to the police station to defend ourselves against this vile accusation and all because you didn't do your job properly.'

Mary let out an involuntary cry, certain he was going to hit her. 'I don't want to talk to you until this whole bloody mess is over.'

The next morning they awoke, dressed and got in the car. They drove to the station in silence, each bound by their own fears, scared of what would be asked and how the other might respond. Mary became increasingly jittery the nearer they got. Her pulse quickened, her stomach churned, nausea rose and faded away. She felt Stephen grow increasingly morose, his hackles rising in preparation for an interrogation. They had never before needed to talk to each other more, and yet they couldn't speak to one another.

'We are Stephen and Mary Johnston,' said Mary to the desk sergeant. 'We're here to see DI Brown.'

'Mr and Mrs Johnston, thank you for coming down,' said Brown, 'Mr Johnston, please come this way.' While Stephen was taken to an interview room, Mary sat where Ross had done only a few months earlier.

Ninety minutes later, he emerged, dishevelled but defiant. 'Would you like to wait for Mrs Johnston, or if you want an officer can drive you home?'

'I want to be driven home.' Stephen followed a uniformed officer out to a waiting car, without looking at Mary.

'Mrs Johnston,' the inspector turned to her, 'shall we?' He led her through to the same room. It was a small and square shaped, with a table in the middle. On one side were two chairs for the inspectors, and on the other side a single one for her. The room was so familiar, she'd seen it hundreds of times on the crime dramas she watched. They'd each looked like this room, and in some strange way it was comforting. It put Mary a little more at ease. She waited while Brown and Morton settled themselves, switched on the recorder and began with familiar words.

'DI Brown and DI Morton interviewing Mary Johnston. The date is October 7th, and the time is 9.56a.m..' Morton looked at Mary and paused, indicating that the interview was beginning. 'Mrs Johnston, how long have you been married to Stephen Johnston?'

'Forty years now.'

'And how old were you when you married?'

'Twenty-two.'

'How many children do you have?'

'One. Nicola. We tried for more, but it wasn't to be.'

'How old is Nicola now?'

'She's forty. I got pregnant very quickly after the wedding.'

'Do you have a good relationship with Nicola?' She knew their relationship would reflect badly on her and didn't want to add fuel to the fire, but she couldn't deny things were less than perfect.

'No, Inspector. As you well know we don't. It hasn't been good for some time. Nearly five years, to be precise.'

'Can you tell me what went wrong between you?'

'To be honest, no, I can't. She's always kept herself to herself, she's never been one to confide in me or Stephen. And, of course, when she disappeared, well, we didn't know it then, but that seems to be have been the end of any contact, until now.'

'Okay, let's take a step back in time. What was Nicola like as a child?' Mary paused for a few moments, remembering her daughter as she used to be.

'She was a very easy baby, I remember that. She slept through the whole night from an early age, which was an enormous relief. Some babies can take months to settle at night time. And she never had colic, so there were no long stretches of crying. Yes, she was an easy baby, a delight. My friend, Jeannie, her baby cried non-stop for six months. She was a wreck, poor thing.'

'And what about as she got older?'

'She was happy enough. She was good at keeping herself busy when I was doing the washing or the cooking or whatever. Yes, I remember she was a happy wee thing.'

'Did you feel she distanced herself from you at an early age?'

'Oh, no, she loved cuddles. She was so sweet, always drawing little pictures for me, you know, as gifts. I've still got some of them.'

'At what age do you think, did she become distant, withdrawn?'

'When she was about five or six. I don't remember exactly.'

'How did it manifest itself?'

'What do you mean?'

'How did her behaviour change? What was it you noticed that was different about her?' Mary needed time to think, but realised there was no specific change.

'It was lots of things, really. She always seemed to be in a bad mood, didn't want to do anything with me or her dad. Stephen used to take her out to the park, or to the library on Saturdays, and I remember she stopped reading, said she didn't like books any more. She stopped talking. It felt like overnight she went from chatting all day to saying not a thing.'

Mary stopped talking. She couldn't look at the inspector. She was torn. She was aware that everything she was saying was damaging, but images of her changed little girl popped through her mind. Images of Nicola sitting silently in the corner of the sofa when they watched telly, of her at the dinner table not eating very much, and suddenly wanting her bedroom light on at night. After a few moments, DI Brown asked, 'What do you think brought on all these changes?'

'I thought it was a reaction to going to school, she'd been at home with me up until then. I thought it was being separated from me. Then I thought it was the school, that she didn't like her teacher or hadn't made friends. I remember asking Stephen whether or not we should move her, but he said no. He said she was just looking for attention.'

'Is that what you thought?'

'I didn't know what to think. I just hoped she'd settle in, eventually.'

'Tell me, Mary, has Stephen always had the final say on big decisions? Is he the decision-maker?'

'Yes, he is. It may sound odd to you, you're young. But Stephen and I have always had a very traditional relationship. He goes out to work, I look after the home.'

'Within that remit, what are your responsibilities?'

'Raising Nicola, of course, maintaining the home.' She struggled to think of what else she was in charge of.

'Anything else?' asked Brown.

'Food shopping,' Mary grasped, annoyed at her mind going blank at a time like this, and at Brown for pushing her on such an irrelevant subject. 'Why do you need to know this?'

'I'm trying to get a picture of your domestic life, the environment that Nicola grew up in. Would you say you have a happy marriage?'

'Yes, of course,' Mary snapped, and immediately wished she hadn't, realising all too late how it came across. 'I'm sorry, these are very personal questions.'

'It's a very personal allegation that's been made.'

Mary looked at Inspector Brown straight in the eye and for, perhaps the first time, felt how serious the situation was, that it wasn't going to be thought of as some family misunderstanding.

'My marriage,' she began, 'has not been what I expected it to be.' Mary looked behind her a little, as if checking there wasn't someone behind her. 'Even before all this business with Nicola, he wasn't an easy man. Not an easy man, but a good man. A man who has worked hard to provide for his family, who has made difficult decisions on behalf of us all. He's the only man I've ever loved. So even though he's a hard man to live with, even though he can be thoughtless and selfish, he's a good man and not the sort to do what Nicola's accusing him of. If he had done, I'd know, wouldn't I?' Mary looked at Brown for confirmation, but she didn't answer immediately.

'Often we see what we want to see,' Brown said quietly. 'If the truth is too difficult or if we're frightened, we can blinker ourselves into seeing what is acceptable, adjust our ideas of right and wrong. Would you like a cup of tea?' Mary nodded absently while memories and half-memories flitted behind her eyes, each one evoking a confusion of mixed emotions. Her brain was tired with concentrating on telling the truth, but not saying anything that could be taken the wrong way or twisted out of context.

The room that had felt so familiar and secure when she'd first arrived now felt small and constraining. All too soon the inspector returned with vending machine tea, which Mary would normally have rejected, but when it was offered she realised how thirsty she was and accepted it gratefully.

'Let's continue,' said Morton.

It was an hour later when she emerged from the room, tearful but holding herself together, but once in the car, she allowed herself to break down, running over and over the questions she'd been asked. How did the relationship between Nicola and Stephen appear to you, Mrs Johnston? Did you ever see Stephen touch your daughter in an inappropriate way? Did your husband ever have sex with Nicola, Mrs Johnston? Mary was horrified. The things they'd accused him of were repulsive, misconstrued.

The police, or Nicola, had twisted all of Stephen's kindness and affection into something monstrous. She opened the car door and vomited. A passer-by stared at her, completing Mary's humiliation. She drove home, back to her kitchen where she could hide.

Feeling abandoned and ashamed by Stephen's accusations of failure, Mary did not reach this time for the kettle and ginger biscuits, but for the sherry she kept buried in the back of a cupboard. As she sipped, she replayed the police interview, quizzing why she was asked each question, analysing her response and whether she could have, should have, answered differently.

The sherry was addling her brain and making her tipsy. For once she didn't care, she wanted to feel this way, and worse. She wanted to finish her bottle of sherry, fall asleep on the sofa and awaken to a new life, a life in which Stephen loved her, Nicola loved her, Sam loved her. She wanted to wake up to a life with laughter in it. She remembered Nicola as a toddler, running around the kitchen shouting, 'Get me, get me,' in a bid to lure Mary to play chase. Mary remembered the fun they'd had building block towers and knocking them down, Nicola squealing with delight as they crashed to the floor. Imperceptibly, that noisy child had faded away and left in her place a quiet, obedient girl who rarely laughed. She thought of her teenage daughter who closed herself in her room, emerging sullen faced only when forced.

Mary pictured them sitting at the dinner table, her listening attentively to Stephen while he talked at them. He asked questions only when he noticed how unresponsive Nicola was, her eyes focused squarely on her plate.

'Look at me when you answer,' Stephen would bellow, slamming the flat of his hand on the table, startling them and making the crockery rattle. At the time, Mary had put Nicola's behaviour down to being a teenager, but as her memories of those years forced their way forward, she allowed herself to wonder if Nicola's accusations had any truth.

'Don't be daft, Mary,' she said aloud, 'that's the sherry talking.' She swayed into the living room, bottle and glass in hand, pouring as she went. The sherry glass was small and filled up quickly, overflowing onto the carpet. 'Oopsie!' she said, amused at her own lack of concern.

Her drunken swaying took on a rhythm and Mary thought back to her dance hall days; the smell of tobacco and sweaty bodies as couples twisted and spun. She remembered how clammy she felt after two or three successive dances, her stilettoed feet pinching, but her body energised by the music and movement. They'd been carefree days, and momentarily she felt that way again. She tried a spin, but lost her balance a little and staggered, the glass and bottle still in her hands.

'You're drunk.' Stephen was watching her from the door, his disgust all too evident.

'Yes I am,' said Mary, 'and it feels good.' She sashayed her way over to him, inviting him to join her. 'Dance with me.'

His hand slapped her hard on the cheekbone. The strength and shock of it forced Mary backwards, and she dropped both the bottle of sherry and the glass. She stumbled and fell, hitting her head on the corner of the display cabinet. The ornaments inside clinked as it moved with the force of her fall. She feared she'd cut her head open and felt for blood. Sure enough, her hair felt wet and when she looked at her fingers, they were stained red. She lifted her face to Stephen, as if to say, Look what's happened. He was unapologetic.

'Get up, you drunk,' he said.

Mary slowly got herself up from the floor. Her head had begun to throb, and she was a little dizzy from both the fall and the alcohol. She steadied herself against the display cabinet. 'Stephen, please,' she beseeched him, 'this has to stop.' The look he gave her made it all too clear he didn't want to hear another word on the subject. It was a look she'd seen many times over the years, but today it brought with it a specific memory.

Mary had gone to bed, but had woken, for some reason, a few hours later. Stephen wasn't beside her and she wondered where he was. She'd gone onto the landing, but no lights were on downstairs, so he wasn't in the living room or kitchen. She moved to check the bathroom, but, as she did so, Nicola's bedroom door opened and Stephen stepped out. He saw her quizzical expression, but, before she could say anything, he slapped her, hard, so that she'd staggered and had to rebalance herself. 'Get that filthy idea out of your head,' he said, striding into their bedroom.

She'd shut herself in the bathroom for a long time, talking herself out of what she thought had happened.

And here Mary found herself again, thirty years later, still being slapped and still being told to shut up, only this time she didn't lock herself in the bathroom. This time she was confronted by the understanding that Stephen had, indeed, loved his daughter, but had loved her in the way a man should never love a child.

The look Mary gave Stephen was enough for him to lower his gaze before shuffling to the living room window.

'I'm looking at you,' said Mary calmly, 'the man I have loved all these years, the man who has stormed and sulked through the best part of our marriage, but who I have still loved. I'm looking at you, trying to understand, but I can't. Why, Stephen, explain to me why?'

He didn't answer.

'You bastard,' she said, hurling herself at him, thumping her fists on his back as hard as she could.

At first, he didn't repel her, but thump by thump, his hackles rose until he pushed her as hard as he could. She landed almost on the other side of the room. She was shocked and winded, but unrepentant. She gathered herself up and went for him once more. 'My baby, she was my baby.'

Again, Stephen pushed her away and, again, she went for him. But, by now, she was tired and her initial venom had subsided. She collapsed in a chair and wept. She wept for his wickedness and for her own cowardice.

The image of Stephen coming out of Nicola's room all those years ago played on a loop inside her head, which by now was pounding from the alcohol, the cut on her head and the adrenalin pumping round her body. She took another look at her husband before going into the kitchen.

Calmly, she drank a glass of water, swilling down two aspirin. She put her coat on and gathered her handbag and keys.

'Where are you going?' Stephen asked.

'Oh, you're talking to me now, are you?'

'Where are you going?'

'The fog has lifted Stephen. I see you clearly now, for what you are. You've bullied me our entire married life, and you bullied Nicola until she went mad.' Euphoric with her newfound courage, Mary forged ahead, oblivious to the panic taking over her husband. 'Well, not anymore. I've protected you when I should have protected Nicola. She had nobody to protect her except me, and I failed her. I won't fail her any more. I'm going to the police to tell them what you did. They need to lock you away for what you did. You're a monster.'

She strode towards the front door, but Stephen pulled her back.

'Don't be stupid, woman. Do you think you'll get away scot-free? No. After all, you said it yourself, you protected me. You knew all along. And you never said a word. You lied in your statement. If I go to prison, you'll be coming with me.'

'It's where I deserve to be. I always thought that I was such a good person, such a loyal wife, a Christian person, but I couldn't have been more wrong. I was weak and pitiful and deserve whatever comes to me. What we did was wrong. We must be punished.'

'Oh, no, you don't.' Stephen grabbed a hold of Mary and dragged her halfway up the stairs. 'Get up there now and calm down. You're making a fool of yourself.'

'No, I won't.' Mary fought back, kicking and hitting, starting and pulling away from him. She felt Stephen's grip release and, for a moment, she was triumphant. But when she felt herself fall backwards and unable to grab the banister, Mary's last emotion was of disappointment and sorrow that once again she'd failed her daughter.

Stephen watched Mary fall. He'd simply let go of her and she did the rest. Just as she hit the ground, his legs gave way, and he slumped onto the stairs. He couldn't take his eyes off her. He almost laughed with the surprise at how easy it had been, just to let her slip out of his grasp, to let her head hit the floor. The smile soon disappeared as remorse galloped in.

'Mary,' he said, running down the stairs. 'Wake up, Mary, are you alright?'

He shook her, slapped her face, trying to elicit a response, but none came.

Chapter 28

'Goodnight, Nicola,' called Simone, an Italian Hotel Management graduate who was with us for her sandwich year. Like so many others, she'd struggled to understand Glaswegian when she first arrived, but, after five months, she not only understood most locals, but had developed her own hybrid accent, some sounds musically Italian, others broad Scots.

'See you tomorrow, Simone.'

I stepped out onto the street just as Brown and Morton were getting out of their car. I hoped they had a response from the Fiscal, but figured they would have let me know with a simple phone call. Their being here was not good news. It was eight o'clock on a Wednesday evening. The street was quiet, the home time rush-hour traffic had been and gone.

'Can we go somewhere to talk?' asked Morton. No pleasantries, this was serious. I led them into one of the hotel's small function suites. It was being set up for an event the next day, but was more private than the hotel café or bar. We sat down.

'Nicola, I've got some bad news,' said Brown.

'It's the Procurator Fiscal, isn't it? Have they rejected the case again?'

'No, it's not that.' I waited, looking expectantly at them. 'It's your mum.'

'Has she backed out?' I tutted and swore under my breath.

THE DAY SHE CAME HOME

'Not exactly,' Morton said.

'What then?' Morton and Brown glanced at one another, deciding Brown should speak.

'Nicola, your mum passed away this afternoon,' she said. They both stared at me, waiting for a response.

'She died?'

'There was an accident. Your mum fell and I'm sorry to say she passed away.'

'An accident? At home?' Brown nodded. 'Oh, my God, poor Mum.' I was dumbstruck, immediately thrown back to our dinner together only a few nights before. I pictured her face, the worried expression that never left. I saw her smooth skin; she'd always had good skin, clear and young looking. I was devastated. Of course I was, she was my mum, and yet, there was something about her death that seemed inevitable. I realised I was surprised it hadn't happened sooner. 'Was it Dad?'

'Why do you ask that?' Morton said.

'Oh, I don't know, just a feeling, I guess. Probably because she made a statement against him. Is that why he did it?'

'She made a statement,' said Morton, looking confused, 'but I'm afraid it didn't corroborate yours.'

'Did she tell you she was going to?' Brown asked.

'No, but I thought…' It was my turn to look confused. 'You said a couple of witnesses had come forward. Wasn't Mum one of them?'

'No, she wasn't one of them,' said Brown. 'Why did you think she was?'

'Because I went to see her, and we talked about it. I was sure she would.'

'If she was planning on changing her statement,' said Morton, 'I'm afraid she didn't before she died.'

'You're sure?' I asked. 'You're absolutely positive she didn't come to the station or phone you or anything and say she'd changed her story?'

'Positive.'

I was devastated. 'Why didn't she?' Tears exploded, I bashed clenched fists against my temple in frustration with myself for ever thinking Mum would have the courage to go against Dad. The swing of a door and the rattle of a trolley coming into the room brought me back to the here and now. Whoever it was that came in guessed something was going on, so they apologised in a quiet voice and scuttled out again.

'Tell me again,' I said, trying to compose myself, 'you said she had an accident?'

'Yes, it seems she slipped on the stairs,' said Brown. 'She turned around to talk to your father, who was standing at the bottom of the staircase, lost her footing and fell.'

'Did she suffer?'

'No, it was instant.'

'Poor Mum. Poor, poor Mum.' I felt so mixed up. Our relationship had been less than close, but there had been some good times and I did love her. At the same time, she had let me down again and again by staying with Dad and not finding the strength to rescue either herself or me.

After a while, Brown asked, 'Are you alright, Nicola?'

'Yeah, I think so. I don't know.'

'We'll give you a lift home.' They stood up, and I followed suit. In a daze, I trudged to the car and got in the back.

'I'm moving soon,' I said when we pulled up outside my flat, making no effort to get out of the car.

'Oh, yeah?' said Morton.

'Yeah.'

'Where are you moving to?' asked Brown.

'To Bearsden. I've found a two-bed flat near to Sam's school. He'll have his own bedroom. I need to ask him what colour he wants me to paint it. I think he'll choose blue. Ross says that's his favourite colour.' Brown and Morton got out of the

THE DAY SHE CAME HOME

car. Brown opened my door to encourage me out and followed me up to the flat.

'Is there anyone we can call for you?' Morton asked. I shook my head.

'There's nobody,' I said. They hung around for a while and tried to get me to talk, but I just wanted to be alone. Eventually they took the hint and left.

As soon as they'd gone, I took my bottle of vodka out of the freezer and downed two shots in quick succession, before putting it back and lying on my bed. I felt I ought to have a reaction of some sort. Isn't that what people do? They cry and wail, or get angry and break things, or retreat into themselves unable to face the grief? But I felt none of these things. I felt absolutely nothing.

I phoned Ross.

'The police came to see me at work today.'

'Oh, yes.'

'Mum died.'

'God, Nicola, I'm so sorry. Are you okay?'

'Yes, I'm fine. I feel confused and a bit numb, but other than that I'm fine. Brown and Morton hung around for ages waiting for me to collapse or something, but I didn't.'

'Do you want me to come around?'

'No, there's no need.'

'What happened to her?'

'She fell down the stairs. She led a disappointing life and died a disappointing death.'

'I know your relationship had its ups and downs, but, still, I'm sorry for your loss, Nicola.'

'Thank you. Tell me about Sam. Did he have a good day?'

'Yeah, I guess so. He fell out with his friend, Ewan, at break-time, but they were friends again by the end of lunch. I got his report card last week. He's doing well in English and Art, but struggling a bit with sums.'

'Just like me.' I said.

'Yeah,' said Ross, smiling, 'you were never good with numbers.'

'What else?'

'He wants to go for a sleepover at Ewan's house, but I'm unsure. I feel he's too young to be having sleepovers.'

'He's nearly seven. What are you worried about?'

'What if he wakes in the night and gets scared?'

'Does he often wake in the night?'

'Sometimes. What if they do things differently and it freaks him out?'

'He'll be fine. Kids are adaptable. He'll get used to it, just like when he comes to stay with me. That'll be new for him too, but he'll get used to it.' Ross didn't respond. 'Ross, you still there?'

'Why would he be staying at your place? You don't have room for him.'

'I'm moving.'

'When?'

'In a couple of weeks. I've found a place near Sam's school. To make things easier.'

'Nicola, you're not...' he stopped himself. 'Let's not talk about that. Again, I'm sorry about your mum. Give me call if you need anything.'

'But we're going to need to work something out.'

'Goodnight, Nicola.' He hung up.

I sat with the phone in my hand for a long time, unmoving. I felt utterly alone. I briefly flirted with the idea of going back to the bar and finding the man I'd had sex with, but I knew that wouldn't make me feel any better. If anything, it would make me feel worse, acknowledging I'd sunk to the new low of actively seeking out a man who didn't even know my name. It wouldn't change the fact my mother was dead, that I was getting divorced, or that I might never see my son again.

THE DAY SHE CAME HOME

Eventually, I got up and went into the kitchen with the intention of making a cup of tea, just as Mum always did, but, instead, I opened the freezer and pulled the vodka out again. This time I didn't bother with a glass and slugged the clear liquid straight from the bottle. As it always did, it burned the back of my throat, making me wince. I enjoyed, however, the warmth it spread through me as it worked its way down to my stomach.

I took the bottle with me to the sofa and channel-hopped, keen to take my mind away from how desperate my life had become. I took another swig. At least I have work, I thought. That is the one area of my life that is good. I fit in there; I belong to that world of check-ins, check-outs, tourist information, staff rotas, and all the other little cogs that make up the running of a busy city centre hotel. I was contributing.

I enjoyed talking to our guests, who always had a tale or an adventure to share, whose lives appeared so normal, so abundant in love and friendship. That is what would keep me sane throughout this hideous chapter of my life.

My phone beeped, it was Mags. SEE YOU TOMORROW? I smiled to myself. She couldn't have timed her message better. It was an apt reminder that I was making some new friends. I perhaps hadn't found a kindred spirit, but those at Tony's Heel Diggers were good people. They were fun and wanted to get to know the person I am now, not the wreck I was four years ago. YES! I messaged back.

Mags would never know how important that text message was in restoring my faith in myself.

I put the vodka back in the freezer and, instead, made that cup of tea. While I waited for the kettle to boil, I realised I had no photographs of Mum, not even an old one, taken in better days. I couldn't remember any photos of my parents, except the lone framed photograph of their wedding day. We didn't have the family days out others enjoyed, when somebody took some photos to record the event.

When my family had a day out, we simply tried to make it through in one piece. There was no need to immortalise it on film. I pictured my mother at home, quietly but quickly making her way around the house, cleaning and tidying, cooking and washing, always with one ear listening for Dad, anticipating his moods or how to placate him if she'd forgotten to do something.

I had a sudden memory of her in the kitchen suggesting to Dad I stay at home to catch up on schoolwork, instead of going swimming with him. I had sat mute, watching her face as he shouted and stormed at her, blaming her for ruining his day by not making sure I was on top of my schoolwork. I thought he might lash out, but he didn't and, instead, went swimming by himself. I still remember how both Mum and I relaxed as soon as the door pulled shut behind him.

I wondered how many other times she'd tried to keep me with her, but which I'd forgotten about or hadn't noticed in the first place.

The kettle boiled, and I poured the hot water. As I swirled the teabag around the mug, I considered the possibility that perhaps Mum had made efforts to protect me. They weren't nearly enough, but perhaps she'd done what she felt able to do. I shook my head, bringing me back to the present. Just because she's dead, I thought, doesn't mean she's absolved. No more than Dad would be if his heart attack had taken him to his maker.

Death can change the way we view people. We all too soon forget the bad and remember only the good until eventually they morph into a completely different person. I didn't want to do that with Mum, not yet. I couldn't afford to see her as a victim because I needed my anger. It was what gave me my strength. My anger was what would see me through days like this, days when I wanted to throw my hands in the air and disappear again. Only once the court case was over would I be able to fully grieve for my mother.

Chapter 29

Life seemed to take on a new rhythm after Mum's death. It effectively severed any remaining connection I had with their house and my old neighbourhood. I couldn't yet grieve for that part of my life, I had to stay focused on the here and now until the court case and custody battle had resolved themselves. I had done all I could to bring Dad's history to light. It was now up to the authorities to decide if the case was strong enough.

I had accepted, too, Ross's demand for a divorce. When I really thought about it, did I still love him, or was it the idea of Ross and what I'd left behind that I was clinging on to? Our relationship had deteriorated before I left, and the intervening four years had changed us both. I was certainly not the woman he had fallen in love with a decade before. When I finally admitted this to myself, it was amazing how much pressure I removed from my life. I was able to focus instead on my imminent move to Bearsden.

Work continued to go smoothly. We had a great team of staff who worked well together and produced a cheerful, efficient environment that rubbed off on our guests. Dawn, my manager, had come through for me and agreed we could work my shifts around the days Sam stayed with me, as long as those days were fixed. It felt like everything was coming together.

'Morning, Simone,' I called from the reception desk, where I was checking our upcoming bookings.

'Hi, Nicola, how are you?'

'Fine, thanks.' Something about the way she asked struck me as odd, but I couldn't put my finger on why. Before I could ask, though, she'd disappeared upstairs.

I went through to the kitchen, in need of a caffeine pick-me-up. The kitchen staff were prepping for lunch. It was ten thirty in the morning, but all too quickly it would be midday and the restaurant would get busy. Again, I was aware of strange looks. I ignored them as long as I could.

'What?' I demanded, self-consciously checking my hair and my suit, wondering if I'd made a mess of getting ready that morning. Jarek, one of the sous-chefs, came over to me and placed a newspaper on the counter in front of me.

There on the front page, below an advert for an M&S discount voucher, was a school photograph of me as a child. Next to it was one of my father as a young man. The headline read, 'Missing Woman: Paedo Dad's Reign of Terror Nearly Over.'

I looked up, and all eyes were on me. Humiliated, I grabbed the paper and hid in the ladies' toilet to read the article.

It outlined everything; the abuse, my disappearance, Sam, Ross divorcing me and even Mum's death which they'd labelled as 'suspicious'. I felt sick. How could this have happened? Who would have told them all this? Then it said a court date had been set. Was that true? If it was, why hadn't I been told? I couldn't read any more and put the paper in the bin.

I looked in the mirror, my cheeks were pale and my eyes looked wild. I splashed water on my face, trying to revive myself. My hands shook more violently than I'd ever have believed possible. I didn't want to leave the safety of the toilets, but what was I going to do, stay in there all day? I'd just decided I would leave when one of the receptionists, Kirsty, came in.

'Nicola, there's someone at reception asking for you.'

'Who is it?'

'He didn't say, but said it was important.'

Convinced it must be DI Morton, I followed Kirsty through, but it was a man I didn't recognise.

'Can I help you?' I asked him.

'Yes, you can. My name's Stuart Graham and I'm a reporter for The Herald. Would you like to tell your side of the story of your disappearance? Our readers would like to understand your motivation behind leaving your son who was only, what, two years old at the time?'

'Get out,' I said. 'Get out or I'll call security.'

'There's no need for that, I just wanted to give you the chance to tell your side, it's only fair you have your say.'

'Get out, get out, get out!' I heard my voice getting louder and louder, but was utterly unable to contain my panic and fear. I was completely out of my depth and didn't know how to handle a door-stepping journalist. I must have looked like a banshee because that was the moment a photographer decided to appear and take my picture, compounding my horror and humiliation.

Two of our porters turned up and escorted the men out. A few guests, startled by the outburst, stopped to watch what was unfolding. I felt as though I were in a cage, an exhibit for wonder and speculation. I couldn't stay here, not after what just happened.

I snuck out the back entrance and practically ran the whole way home, stopping only at my corner shop to buy every newspaper with my photo or name on it. The stories all outlined, with very little truth, my breakdown, my 'years in hiding' on Shetland and my futile attempts to win Ross back. There was also a photo of me, blurred and taken from a distance. This meant someone had been following me, photographing me anonymously, and it made me sick to my stomach to know I'd been spied on.

Throughout it all was the mention of Sam, so cruelly abandoned by his mother. What sort of woman, they asked, could leave her child, never make contact and start a new life? I had a horrible image of Sam seeing the headlines or somebody saying something. It terrified me to think of the effect this might have on him. The articles mentioned a source, but the source was never named. They had even supplied a school photo of me. Had they also supplied the photo of Dad? I ran through possible names in my head, suspicious of everyone, including Ross. Had he done this as revenge? He certainly knew the whole story and had access to photographs. But, no, even if he hated me, he'd never do that to Sam.

What about Claire? Maybe she needed whatever cash payment the papers were offering. No, I couldn't believe her capable. If I carried on this way, I'd drive myself crazy.

Only now did I hear my phone buzzing in my bag. I pulled it out and saw I'd just missed the last of five missed calls and five voice messages, all from Ross. I dialled my voicemail.

'Call me,' said his first message. 'Have you seen the papers? Call me,' said the second. By the third message, he was angry, 'For Christ's sake, Nicola, pick up. I've had reporters here and everything.' I didn't need to listen to any more and called his mobile.

'Did you tell them?' I immediately demanded, all rational thought gone.

'Of course, I bloody didn't.'

'Then who did?'

'I've no idea, but it's a nightmare.' I think we both felt a lot better after our outbursts, but it didn't answer the question of who the source was.

'I suppose it doesn't matter who told them,' I said, 'it's done now. Why they're interested is what I want to know.'

'Fucking tabloids, they love other people's misery. Have the police been in touch? Do they know who did this?'

'No, they haven't. You'd think they'd at least have called.'

'They probably did, but you didn't pick up,' he said, unable to hide his sarcasm. 'You should call them, find out what's going on.' As soon as we hung up, I called DI Brown.

'We're on our way to you now,' she said when I called. 'We went to the hotel, but they said you'd gone.'

'A reporter turned up. It was too humiliating, I couldn't stay.'

Brown and Morton arrived shortly after and asked me if I had any idea who the story had come from.

'None, but if they won't give their name, doesn't that suggest it's someone official?'

'Not always,' said Morton. 'It could be someone who just doesn't want it to be public knowledge they've sold you out.'

'Is there anything we can do to stop it?' I asked.

'Not now it's in the public sphere,' said Morton.

'We can manage it though,' said Brown, 'by simply not responding to them, not giving them any reaction or comment. Eventually, they'll lose interest and another story will be front page.'

'They turned up at my work, took a photo and everything.'

'Did you say anything to them?' asked Morton.

'Only to go away.'

'Be aware,' said Brown, 'they will turn up here, it won't be hard for them to find out where you live.' She got up and looked out the window and tutted.

'They're already here,' said Morton, joining her at the window.

I cringed further into my seat. I didn't want to face what was out there.

'What do I do?'

'Carry on as normal. We'll post a man at the hotel entrance to stop any journalists coming in.'

'Is there a back way out of your building?' asked Morton. I shook my head.

To Brown, he said, 'That could be a problem.' She nodded.
'Why?' I demanded. 'What do you mean?'
'There's always the risk they'll follow you to work.'
'Brilliant,' I said to nobody in particular.
'It won't be as bad as you think,' Brown reassured me. 'It just means they'll follow you for a while, but if you don't acknowledge them, they'll soon give up.'
'Have you really no idea who's done this?' I demanded.
'Not yet,' said Morton, 'but we will do and whoever it is will wish they'd never been born. It makes everything so much harder.' He paced around the room, clearly pissed off with this development.
'Will all this media attention affect the case, or my custody of Sam?' I asked.
'No,' said Brown, a little too quickly, 'it won't. The jury has been carefully chosen and they'll be shielded from any future tabloid coverage.'
'It says in the paper a date has been set, is that true?'
'Yes, that's the date we've been given. It's been leaked before we had a chance to tell you. You'll get a letter through telling you the day and time you're needed.'
'I feel like I'm in a nightmare,' I said. 'Ross is furious, he says the press are at his house too.'
'You're both going to have to be patient,' said Brown. 'This sort of story sells, but as soon as the case is settled, they'll leave you alone and you can go back to normal.'
'Things will never be normal,' I told her. 'Everyone will know about Dad and what he did to me. People will look at me and say, "That's the woman who abandoned her child." I'll never live it down.' Brown crouched next to me and took my hands in hers.
'It doesn't matter what they say,' she said. 'What matters is that you survived. What matters is that you know it wasn't your fault. What matters is that you love your son and are fighting to

be with him. In Sam's eyes, the fact that you're going through all of this to be with him will mean more than the fact you left in the first place.' She looked me in the eye. 'That's what matters.'

Chapter 30

There were only three weeks left until the court case started, and each day was a struggle. A near constant stream of reporters were camped out on the street outside my flat, so that I had to keep my curtains permanently shut. Every time I came or went they stuck cameras and microphones in my face, shouted questions at me and said the most horrible things in order to get a reaction. Some even followed me for a full block before giving up. It was a horrendous experience.

Being at work was a salvation where, for the most part, I could escape reporters and questioning looks. True to their word, the police stationed a man in the foyer for the first week, by the end of which the press had stopped coming in. After a while, my furtive scurrying between home and work became the new normal, and I got used to pushing past the reporters at my door.

My neighbours, on the other hand, didn't. Snarly comments were thrown my way about my disappearance or the nuisance the press were making of themselves. By the end of the second week, I was able to move into my new place in Bearsden, which only fuelled the tabloid fire. They couldn't get enough shots of my scant possessions being put into the smallest of removal vans. Commentary was made about how little I owned and how poor I was now that I'd left my husband. They made imaginary comparisons between my tiny one-bed flat and the supposedly luxurious semi-detached palace I'd left behind. It infuriated me that they reduced my abuse, my breakdown, and my broken family to a lifestyle choice. I'd hoped for respite when I moved to the new flat, but when I was stopped by a familiar reporter on my way to work, my heart sank and I wanted to lash out with frustration. I was a prisoner without walls.

Throughout this time, Brown and Morton kept in regular contact. I began to get the feeling that, as their star witness, they wanted to make sure I didn't abscond just before the trial began.

'You need to have a think about whether you want to give your testimony in person or by video link up,' said Brown for the umpteenth time. 'A lot of witnesses in such cases would rather not be face-to-face with their abuser, and that's absolutely fine'

'No,' I said straightaway, 'I've told you, I want to be there, I want to hear what he has to say for himself.'

With all the craziness that was going on in my life, the few hours a week spent with the Child Abuse Support Group was the place I felt most normal. I tried not to miss a single one because it was only there, when I spoke about what had happened as a child, or how I felt now, that there were no tilted heads of pity or gasps of shock. Instead, there was recognition and understanding. I told them about Mum dying. 'It happened weeks ago now, but still I feel nothing, not happy, not sad, nothing. It doesn't seem normal.'

'It could be you've so much else going on that you can't cope with another tragedy at the moment,' said Hayley.

'My mum died when I was going through my court case,' said a young man a few seats down, 'I just couldn't handle it, so I shut it out, didn't think about it at all. It wasn't until about two years later that it hit me. You need to give it time.'

'When my mum died,' said a woman opposite, 'I didn't know how I felt, so I felt nothing. I had been so angry with her for so long for not protecting me from my brother that I blamed her almost more than I blamed him. But she was still my mum. It took me a long time to figure it all out.'

I listened to these shared experiences, and already the weight of confusion was beginning to lift. I wasn't alone, others understood these complex states and the emotional void where feeling should be. It was such a relief that I couldn't stop myself from crying. 'I'm sorry,' I said, 'I can't stop crying these days.'

Hayley smiled and said that no apology was needed and moved on round the group.

The next day I got a surprise text message from Ross, asking if he could come over when I got home from work. It was half-past eight when the bell rang. I'd been on edge all day, still hopeful Ross had changed his mind about fighting me over custody of Sam. I knew it was wrong to get my hopes up, but, like a glutton for punishment, I couldn't help myself. It was the first time we'd been face-to-face since the newspapers broke the story.

I showed Ross around the flat, emphasising how clean and modern it was, which bedroom was Sam's and how close it was to Sam's school. I really wanted him to like the place and to see I was serious about being a responsible parent.

At last, we sat down, and I poured us some wine. We made chit-chat, but all the while, I was desperate to get to the point of his visit.

Eventually he said, 'Sam saw your picture in the paper and recognised you.'

My first thought was that Ross was trying to turn Sam against me before we'd even met.

'Why did you show him?' I asked.

'Don't be daft, I didn't show him. Your story and your photo are everywhere.'

'What did you tell him?'

'The truth.'

'The truth? All of it?'

'Not all, but a lot of it. I told him you'd not been well and had to go away, but now you are back and feeling better. Don't worry, I haven't told him anything about your dad.'

Slowly, it dawned on me that now Sam had seen my picture, he knew his mum was back.

'Did he ask to see me?'

'Yes.'

'And?' I couldn't keep the desperation out of my voice.

'I said, not yet.'

'Why not yet?' I demanded. 'You can't keep me hidden away forever.'

'I know I can't, but I'm not ready.'

'Not ready for what?'

'To share him,' Ross said, avoiding my eyes. 'It's been just the two of us for so long I can't – I'm not ready to be separated from him.'

'But you won't be separated. I don't want to take him away from you. I just want to be part of his life, both of your lives.' We were onto our second glass of wine and tongues started to loosen.

'If I'm honest, there's a part of me that doesn't trust you not to disappear again.'

'That's not fair, I'm doing everything I can to show you I'm well and healthy and here to stay. It's you that keeps pushing me away.'

'Do you blame me? You disappeared, Nicola. I don't know how to make you understand what damage that did to me. I know we were having problems, but you took everything to a whole new level. It's taken me a long time to come to terms with the fact you're back.'

Ross was up and pacing, clearly frustrated with me. He settled by the window and pulled the curtain a little to look

THE DAY SHE CAME HOME 217

outside. I refilled our glasses and took his over to him. A peace offering as I didn't want to argue.

'Look,' he said, accepting the glass. 'Now Sam knows you're around, I know I can't keep you from him forever. Just give me a bit of time to get used to the idea.'

To hide my temper, I downed my glass and went to the kitchen for another bottle of wine. How could he say that to me? He'd had months to get used to the idea, I'm the one who'd had to be patient, holding myself back from turning up at the school gates and saying, "Hi, Sam, I'm your mum."

It was clear Ross had thought I'd either leave again or that I'd never get myself together enough to be granted access. I think he was only now realising I was here to stay and that custody might just go my way.

'It's only a week until Dad's court case,' I said, topping up our glasses, before sitting back down on the sofa.

'It's come around quickly.'

'It's felt like an eternity to me,' I said, taking a swig of wine. 'I'm going to testify in person. I don't want to do it via link up. I told the police, I want to hear the judge tell him he's going to prison.'

'Do you want me to come with you for support?' asked Ross, sitting next to me.

'Yes, I really do.' I smiled at him, grateful that he still cared enough to do that for me. I reached out my hand and, for a moment, put it on his. Then I said, 'It's Mum's funeral next week too. I can't decide whether or not to go.'

'You should,' said Ross, 'I know things were complicated, but she was your mum. The funeral might offer some sort of closure.'

'Yeah, it might.'

'Your dad will be there.'

'Maybe that's what's stopping me. What if he tries to talk to me, or worse, causes a scene?'

'Surely even he wouldn't do that at your mum's funeral.'

We reached for the wine bottle at the same time. Our hands touched and then our fingers entwined. It felt nice to be sitting there next to Ross with, for once, no animosity between us. I felt closer to him that evening than I had done in a long time, well before I even left for Shetland. Ross must have felt the same because it wasn't long after that we began kissing. Our kisses were passionate and urgent and led us to my bedroom.

Our lovemaking was, in turns, gentle and caressing, then strong and forceful. It felt as though we were reacquainting ourselves with each other's bodies and enjoying the familiarity, but were then taken over with frustration at what we'd done to our marriage and how much we'd hurt each other.

When we finished, I lay in Ross's arms and cried because it felt so natural and right to be there with him, and yet I knew it was the last time I would be so. I understood we had just said a very personal and spiritual goodbye.

Chapter 31

'You slept with Nicola?' Claire thumped a newspaper down on the café table.

Ross looked at it and, recognising a composite photograph of himself entering and exiting Nicola's new flat, quickly hid it under the table. He'd arranged to meet Claire for lunch because with everything that was going on, they hadn't seen each other in over three weeks.

'Not so loud,' he said, looking around.

'Is she still in love with you? What were you thinking?' Claire paused before her expression suddenly lit up, 'Are you getting back together?'

'Slow down, no, she's not still in love with me and we're not getting back together. I went round to tell her Sam saw her photo in the paper.'

'You showed him?'

'No, of course not, Jesus. He saw it outside the corner shop. He recognised her from the photos at home and, when he asked why Mum's picture was in the paper, I had to tell him.'

'I guess you couldn't keep her hidden forever.'

'Claire, I wasn't trying to keep her hidden,' Ross couldn't keep the irritation out of his voice. 'But nor was I going to welcome her back with open arms. She left us, don't forget.'

Claire had picked up a menu from the middle of the table and perused it. Without looking up, she said, 'You had to go to

Nicola's flat to tell her this? You couldn't do it over the phone?' Ross blushed, he felt like he'd been caught out at something.

'Of course I could've, but I wanted to see her flat. Claire, I think she's going to take Sam away from me, I really do.' His voice trembled enough for Claire to look up from the menu, giving him her full attention. 'Her flat is lovely, she's got a good job, she seems totally together now, not like before. She's even won you over.' Ross stopped himself from saying any more because he felt his throat catch.

'Ross, she's not going to take Sam away from you.' Claire reached over and put a hand on his arm.

'You don't know that,' he snapped.

'I do.'

'The courts always favour the mother, you know that.'

'Not anymore they don't and, anyway, they're hardly going to remove him from a steady and secure home and put him full-time with Nicola who, let's be honest, still has a lot to prove and who Sam doesn't even know. Yes, she's his mother, but she's also a stranger.' They sat in silence for a while, then Claire asked, 'Is that why you slept with her? So she wouldn't take Sam away?'

'No.' Claire looked at him doubtfully. 'Honestly, Claire, do you really think I'd do that?'

'I think you might be panicking enough to do it, yes.'

'Well, I'm not. I didn't mean for it to happen, but we were chatting, there was wine, and it felt really nice being with her.' He shook his head slightly, as if he couldn't believe what he was about to say. 'I like this new, strong Nicola. Sometimes, it feels like I'm meeting her for the first time, just getting to know her, and I'm reminded of how much I loved her and of the good times we had together.' Ross looked up and saw Claire watching him with an amused sadness. 'What?' he asked.

'You still love her. You still love Nicola. Can't you give it another go with her?'

'I've thought about it,' he said, shaking his head, 'but I can't. I do love her, and I always will, but not enough to be able to forget everything that's happened and start over.'

A waitress came and took their order. When she'd gone Claire asked, 'Will you share custody with her?'

'I don't know. Since it all came out about her dad, everything makes sense. I mean, I'm amazed she held it together for as long as she did. If my father had done that to me, I'd be behind bars by now.'

Claire nodded in agreement.

'What's stopping you?' she asked.

'What's stopping Nicola from leaving again?'

'Ross, come on, she's not going to leave again, is she?'

'That's the thing, Claire, I don't know.'

Ever since the truth about Nicola's abuse had come to the surface, Ross had gone back and forth in his mind about whether to contest Nicola's application for joint custody or not. On the one hand, Ross felt every child needed a mother and that the time would come when Sam would want to search for her. If he ever found out Ross had kept Nicola from him, Sam would not see it as a kindness. He had to admit, too, that it would be nice to have a bit more free time, as being a sole caregiver takes its toll.

On the other hand, Ross couldn't bear the thought of Sam and Nicola getting so close that Sam would want to go and live with her full time. That would break his heart. Nor did he think Sam's heart could take it if, for whatever reason, Nicola decided to take off again. When he thought back to how much Sam had cried in that first week, how long it took him to settle at night without his mother there, Ross knew he was doing the right thing.

'For what it's worth,' said Claire, 'I really don't think she'll leave again. She's invested too much and, as you say, she's a different person now.'

Ross pulled the newspaper back out from under the table and looked at the photos of himself. 'I can't believe they were there all that time,' he said.

'Nicola says they never leave. She's seen them there at 2a.m. before.'

'Do you see much of her?'

'About once a week.'

'God, Claire, how did this happen?' He bashed his hands against the sides of his head.

The waitress came back with their food. 'I don't blame you,' she said. 'What that woman did to you and your son is a disgrace, a pure disgrace.'

The woman's words shocked Ross into silence and unable to come up with a suitable response he simply said, 'Thank you.'

They ate their lunch quickly and quietly, aware they were being scrutinised by the staff, if not the other diners. After they paid, they stood on the pavement.

'I'll walk you to work,' said Claire. 'Has Jamie been in touch? I know he wanted to see you.'

'Yes, he messaged me yesterday and we're going to meet for a drink next week.'

'He's still angry with Nicola. He said if I ever did that to him he'd be unable to forgive me, regardless of my childhood.' Ross didn't say anything. 'I said that was heartless, and I didn't believe him.'

'That's pretty much how I felt.'

'But you don't now, not now you know about her past.'

'That's true, but I'm still wary.'

'You're right to be, and so would Jamie be, but to be so unforgiving seems too much, don't you think? I told him he'd be punishing the kids more than me. They'd want to know their mum after all.'

'Claire,' Ross gently reprimanded his friend, 'don't try to persuade me one way or the other.'

'I'm not, honest, I'm just telling you about a conversation Jamie and I had. I think one of the things he finds so hard about the situation is that it reminds him of his own family. His parents divorced, and she remarried. I think his father convinced him his mother loved her new family more, and Jamie believed it.'

'What do you think?'

'I think she loves him just as much as the others. That said, Jamie does make it difficult for her. I think he's still angry about the divorce, but they're not a family who talk about things, so it'll probably never get resolved.' Claire laughed to herself, 'He hates it when I try to talk about relationship stuff with him, it freaks him out.'

'It's funny isn't it, you think that when you grow up, you won't make the same mistakes your parents made, and sometimes you don't. Instead, you make your own fresh mistakes. My parents have a great marriage, there's never been any dark secrets-'

'That you know of,' teased Claire.

'Oh no, there're no skeletons in our cupboards, my family are too boring and normal.'

'Is any family normal and boring when you dig a little? I'm not so sure.'

'Trust me, mine are, and I think that's one of the reasons I've found this so hard. I feel I've let them down by, I dunno, choosing the wrong wife or not being a good enough husband.' Ross hung his head. 'Something like that, anyway.'

'Do you think you weren't a good enough husband?'

Ross nodded his head, unable to meet her eye.

'Marriage is hard,' Claire said matter-of-factly, 'even for normal and boring couples like your parents.' She put her arm through his and they walked on in silence for a while. 'Do you think we're being watched by the paparazzi now?'

'God, I hope not,' Ross smiled, 'they'll think I'm having an affair with you as well.'

'I should have put some make-up on, if I'm going to be on the front pages.'

'How are the kids?' Ross asked, keen to change the subject.

'They're fine, same as ever. Lots of squabbling and they refuse to eat any food I make them. Every day there's something new they don't like, which they insist they've never liked and swear they told me about. It drives me up the wall. You don't know how lucky you are with Sam. Whenever he comes over for dinner, he eats everything that's put on his plate, no arguments.'

'That's because my cooking is so awful he's relieved to be somewhere else.' They laughed before falling into another silence.

'Are you going to the trial?' Claire asked.

'I said I'd go on the day Nicola gives evidence. Are you?'

'I can't, unfortunately, but, to be honest, I don't know if I want to know what happened. I'm scared that if I do know I'll always see her in terms of her abuse, not for the person she is now.'

'Isn't that a bit...?'

'Selfish? Yes, it probably is, but I can't help it. I'm not sure I can listen to the details of what happened. It makes me sick to think about it. I imagine someone doing that to Alisdair or Eilidh, and it makes my blood boil.'

'I understand.'

'Do you think I'm a bad person?'

'No, of course not.' By now, they had arrived at Ross's office and they said goodbye.

'Look after yourself,' Claire said, 'I'll speak to you soon.'

Ross found it hard to concentrate for the rest of the working day, and he went through the motions until it was time to leave. He thought hard about his conversation with Claire, and how extreme Jamie's response was to Nicola's disappearance. He'd never talked to Jamie about his parents because Claire was right, Jamie didn't like what he'd call 'touchy feely' stuff. He did know that Jamie's relationship with both his parents was tricky. He also knew he didn't want that for him and Sam, but it was hard to know what the best thing to do was. He wanted to protect Sam by keeping Nicola, and any future hurt, out of his life, but in doing so would he harm his son even more?

Chapter 32

I don't know why I questioned it because, of course, I went to Mum's funeral. How could I not? Despite everything, she was still my mother and there must have been a bond at one time and Ross was right. The service might be a way of saying goodbye and achieving some closure. The only promise I made to myself was that I would leave straight away and spend the rest of the day at home, quietly by myself.

It was a damp, wintry day. It wasn't actually raining, but moisture draped the air like a heavy curtain. The clouds were fat and threatening. I went to the service by myself. Both Ross and Claire had offered to come with me, but I wanted to go alone. I didn't want to be distracted from whatever I was feeling about her death. In fact, I wanted to know what it was I was feeling because it was still a mystery even to me.

The press were expected to make an appearance and so there was a police presence was to stop them coming up the driveway to the Glasgow Crematorium chapel. As I waited to enter, I looked down to the gates and watched them all milling about, zoom lenses primed and ready. I thought how cold they must be standing out there, the wind whipping around them. How much would they sell these shots for, I wondered, and was it worth waiting in the cold?

The wind swirled around me too, fallen leaves lifting in the gusts. I shuddered at the cold, but also with nerves at how the next half hour would pan out. I walked in and took a seat at the front of the chapel. I kept my head facing forward; I didn't want to speak to anyone. Before long everyone took their seats and the service began.

There was no music as the coffin was carried in. Dad followed behind, looking pale and withdrawn. His usual demeanour lacked its previous power. He caught my eye, and I thought he was going to say something, but, whatever it was, he thought better of it and looked away. He sat down at the front of the chapel, but on the opposite side of the aisle to me. I was thankful for that small mercy. If I didn't turn my head, I didn't need to look at him.

The minister began his address, recounting Mum's life. It didn't last long. When he invited Dad up to give his eulogy I held my breath, wondering what he would say about a wife he'd never loved, had barely liked.

'As you all know,' he began, 'Mary was a very special woman. She had a gentle nature, a kind heart, and never a bad word to say about anyone. She was loyal, loyal to me and to her friends. She lived a simple, Christian life, she didn't strive for the world, but made the most of what she had here in the city of her birth, surrounded by a life of comfort and simple pleasures. Mary was my partner in life for over forty years. Every day, she gave me strength and courage. I don't know what I'm going to do without her.'

That was it. He sat down. I don't know what I'd thought Dad would say, but I suppose that was about right. No mention of love, only how she'd served him. No word about me or Sam. Dad could not have made it any clearer we were cast out, that my accusations were false and I was a Judas.

The minister led us in a prayer as the curtain closed on the coffin. I began to cry for the mother I wished I'd had. I wept for the loving, embracing, protecting mother I should have had, that I, like any child, deserved. When Mary died, so did any chance of finding that mother. I wept too, for my own part in her death. If I'd tried harder to make her leave him, maybe things would have been different.

The chapel doors opened, and cold air rushed in, drying my tears as they fell. The minister and my father stood by the door to shake hands with mourners as they left. There was to be no wake. In time, I made my way outside, careful not to catch the eye of either my father or the minister. Now it was over, I wanted to leave as soon as possible, but I was stopped almost immediately by a woman who looked to be about my mother's age.

'Nicola,' she said, 'I'm sorry for your loss. You won't remember me, but your mum and I were friends a long time ago when you were just a wee thing. You and my Donna are the same age and used to play together.' I looked closely, but didn't recognise her. 'Well,' she said, coming closer, 'your dad didn't like your mum having friends he didn't know and soon stopped us seeing each other.' She looked around, checking nobody could hear us. 'I saw the papers, and it doesn't surprise me. He was always a bully, and I felt sorry for you and your mum. But what could anyone do? She loved him.'

I didn't know what to say. She was the first person from my past to speak to me and I felt a floodgate was about to open, but before she could say any more, another woman came over.

'Reenie?' she asked the woman. 'It's me, Janice.'

'Oh, my God, Janice, so it is. Do you remember Nicola? I was just telling her, what her father did doesn't surprise me, he was always a bully. Poor Mary.'

'I'm sorry for your loss,' said Janice. 'None of us knew what she saw in him,' Janice confided. 'He was such a bully, he stopped her from seeing any of her old pals, didn't he, Reenie?'

'Oh, aye,' Reenie agreed.

'But what he did to you Nicola is shocking, absolutely shocking. I had no idea, did you?' she asked Reenie.

'None. If we'd known, maybe we could've helped, but Mary never said a word.' They both looked at me, heads tilted to one side, waiting for me to say something.

'How did you know Mum?'

'We used to live on the same street,' said Reenie, 'grew up together.'

'Did you know her brother, Callum?'

'Oh, God, wee Callum, I'd forgotten all about him.'

'He was younger,' said Janice, 'went away to sea. Did he ever come back?'

'I don't think so,' I replied. 'At least, I never heard that he did.'

'He did,' said a man with a broad Scots accent. The three of us turned to look at him, surprised by his interjection.

'Did you know him?' I asked. I was beginning to feel bombarded by all these strange people who knew my family, but of whom I had no recollection.

'I am him,' said the man. I felt everything stop as I stared at him, looking to find a resemblance to my mum, but I couldn't see it.

'You're Callum?' I asked.

'I am, but when I saw Mary's picture in the paper and read about what had happened, I took the first flight I could.' He pulled an envelope out from his coat pocket. From out of the envelope, he pulled a black-and-white photo of a young man and woman. The woman was unmistakably my mother.

'That's me and your mum. Before I left for overseas, we went up to the Trongate and had this photo taken. We didn't have any from when we were kids and I didn't know if we'd ever see each other again.' He rubbed his thumb over the picture of Mum and I could hear emotion in his voice. 'Turns out we didn't.'

Reenie and Janice looked at the photo. 'Well, I never,' said Janice, 'so it is, that's Mary alright. And that's just how I remember you, Callum.' They looked at him with renewed interest, as did I. He was the only family I had ever met, my only link to the past.

'Can I take you for a coffee?' Callum asked me. I nodded, fascinated by this man who was my uncle and who had appeared like an apparition by my side. Before anything else could be said, we watched in silence as the squad car pulled up. Blue lights were flashed, but no sirens blared. Dad was helped into the back of the car and, I assumed, taken home. Everybody watched in stunned silence. The only sound to be heard above the wind was the click, click, click, of the cameras being blown in our direction. As soon as the car was out of sight, the mourners resumed their chatter.

DIs Brown and Morton materialised, unexpectedly, beside me. Janice and Reenie made their excuses and wandered away. 'Who were they?' asked Morton.

'They were friends of Mum's before she got married.' I said. Morton looked at Brown, who gave him a nod, and then he followed Janice and Reenie. I watched him show them his ID and ask a question before I noticed Brown querying how Callum knew Mum.

'I'm her brother, Callum.' Brown's eyes widened when she heard his name. 'I saw on the news what had happened and took the first flight over.'

'You're the brother in Australia?'

'That's right.'

'I'd be keen to ask you some questions.'

'Absolutely,' said Callum, 'but I don't know what I'll be able to tell you. I haven't seen Mary since I was sixteen.' He showed her the photo he'd brought.

As he did so, I looked again at my uncle. He looked youthful and tanned. I pictured him in a spacious bungalow with a pool in the back garden and a large deck and barbecue where he grilled fresh fish and seafood. Did he have a family, I wondered?

'Do you have time to come to the station now?' Brown asked.

'I was going to take Nicola for a coffee.'

'I'll drive you both to the station and you can go on from there,' she said. When we arrived, I waited in reception while they took Callum to the interview room. Time dragged, but eventually the door opened and Callum appeared looking drained. Was that simply jet lag, I asked myself, or as a result of being interrogated? I took us to a nearby café. We ordered at the counter and found an empty table.

'How was your flight?' I asked as a way to break the ice. This man was a stranger to me, after all, and I felt awkward in his presence.

'Long,' he said. 'I wanted to get here as quickly as possible and find out what was going on. I couldn't believe what I was reading in the press. It sounded so incredible.'

'I can't believe it was on Australian news.' I said.

'It wasn't, but I regularly check online to see what's happening over here. It's front page news here.'

'You haven't lost your accent,' I said.

'You're right,' Callum laughed. 'I've got British friends at home who, within a year, sound born and bred in Oz. I've been there for forty years and still sound right at home here.'

He pulled out some snapshots, modern ones in full colour, contrasting with the old black and white studio shot of him and Mum.

'This is my wife, Kim,' he said, pointing to a slim, athletic woman. 'It was taken on holiday in Margaret River.' He pulled out another from behind it. This one was of two men, who looked to be in their thirties. There was no question they were his children. One looked exactly like Callum and the other looked so like my mum it was eerie.

'These must be your sons,' I said.

'Yes, that's right. Colin and Simon. Colin is thirty-nine now, got his own plumbing business. Simon is thirty-six and an academic. What he studies, I've no idea. All I know is that it's something to do with lasers.' Callum chuckled to himself before saying, 'I'm sure it's nothing to do with light sabres. He's no Jedi warrior, that's for sure.' From the way he told his joke, I could tell it was a family favourite, and he'd told it many times. Behind the mockery was an ill-concealed pride at his clever boy. I ran a finger over the image of Simon.

'He looks just like your mum, doesn't he?' I nodded. 'Do you have any photographs of your mum?' he asked, 'Recent ones?'

'No, I don't,' I replied. 'I was just thinking about that the other day. We didn't take many when I was a child. Any we do have are with Dad. I didn't want any when I left home.'

At the mention of my father, we both looked away. I didn't know how much this man knew, nor how much I wanted to tell him. He was still a stranger.

'What did the police want?' I asked.

'I think they wanted to check I am who I say I am.'

'Are you?' I don't know why I was being so curt with him. Perhaps I expected him to throw another family skeleton in my face. Perhaps I was still suspicious about who he said he was, though why I should be, I don't know.

'Yes,' he said gently, 'I am.'

'Tell me about my mum,' I said. 'What was she like when she was young?'

'She was such a gentle girl. After the others were taken away and Mum got stuck into the drink, Mary looked after me. She didn't have to, she could have moved out, got on with her life, but she didn't. She raised me really, even though she was only a few years older.'

'You must have been very close?'

'We were. She really was a mother to me. I remember she got a job in the glove department at Copland and Lye. She loved that job, and she looked so glamorous in her fancy dress and heels. Mary always looked after herself. When she brought home her first wages she took me out for an ice cream. It was amazing.'

'I didn't know she'd had a job. I thought she met Dad straight out of school.'

'No, she left school at fifteen and had a few casual bits of work before getting the job at Copland's. She'd been there a couple of years before I joined the navy and went overseas.'

'Why did you leave her behind?'

'What makes you think I did?' Callum looked at me, perplexed.

'You left as soon as you could. You could have stayed and got a job here.'

'There was nothing for me here in Glasgow. I didn't want to stay on at school, I had no skills, an alcoholic mother and an absent father. You're right, I left as soon as I could.'

'You abandoned her.'

'Is that really what you think?' He was clearly hurt by my accusation. 'As soon as I settled in Australia, I wrote for her. I told her how good life was there, that we could start a new life together, away from Glasgow and the poverty and the cold.'

'So why didn't she go?'

'You would have to ask her that,' he sighed, shaking his head. 'All I know is that by then she'd met your dad and thought she was in love.'

'You don't think she was?'

'Oh, I'm sure she was. Why else would she have stayed with a man like that?'

'You knew about him?' I was shocked. If he had known why hadn't he done something?

'I knew he was a bully and that he kept Mary on a short leash, but I had no idea of the violence or,' he looked at the table, clearly embarrassed to mention my abuse, 'what he was doing to you.' He reached a hand over and put it lightly on my forearm. I, too, was embarrassed and couldn't look up. 'I had no idea.' he said. 'If I had, I would have come to get you both.'

'Did you keep in touch with each other?'

'I wrote, and she replied for a few years, but eventually she stopped. I think I heard from her only two times after she got married. The first time was after the wedding. She said it had been quiet and beautiful, and that she was very happy.'

'A shame it didn't last,' I said, unable to keep the bitterness out of my voice. 'What did she say in her second letter?'

'She wrote to tell me about your birth. She said it had gone smoothly, and she loved you very much. She was over the moon, I could tell from her letter. She said Stephen was delighted too and had been back to his loving self. She said they doted on you.' Callum hesitated before saying, 'I noticed though that her tone was different. I don't really know how to describe it, but she seemed altered. Her voice wasn't coming through. Does that sound daft?'

'No, not at all. The more I think about her life, the more I see how lost she was. I think she gave up on herself, or a life without Dad. She might have wanted to leave him, but she didn't feel able. She'd lost sight of herself and we both suffered for it.' I stirred my near empty coffee cup. 'Didn't she say anything about what Dad was doing? Is there anything you can remember that can be used in the court case?'

'I'm sorry, Nicola,' he said, 'there isn't. I never met him, never even saw a photo of him.' I'd known that would be his answer, but it was still disappointing. 'I'm sorry, Nicola,' he said again. 'Can I maybe take you for lunch or dinner? You're all I have left of Mary, of my life here. I'd like to get to know you.'

'That would be nice,' I said, and meant it. Outside the café, I asked him, 'Where are you staying?'

'I got a cheap room in a budget hotel, which is where I'm heading now. Jet lag is kicking in. I only arrived yesterday and haven't adjusted yet.' He pulled out a business card and on it wrote down his UK mobile number. 'Call me tomorrow,' he said, 'and we can arrange something.'

'Okay, Uncle Callum,' I said, laughing at how strange it sounded.

'Less of the uncle,' he said jokingly, 'it makes me sound older than I feel.'

Chapter 33

It had recently been Claire's birthday, and I'd promised to take her out to lunch. I'd booked a table in one of the nicer restaurants in Princes Square. It was at the top of the shopping galleries and, with the glass roof letting in the sunshine, the atmosphere was warm and summery. I ordered a bottle of champagne to toast her good health.

I'd been there half an hour, and she still hadn't arrived. I'M HERE, I messaged, ARE YOU ON YOUR WAY?

I got no response and worried that there had been a mix-up in communication. I was just about to call and check on her when Claire appeared at the ma"tre d's station and was shown in my direction. I stood up to hug her and noticed her eyes were red and blotchy, and her face was pale.

'My God, Claire, what's happened?' I asked.

'I've had a huge argument with Jamie, but let's not talk about it.'

'Was it about you coming to lunch? I know he's still angry with me.'

'No, nothing like that, honestly. Let's order, I'm starving.'

A waitress came to the table, poured the champagne and took our order. 'Sláinte,' we said, clinking glasses.

'How are your various legal battles?' Claire joked before I could probe further. I couldn't help but laugh. It did seem this was my year of police interviews and solicitors and court appearances.

'I've had a letter from Kwame Martins telling me a date is set for the divorce and custody hearing. I don't know what to concentrate on first,' I told her.

'It doesn't rain, but it pours, eh? I'd think about the custody hearing, that's more important. Your dad is part of your past, a past you don't want. Sam is your future, with or without Ross. That should be your focus.' She was right, of course.

Regardless of how Dad's court case went, my future lay with Sam. Dad was part of my past and once the case was over, I need never see him again.

'How is Ross?' I asked her. I had had no contact with him since we'd slept together.

'He's alright, I think. He's as nervous as you about the hearing. He's terrified at the thought of losing Sam.'

'I keep telling him he won't lose Sam,' I reassured Claire. 'Nobody wants to separate them, especially not me. I just want the chance to make up for what I did, and for what I've missed out on.'

'Listen,' said Claire, 'I talked to Ross about shared custody.'

'Do you think he'll change his mind?'

'I don't think he's trying to punish you, I think he fears being hurt again.'

'Every time I think about the hearing, it makes me feel sick to my stomach, I'm so nervous.'

'Tell me about your uncle – him turning up like that must have been such a shock?'

'A huge shock,' I said. 'He appeared by my side so unexpectedly I didn't believe him at first.'

'How did he even know about the funeral?'

'The internet.'

'Of course,' Claire rolled her eyes. 'What did we do before the worldwide web?'

'Once I got over the surprise, we chatted and he seems nice.'

'Did your mum ever tell him anything about your dad?'

'No, she only wrote to him twice and didn't mention anything.'

'I hoped he might be another witness for you.'

'That was my first thought as well but, no, he can't help. He's told me more about their childhood, though. Mum never really talked about it, but their mother was a drunk and regularly lashed out at both Mum and Callum. I think that being beaten was normal for Mum. Maybe she even saw it as a way of showing love.'

'Did she ever hit you?'

'No, never.' Claire's question prompted a vague, unremembered echo of being sent to my room or into the garden to play. 'She took the beatings for me.'

'Your poor mum. First her mother, then her husband. No wonder Callum took a fast boat out of here.'

'Yeah, I guess,' I laughed, but faltered abruptly. 'He says he asked her to follow him to Australia, but she said no. By then she'd met Dad.' I shook my head like a dog freeing itself of water. 'Enough of this sad talk, it's your birthday, let's talk about you. Did Jamie buy you a birthday present?'

'Yes, a couple of books I'd asked for.'

'What about the kids?'

'The usual homemade card and Eilidh wrapped something of hers that she thought I'd like. It was very sweet but I'm not really into Hatchimals.' We both laughed, but Claire's tone was low and dull. There was none of her usual energy and enthusiasm.

'Claire, what's wrong, you don't seem yourself today. Has Jamie upset you?'

'I'm pregnant,' she announced, taking a large drink of her champagne.

'Is this good news?' I asked cautiously.

'No, it's not,' she said with forced cheerfulness. 'It's terrible news and I'm not keeping it.'

'Is that what you were arguing about?'

'Yes. He wants to keep it, but we can't afford it financially and I can't afford it mentally.'

'What do you mean?'

'I can't go through it all again. Alasdair and Eilidh are past that baby stage, they're both at school and on their way to being independent. I want to go back to work. Being a stay-at-home mum has not been easy for me, but we couldn't afford a nanny. Me being at home was the most sensible solution, given Jamie earns so much more.

'I love the kids, but it's not how I saw my life panning out. If we have another baby, that's another six or seven years of my life consumed with sleepless nights, nappies, bottles and playgroups. I've just sold the buggy, for Christ's sake. It would destroy me to have to start again.'

'Claire, I had no idea you felt this way. I'm so sorry, there's me going on about how bad I have things and you're having your own battle.'

'Don't apologise, honestly. I was never depressed or anything like that, I just feel my time at home is nearing an end and I can't wait.' She raised her glass, and we toasted to nothing in particular. I got the impression this had been a hard decision for her to reach, and she didn't want to be dissuaded.

'If you were to go back to work, would you be able to afford childcare?'

'It's possible, but I'm not sure it's worth the stress. I've seen the other parents at school and their lives seem to consist of running from home to school to work and back again. I get the feeling they're constantly chasing their tails.'

'Might that be worth it if it meant you're back at work?'

'I can't decide. It feels like I'll either be miserable at home with a baby but not racing all over the city every day, or at work with other grown-ups and contributing to the world, but stressed out and grumpy with everyone.'

'When you put I like that, it doesn't sound much of a choice.'

'Or, I don't have the baby and go back to work. For me that seems like a win-win situation.' She took another drink.

'What about a nanny?' I asked.

'We really can't afford that. Nursery is expensive enough, but a nanny is beyond our budget.'

'You need a lottery win.'

Claire crossed her fingers on both hands and laughed. The waitress brought over our food, and it looked and smelled delicious. 'I'm starving,' Claire said, 'thank you for lunch, it's a real treat to come into town and eat in a nice restaurant. Most of the time we go only to places that serve their food on plastic plates and don't mind that the kids throw half their meal on the floor.'

'How does Jamie feel about having a third child?'

'He thinks it's amazing and that we should keep it. But that's because he's out all day, his career hasn't taken a nosedive. If anything, it's skyrocketed over the past couple of years. He's great at his job and deserves to do well, but I wish he'd take my professional life as seriously. I wish he could see that being a mum is not a career.'

'Claire,' I said, 'I'm really sorry. I know this must be a hard decision.'

'You have no idea. Jamie wants to keep it, but even if I did too, we really can't afford it, not on one salary. Having a baby is expensive. I've told him he's having the snip. We can't risk this happening again.' She sipped her drink, deep in thought. 'If it had happened when Eilidh was still little, then maybe, but not now.' I could tell she was replaying arguments with Jamie in her head.

'Does he think you can afford it financially?'

'He knows money is tight - you spend what you earn, right? But he seems to think we'll find the extra resources somehow. He talked about tightening our belts, but I know him and that's something he can't do. He loves being able to buy whatever he needs, immediately, online. He doesn't like to budget.'

'When are you, you know?'

'Next week. It's all done by pill these days. I take one next Monday, then the second one on Wednesday. And that's it, apparently. Happy birthday, me.' She poured another glass and took a swig.

It was my turn to comfort her, and I put my hand on hers and gave it a squeeze. I wished I had some words of wisdom for my friend. 'We're both so miserable,' she said, and wiped away a tear before it spilled.

'Let's order some cake to soak up the champers.'

As I walked home after lunch, I couldn't help but feel dreadful for Claire. She had made such a difficult decision, made even harder by the fact Jamie didn't agree. I hoped it wouldn't put a wedge between them, and that in time it would work out to be the better decision.

My phone beeped. It was a message from Callum. ARE YOU FREE FOR DINNER TOMORROW?

We arranged a time, and I was surprised by how much I was looking forward to seeing him again. I wondered what else he might reveal about Mum's childhood. It also prompted thoughts of Dad's court case, which was in just two days' time. I'd had my letter summoning me to testify in the case of the Crown vs Johnston. Reading the summons, with its impressive letterhead, brought what was happening into sharp focus. This was it, the anguish of my childhood and the pain of the past four years was coming to a head and, I hoped, this case would put all my ghosts to rest.

The prospect of standing in the witness box, under oath, made my first visit to the police station feel like morning coffee.

Sitting in a quiet room with only DI Gail Brown scribbling down a few notes was far less intimidating than being questioned in an open court in front of a jury, a public gallery, and the press. The nerves that had, until now, been low lying, began to take hold.

Chapter 34

The following day, Callum met me after work and we went for dinner at Café India in the Merchant City.

'I hear curry is Scotland's national dish these days,' he said. 'It's taken over from fish and chips.' He perused the menu. 'I'm going to have the works,' and, before I could answer, he went on, 'it's on me.'

We ordered poppadoms, their haggis pakora, prawn biryani, lamb kabab and naan bread, all to be washed down with Kingfisher lager.

'Let's see how it's done in Scotland,' Callum said after we'd ordered, clearly pleased with his choice. 'You know, when I left Glasgow, we didn't have any foreign restaurants. Italian ice cream was about as exotic as it got.' He sat back and took a large drink from his beer, which the waitress had just brought over. 'I had one today, actually, at Jaconelli's. I couldn't believe it's still there. We used to go there as kids, for a treat, you know? It hadn't changed a bit. I sat in there with my bowl of ice cream and all these memories came flooding back. I remembered I once found a halfpenny on the street. I couldn't believe my luck. I didn't say anything to anybody, but headed straight round to Jaconelli's and bought an ice cream.' He laughed as he told me. 'Mary saw me in there and thought I'd stolen the money from Mum. She was livid at first, but when I told her I'd found it, she stopped being angry and demanded a bit.'

I had never been to Café D'Jaconelli as Dad had favoured the University Café, but I knew of its reputation as being one of the original ice cream parlours in Scotland and for the fact that neither the café nor its recipe had changed since the 1930s.

'You took a visit to Maryhill?' I asked my uncle.

'Yes, I wanted to see my old stomping ground.'

'Has it changed much?' I asked. Callum thought for a moment, pushing a hand through his hair while he searched for the right words.

'Shops have changed hands, cafés have closed, and there are posh coffee shops now. My old school has turned into flats.' He shook his head, incredulous.

The poppadoms arrived, and we hungrily broke them up, dipping fragments into the various sauces they came with. 'But,' Callum continued between mouthfuls, 'at its heart, it felt the same. The flat me and Mary lived in with our mother is still standing, but it's got PVC double glazing now, not the old rotten wooden windows we had. The Close has a door on it with a buzzer entry system. I left in 1967 so, of course, things have changed, but it's strange to see it in the flesh, so to speak.'

'Could you ever see yourself moving back here?' He shook his head sadly.

'No, I couldn't. I've been away so long I don't fit in anymore. I could tell that just by walking the streets and listening to people talk. I don't think in the same way. It's strange, but I feel more Scottish in Australia than I do here. I might not sound it, but I feel like a foreigner here.'

'That's sad,' I said.

'Och,' he replied, 'it's the way of things. We all move on in our own directions.'

The main course arrived, much to Callum's obvious elation. There were a lot of appreciative sighs and exclamations of delight, which pleased the waitress no end. We dished up and ate in silence for a while.

'I suppose this is what the court case is for you?' my uncle asked me. 'A way to move on.'

'I think in many ways it is. My time on Shetland gave me the headspace to evaluate my life to date, and it wasn't going the way I'd hoped.'

'What were your hopes?'

'The same as anybody else, I suppose. A good job, a family, to feel like a grown-up.'

'And you didn't?'

'No. I felt like I was play-acting, or that I'd run away from home and, at any minute, Dad was going to appear and drag me back kicking and screaming.'

'I was curious. Why did you stay in contact with your parents when you left home? If it was me, I think I'd have wanted nothing more to do with them.'

'I find that the hardest part to explain.' It was a question I'd been asked many times, by Ross, by the police, by Claire and by the support group. 'Dad was my abuser, but he was also my father. He did unspeakable things to me, but we also had fun times. It was him that took me to the cinema, or for ice cream. It was Dad who taught me how to ride a bike or would take us to the beach. Mixed in with the bad stuff was a father who guided me, taught me right from wrong, and who, for many years, was the biggest influence on my life.' I hesitated, knowing how absurd to an outsider it sounded. 'I loved him once.'

Callum looked at me with scepticism, but I could only shrug. It was the way it was. 'You said the court case was only part of the reason you reported your dad. What's the other reason?'

'I had to prove to Ross that my disappearance hadn't been for nothing. I had to show him that I've changed, that I've dealt with, or am dealing with, my past. He needs to trust me again. He needs to trust me for his own sake, but also for Sam.' Talking about Sam still made me well up, no matter how often I did it. I took a moment before I carried on. 'I damaged Sam when I left.

Not in an obvious way, but deep inside him. He may always feel I abandoned him, as others see it, and he may never trust me again, not entirely. Confronting Dad and going through with the court case is part of that.'

'Did you want to reconcile with Ross?'

'At first, yes. I had a fantasy whereby he forgave me everything and we went back to the way we were before.' Callum smiled sympathetically. 'But as you say, everyone moves on. Ross included.' I thought back to my first visits to the house after my return, how like a time capsule the house had felt. Then later, after Ross found me, he removed all trace of me and he moved on.

'Has Sam seen you since you returned?'

'Only on the front of a newspaper.'

'Ouch,' said Callum, 'I bet that raised some questions.'

'It forced Ross to tell him about me.'

'He hadn't already?'

'No.' I sighed. 'He'd been trying desperately to keep me at a distance for as long as possible. I was angry at the time, but I do understand why he did it. Fear is a powerful driver, I know that more than most. It makes us do crazy things.'

'Would you like some more drinks?' the waitress asked, tipping the last of the Kingfisher into our glasses.

I declined. The court case was the next day, and I didn't want to be distracted with a hangover.

'Can we have some water, please?' Callum asked.

The waitress nodded.

'How was the food, sir?'

'Delicious, absolutely delicious. I really loved the lamb dish. Can I have the recipe?' They both laughed before she left to get our water. 'It really is, you know,' he said, pointing at the food, 'bloody gorgeous.'

'Are you coming tomorrow?' I asked, suddenly fearful he wasn't. I had only just met this man, but I was scared he would return to Australia while I wasn't looking.

'Damn right I am. I want to understand what's been happening to my sister and you all these years and why he did what he did.' I watched Callum as his eyes lit up with excitement, which took me aback. Nervous energy was one thing, but he appeared almost happy.

'Am I missing something?' I asked. He took a deep breath.

'Over the past few years. I've been doing a bit of family history research.'

'Go on.'

'I've found two of my younger siblings and we're going to meet tomorrow after the court case.' I was gob smacked.

In the last few months, my mum's family had expanded beyond all belief. She'd gone from being an only child to one of seven, and now three of them had turned up out of the blue. I couldn't take it all in.

'When did you find them?' I asked. 'And how? Mum said they were taken into care.'

'They were, and some of them stayed there, but some were adopted. I found out one was sent to Western Australia and still lives there. I don't think he had a good time there as a child. He's written, but he's not ready to meet.'

'Australia? You mean he was one of those kids shipped out to work on farms and stuff? Child labour?' Callum nodded. 'Poor thing. It's only sad stories you hear about that.'

'I'm sure there were positive outcomes for some kids, but you're right, a lot of negative ones too.'

'What about the two you're meeting tomorrow? Did they stay in Glasgow?'

'They went into care homes and didn't leave until they were sixteen.'

'Who are they? What are their names?'

'There's Robert, who's seven years younger than me. I get the feeling he's drifted a bit. He hasn't mentioned a family, so don't know if he's got one or not. Then there's Elizabeth. She calls herself Lizzie and is five years younger than me. I know that she's married, got two grown-up kids.'

'Wow, Callum, that's amazing. It must feel like a miracle to have found them.'

'It's incredible. I can't wait to meet them. I was only, what, eleven or twelve when they were taken away, but I feel like I know them still. They've been part of me for so long.' He put a hand to his chest.

I wondered if Mum had felt this way about her lost siblings. Did she think about them often? I doubted she ever looked for them as Dad would never have approved, but did she still have a sense of them? Did she know in her muscles that she was one of seven, or after all these years did she feel like an only child?

'I wonder what they look like,' I said, 'if you all look similar.'

'They've sent me photos and there's definitely a family resemblance. I'm pretty sure I'll recognise them tomorrow.'

'Where are you meeting them?'

'Outside the court at 5 p.m.'

'Do you think they'll come into the court?'

'They might do. I'd written to them about Mary so they may recognise her from the media coverage.' The waitress brought us the bill and while Callum paid, I thought about whether I wanted to meet them tomorrow as well.

'I'll walk you to your hotel,' I said, and we sauntered through the Merchant City, each filled with tasty food and thoughts of the next day. 'I'm nervous about tomorrow,' I said at length. 'What if he gets away scot-free?' Callum put a comforting arm around me. It was strange how familiar he felt after only a few days.

'If he does, you'll carry on because that's all we can do. We can look ahead to the future. You can focus on your new life that doesn't include Stephen.'

'And, as of tomorrow, you're going to have a new life that does include a brother and a sister.' He gave my shoulders a last squeeze before removing his arm. He did a funny little jig of excitement, as if he had too much energy and it needed to find a way out of his body. It made me laugh, and I thought again how youthful he was compared to my mum, who seemed to have aged beyond her years.

'I'm trying not to get too excited, or think about it too much, but I've waited so many years to meet anyone connected with me, it's hard not to be.' He paused for a moment, his excitement gone. 'I also want to ask them about our parents and find out if they have any memories of them.'

'Jesus, the family we have,' I said, suddenly angry. 'Did they get anything right? Did they teach us anything positive? Our family tree is littered with abuse and abandonment. Will it ever end?'

'Of course it will, look at us. I've neither abandoned nor abused my kids. Have you?' I rolled my eyes at him. 'Have you abused your child?'

'No.'

'Have you abandoned him?'

'You know I did,' I said, welling up again.

'No, you didn't. You're here, you're fighting very hard to be with him. You've got to stop beating yourself up about this. You were ill, you didn't wilfully neglect him. There's an enormous difference. As someone who was genuinely abandoned by one parent and beaten by the other, I can assure you there is a big difference.' By now we'd reached his hotel and it was time to say goodnight. 'Try to get some sleep,' said Callum. 'I'll see you bright and early tomorrow.'

It was nine o'clock, and I was tired. The food and the beer had made me sleepy, so I opted to take a taxi home rather than the train and, by the time I got into bed, I was exhausted.

Chapter 35

I fell asleep immediately and slept solidly for a few hours, after which I tossed and turned until finally I gave up trying around 4.30a.m.. I pottered about listlessly, drinking gallons of tea to idle the hours away. I had been called to give my evidence at 11a.m., but court began at 10am and there was no way I could have hung about at home until then.

Instead, I made my way to the High Court, grabbing a coffee on the way. I wasn't ready to enter the building, scared of how the day would proceed. I made my way across the road and into Glasgow Green, under the McLennan Arch and towards the People's Palace. It was a cold morning, and I was thankful for the hot coffee to warm me up. A couple of mothers out for a walk, looking for a way to burn off their toddlers' energy, and a few die-hard joggers, passed me by. The air was damp as it had rained in the night. Puddles littered the walkway, and the odd drip still fell from the tree branches that lined the park. I finished my coffee and tossed the empty cup into a bin, heading back towards the courthouse. I was now anxious to get started, but dreading what might emerge and, of course, that the jury would not believe me.

The press were outside, so I hid my face as best I could and ran through the imposing columns that guarded the building. Inside, there was a low-level hum as people chatted. I looked around and saw DI Brown. We made small talk, but I was too nervous to chat for long. Once Morton arrived, I drifted off to be by myself. I didn't notice Ross until he was right by my side.

He put his arm around me and said, 'I told you I'd come,' before hugging me tightly. I needed that.

Before long, Callum also appeared, and he too gave me a much-needed hug. Having spent my childhood with entirely undemonstrative parents and feeling very alone in the world, it was wonderful to have Ross and Callum by my side, holding me in their arms and showing me their support. This is what it must feel like to be part of a normal, loving family, I thought.

'Ross, this is my uncle Callum.' Ross looked at me in surprise and I smiled. 'Callum, this is my husband, Ross.' They shook hands. 'Callum is one of mum's brothers, from Australia.'

Before we could say any more, a clerk appeared and called us through.

'Your mum's brother?' Ross whispered as we made our way into the courtroom.

'I know,' I whispered back, 'and there's more. I'll tell you later.'

Ross, Callum and I sat halfway back. I wanted to be close to the action and hear all that was said, but I didn't want to be too close to Dad. The courtroom was packed. I looked up to the public gallery, and it looked to me like all the seats were taken. There were a number of journalists seated together and even a few of what I took to be sketch artists, with pads at the ready. Just as I was wondering where Dad would sit, two police officers led him in and sat him on a raised platform which was partitioned by glass. I was shocked at his appearance. The tall, dark, brooding man of my childhood had disappeared and had been replaced by a shrunken, grey, old man. I gasped out loud.

'Are you alright?' asked Ross, taking my hand. 'If you want to leave, just tell me.' But I didn't want to leave, I wanted to understand. Had his heart attack, arrest and the knowledge he'd been found out taken its toll, or was it that the veil had been lifted from my eyes and I now saw him for what he was?

'All rise,' commanded a voice that brought me back to the here and now. The judge came in, she sat down and proceedings got underway.

A clerk stood up and asked, 'Mr Johnston, are you ready for the trial to begin?'

He nodded.

In turn, the prosecution and the defence laid out their arguments.

'Stephen Johnston,' the prosecuting barrister said, 'is charged with the sexual abuse of his daughter between the ages for four and fifteen years old, as well as the physical and psychological abuse, and death, of his wife.

'The prosecution will show that he has built a web of abuses, controls and lies around his family, bullying his wife and daughter, both physically and emotionally for over forty years. The systematic and sustained sexual assault of his daughter led to her breakdown and the tearing apart of her family. The coercive control of his wife for more than four decades led to her social isolation and prevented her defending her daughter from Mr Johnston's onslaught. Without friends, family or any other support, Mary Johnston was at the mercy of his every whim.

'Only when she was desperate and couldn't take any more did she stand up to her husband, after which there was there an altercation, the result of which was the death of Mary Johnston.'

The defence, on the other hand, claimed that, 'Mr Johnston is not guilty of the charges laid before him. Mrs Nicola Ramsey has made up the story as a way of absolving herself for abandoning her husband and son. Mrs Ramsey was a loner as a child, preferring her own company to that of anyone else. As a teenager that solitariness took a turn for the worse and she chose to remove herself from a safe and secure home. Having poured nothing but love on his only child, this rejection left Mr Johnston hurt and confused. Despite repeated attempts to maintain a relationship with Mrs Ramsey, he was cut out of her life. All too soon, however, Mrs Ramsey also cast aside her husband and son, spending the next four years as a single woman. She deliberately absolved herself from the responsibilities of motherhood.

'When the whim took her, she returned to Glasgow in the vain attempt to reunite with her estranged husband and child. When she saw how weak Mr Johnston was after his very severe heart attack, Mrs Ramsey saw her chance to exonerate herself from the part she played in the heinous abandonment of her son, and she made up this horrific accusation.

'The defence will illustrate clearly that Mrs Ramsey is manipulative, devious and delusional.'

I was mortified to think this was how Dad's legal team were going to make me out and I could already feel just how easily they could do it. So much of what had happened in my life could be taken that way. A cold shiver spread down my spine.

Once the opening statements had been read out, the first witness to be called was DI Gail Brown. She took the judge through the investigation and I listened intently, hearing for the first time who they had spoken to and what they'd found out. She mentioned old neighbours and colleagues of Dad's whose names came flooding back, bringing with them snippets of conversations I'd overheard as a child, flashes of memories of garden parties and evening dinners, friends of my parents who had children of their own. Where had these people gone? They seemed to have dropped off the face of the earth, and I hadn't thought of them until now.

They next called Joan Murray to the stand, whose name was vaguely familiar, but I couldn't place her.

'My mum and dad were friends with the Johnstons,' she told the court. 'We used to go around quite a lot. Me and Nicola were close in age and used to play together.' Again, some vague memories hidden deep in my brain stirred. 'I had a doll's house that Nicola loved and whenever they came over, that's all she wanted to play with.'

All of a sudden that memory broke free and played itself. I remembered Joan's bedroom. Everything was white. White walls, white carpets, white furniture, white bedding. I remember it feeling ethereal and dreamlike, such a stark contrast to my bedroom with its dark, old-fashioned furniture. When I'd come back from Joan's house, my room always felt oppressive and boring, before it went back to feeling familiar and normal.

'Are you older or younger than Nicola?'

'Older, two years older.'

'So, when Nicola was only three years old you were five?'

'Aye, about that.'

'Why did you stop visiting the Johnstons?'

'Sometimes, I used to stay over. If my mum and dad were going out for the night, I'd stay with them.'

'But that stopped?'

'Yes.'

'Why?'

'I told my parents that Mr Johnston had touched me.'

'Oh, my God,' whispered Callum, 'he's a serial paedophile.' I turned to look at Callum, startled to hear him use that word, but, of course, he was right. I had only thought in terms of my father abusing me, but the fact this had happened to other little girls, even one other, reframed him in my mind.

The newspapers had bandied the word around, but they did it so often that it had lost its meaning. But here in the quiet of the courtroom, hearing Dad described so, the full force of the word and what it meant hit me square in the face. My father was one of those men, one of those men who do unspeakable things to children. You hear about them, you read about them, but you don't think you know them, let alone live with them, and you definitely don't think of yourself as one of those poor children whose future is ruined by those childhood experiences. Yet here I was, one of them.

'What do you mean "touched you"?' the prosecutor asked. Joan Murray described the very same things that he'd done to me. My eyes must have been on stalks because Ross's grasp on my hand got stronger. She was quizzed further, then asked questions by the defence who tried to discredit her, but I knew from her description of what happened she was telling the truth.

All too soon, it was my turn. I shook as I made my way to the witness stand, wishing there was a seat because my legs were weak and I felt light-headed. A glass of water was put in front of me and I immediately gulped it down, grateful for something to focus on.

'Are you Nicola Ramsey, daughter of Stephen Johnston?' asked the prosecutor.

'Yes.'

'Please speak up,' said the judge, 'so we can hear you.'

'Yes,' I repeated, moving closer to the microphone.

'Please will you tell the court about your relationship with your father?' the prosecutor asked.

'It's been difficult,' I began, 'He started to abuse me when I was only four years old.' My hands trembled as I told the court what I had told the police.

Although I had said the words out loud many times before now, saying them in front of my father made it feel like I was doing it for the very first time. My voice broke repeatedly, forcing me to sip so much water I finished the glass they'd given me. I felt as though I was fumbling over my words and Dad sitting there, watching me with no emotion, didn't help.

When I had finished telling my history, the prosecutor said they had no more questions. The horror of my childhood spoke for itself. The defence asked me more difficult questions, exploiting that blurred line between love and hate. I had hated and feared my father for most of my life, but he was still my father and I would have given anything for him to have changed his ways so that we might have had a normal relationship and that he would have been a role model I was proud of.

'Let me ask you this,' said my father's lawyer in his old-fashioned accent that told me he'd gone to a top private school and good university. 'Why did you wait until your father was dying before making this accusation?'

'When I saw him in that hospital bed, I realised that if he died having never taken responsibility for what he did to me, I would never be able to know, in my heart, that his behaviour wasn't my fault. I was a child, and he abused his power. If he didn't answer for that before he died, I could never truly get on with my life. I need closure. I was a child. It wasn't my fault.'

My time in the stand passed in what felt like a few minutes and in a bit of a blur. Before I knew it, I was back in my seat next to Ross.

The judge called for a recess and we stood as she disappeared into her chambers. As soon as her door closed, a murmur rose from the courtroom as people turned to each other to confer. Ross, Callum and I silently made our way out to the foyer. I was still a bit shaky, so Ross went to find us some water and Callum kept me silent company, both of us mulling over what had just happened.

'Do you remember me?' a woman asked. I looked up and saw Joan Murray in front of me.

'Yes, yes, I do and I'm sorry, I'm so sorry he did that to you. I had no idea.'

Being confronted with someone from my distant past, someone who had been exposed to my father's abuse hit me hard. Joan pulled me to her, and we hugged each other tightly. We had a bond, despite not having seen each other for forty years.

'It's not your fault,' she said, 'you didn't do it, don't apologise. In fact, I need to thank you.'

'For what?'

'If you hadn't come forward, I never would have done anything. I've been living with it all these years, and now I've finally been able to tell someone. Thanks to you.'

That was a pivotal moment for me. Joan made me realise this case was not just about me and what I needed. It was for all of us, for all victims of abuse. Our voices belong to an ever-growing army of survivors who refuse to be silent any longer. We refuse to protect our abusers with our fear and our guilt. Our voices are one more nail in the coffin of child abuse and its shroud of shame.

When recess was over, we took our seats again. The prosecution called Barbara-Ann Ferguson. She was tall and slender, with dark hair pulled into a tight ponytail. She wore heavy make-up and had large gold hoops in her ears. She had a strong face that might not be described as beautiful, but handsome. She had a presence, and I found it hard to take my eyes off her. Her name was completely unfamiliar to me and I anxiously waited to hear who she was.

'Please will you tell the court your name,' said the prosecution, 'and how you know the defendant.'

'Barbara-Ann Ferguson. Stephen Johnston is my father.' This time I gasped out loud and looked at my father. His face was impassive, as if he hadn't heard.

'My God!' Callum muttered, momentarily covering his eyes with his hand.

'He and my mum married in 1960, the year I was born.'

'When did they separate?'

'1964, when my mum realised what was going on.'

'What was going on?'

'She realised he was touching me – abusing me – when I was only four years old. She kicked him out.'

To say I was reeling was an understatement. I grabbed Ross's hand to stabilise myself. There had never been any mention of an ex-wife or another child.

'When did the defendant and your mother divorce?'

'They didn't, they couldn't afford to. In those days it was really hard to get divorced and really expensive.'

'Are you telling the court that Mr Johnston was still married to your mother when he bigamously married Mary Kennedy?'

'That's right.' Shock overpowered me, and I had to leave the room. I ran to the toilet and threw up. I didn't think I could take any more revelations that day.

When I eventually emerged, pale and exhausted, from the toilets, Ross was waiting for me.

'We broke for lunch,' he said, putting his arms around me and I wept.

'What a day, eh?' he said gently.

'I know,' I said, half-laughing with the shock of it all. 'What else has he lied about?'

Chapter 36

When we returned after the lunch recess, my father was called to the stand. He made his way slowly, seeming to shuffle, a visible contrast to the strong, purposeful stride I associated him with. A fresh glass of water was put in front of him and he drank from it.

'Mr Johnston,' began the prosecutor. 'How did you first meet Teresa McKay?'

'She worked in my local pub.'

'And it was love at first sight, would you say?'

'I suppose so. We were both very young.'

'Not long after you became a couple, Teresa became pregnant. Is that correct?'

'Yes. I think it was only about six months after we met.'

'So, you married in 1960, the year Barbara-Ann was born.'

'That's right.'

'Why did the marriage breakdown?'

'Because we were too young and got married too quickly.'

'Is that all? I mean, many young couples weather the storms and their marriages continue.'

'We were too young,' he repeated, his face stony.

'Was it not that she accused you of abusing Barbara-Ann, who was only four years old at the time?'

'She was angry with me, she was looking for a way out. She was crazy.'

'Why was she angry with you?'

'Soon after we married, it was obvious we'd made a mistake. We annoyed each other and argued a lot. In the end, we hated each other, and both wanted out.'

This was the first time I'd been able to make myself look at Dad properly, to take in the full image of him as he was now, not as he used to be. His voice was the softest I had ever known it. He sounded tired and broken; slumped in his seat, he looked as though he'd had the fight knocked out of him. I still didn't detect any remorse, however. Maybe he really didn't think he'd done anything wrong.

'Why did you not divorce?'

'We couldn't afford it, so we went our separate ways. I thought we could divorce later on, but she disappeared, I couldn't find her.'

'Did you ever initiate divorce proceedings?'

'No, I told you, I couldn't find Teresa. She'd moved on and nobody would tell me where to.'

'Did you tell your new, young fiancée, Mary Kennedy, that you were married?'

'No.' Here, at least, he looked embarrassed.

'Why not?'

'At first, she didn't need to know, but when we got more serious, I tried to find Terri. When I couldn't find her, I didn't say anything because I didn't want to disappoint Mary.'

'Isn't it, in fact, that you did not search for Terri McKay because you knew that if you made contact she would tell Mary and maybe even the authorities that you had sexually abused your daughter?'

'No, it isn't.'

'Isn't it true that you didn't want to risk Mary Kennedy not marrying you?'

'No.'

'You couldn't risk it because you realised you'd found someone young and naïve, someone so in love with you that you were confident she wouldn't say anything about it when you began to abuse your next child?'

'Absolutely not.' My father began to get worked up and leaned on the stand for support. I saw anger flash over his face, a remnant of his formidable self. 'I did not abuse Barbara-Ann, and I didn't abuse Nicola either. I loved those girls, both of them, but their crazy mothers couldn't see that. They wouldn't let me love them, they wouldn't let me love my daughters.'

'You say you loved your daughters and yet you sexually abused them. You did what no father should ever do to their child.'

'They were my responsibility, it was my job to look after them, keep them safe and fulfil their needs.'

'You weren't fulfilling their needs, you were fulfilling your own.'

'We took care of each other. Both Barbara-Ann and Nicola loved me and it was their mad mothers who were jealous and turned them against me.'

By now, Dad was tired and breathing heavily. He nearly stumbled, and a clerk helped him into a chair. The prosecutor gave him a moment before continuing.

'Mary Kennedy was so besotted with you,' he said, 'and so under your coercive control that she was incapable of defending either herself against your physical abuse or her daughter from your sexual abuse. You weren't going to repeat the mistake you made when you married Teresa McKay. No, this time you were careful to choose a woman much weaker, far more susceptible to your demands and who, crucially, was alone in the world. Mary had no family to support her in her time of need. There was nobody she could run to for protection with her toddler. Mary wasn't able to stand up to your bullying.'

'I never bullied Mary, I never needed to. She loved me and knew her place.' Dad nudged himself further forward in his seat.

'And what was her place? To do as she was told?'

'Absolutely. I was head of the household.' His voice regained some strength. 'I was responsible for all of us, and I took my responsibility seriously. It was my house and so my rules.' He stood up again. He was not going to let anyone question how he ran his castle. 'Mary's job was to keep the house the way I liked it, to take care of Nicola the way she should be and not,' – Dad was on a roll now, his voice booming, just as it had done when I was a child – 'not to disobey me. I don't make decisions on a whim, they are thought out and made for the benefit of everyone. If I'd let either of those hysterical women make the big decisions, God knows where we'd be.' His hackles were up and the prosecutor went with him.

'And when Mary did disobey you and threatened to tell the police about what you'd done to Nicola, isn't it true that you pushed her down the stairs?'

'I didn't push her, I didn't need to push her. She fell, the stupid woman. She never could handle her drink. She was drunk and talking like a crazy woman.'

'Another crazy woman in your life, you seem to be drawn to them,' the prosecutor goaded.

'Yes, she was crazy. The stress of Nicola's return was too much, it tipped her over the edge.'

'Crazy, mad, hysterical. These are the words you use. But I ask you, Mr Johnston, were they crazy? Or did you beat and threaten them into doing things they would never have done if left alone to make their own choices?'

'Mary wouldn't have lasted a day if I hadn't been there.'

'Wouldn't she? Instead, Mr Johnston, did Nicola's return make her finally see you for what you really were – an abuser and a bully – and now she was going to put you behind bars where you belonged. And so you pushed her down the stairs.'

'I didn't push her,' bellowed my father, 'all I had to do was let go, and she did the rest.' The court fell silent, all eyes upon him, but he was oblivious. 'And I was glad, glad to be finally rid of her and her constant chatter. Chatter about nothing. Day in and day out, her voice was in my ear like a mosquito you just can't kill, wearing me down. Her life amounted to nothing and now she's gone and its good riddance.' His outburst left him breathless and sweating. One of the officers tried to assist him, but he shook him off.

'And you,' he forced himself to standing, pointing down at me, 'I gave you everything and you betrayed me. I loved you with all my heart. I gave you all of me and you threw it back in my face.' His cold eyes drilled right into my soul and I felt like a child again, terrified by my father's anger and what he was capable of. I sat rigid, unable to move or respond in any way. 'I gave you everything,' he repeated, but his anger had passed and he broke down in tears. This time he didn't fight the officer who helped him into a chair.

Chapter 37

I went over and over again in my mind what Dad had said, how nasty he looked when he shouted down at me from his pulpit. I was so caught up that I was unaware of what else was being said, and it was only the judge's hammer that brought me back to the present.

'What happened?' I asked Ross. 'Is it all over?'

'For now. The jury have gone to deliberate.'

I watched as Dad was led out the door he had come in from, after which we made our way out. For forty-five minutes, the three of us wandered the hall outside the courtroom, not saying very much, but what we did say was in hushed tones, our faces grave. My stomach wouldn't stop churning. Back inside, I watched Dad be led once again from the antechamber. Then the judge took her place.

'Ladies and gentlemen of the jury,' she said, 'have you come to a decision?'

'We have,' said the forewoman.

'On the charge of continuous and coercive control of Mrs Mary Johnston, how do you find the defendant?'

'Guilty.'

'On the charge of the sexual abuse of Mrs Nicola Ramsey, how do you find the defendant?'

'Guilty.'

The relief I felt at hearing those words is something I'll never be able to articulate fully. I felt vindicated. It was as if I'd been on trial and the jury were determining whether I'd been telling the truth, not whether Dad was guilty. Now the whole world knew I hadn't simply made it up as an act of vengeance, but that it was true. Both Callum and Ross took one each of my hands and squeezed them tight. A few others in the court cheered. I looked across to Barbara-Ann and Joan Murray, and we shared a smile of triumph. The judge banged her gravel and brought the court to order.

'This court finds the actions of Mr Stephen Johnston to be reprehensible in every way. The physical and mental abuse he placed on his wife, Mary Johnston, and his daughter, Nicola Ramsey, showed no bounds. We know from previous testimony that Mrs Ramsey was not his first victim and it cannot be taken for granted that she has been his last. For that reason, Mr Johnston is considered a menace to society and cannot be allowed to remain at large. The longevity of his crimes show him to be purposeful and calculated in his actions. The court hereby sentences him to fifteen years in prison with no opportunity for release for at least ten years. Court dismissed.'

It was the hoped-for result, and as I left the courtroom, I grinned from ear-to-ear.

'Is that it?' Ross asked Inspector Morton. 'It all seemed to happen so quickly.'

'Yes, that's it.' Morton looked at me. 'You can be assured that your father will be off the streets for a very long time. He won't be a threat to you or anyone else.'

'I can't decide if I want to celebrate or sleep,' I said, 'I feel exhausted after so much tension.'

'First things first,' Morton said, 'Let's make a statement to the press so they'll go away. They know the result but will want a comment from you. Are you able to give them a few words?' I nodded, and we walked out of the building into a cacophony of reporters. I stood amidst them, unsure of what to say.

'Today has been a difficult day, but also a positive one. My father, my perpetrator, has been put away for a very long time. He's been held responsible for his actions, not only for my abuse, but for the abuse of others.' I took a deep breath, unsure what else to say. 'Thank you to all those who have supported me. I am eternally grateful. I'm looking forward to rebuilding my life and,' remembering what I'd heard others say on TV, 'ask for privacy at this time. Thank you.' My statement made, the journalists went their separate ways to report back.

DIs Brown and Morton came over to me. 'Congratulations,' said Morton, shaking my hand. 'You did good today.'

'Well done,' said Brown, 'Today was tough, I know.'

'Why didn't you tell me I had a sister?'

'We couldn't, we didn't want anything to jeopardise the case.' She looked at me intently.

'Thank you for not giving up,' I said, 'it means everything to me.'

Gail Brown smiled at me before looking at her phone, which was ringing.

'Take care of yourself,' she said. She answered the call and she and Morton headed off.

I had a moment to myself, there in front of the High Court. The wind still blew, and I took a deep breath, filling my lungs until they hurt, before releasing that trapped air, just as I had been released from my father's clutches. I'd wanted him to be held responsible for what he'd done to me, to my mother, to Barbara-Ann and to Joan Murray. Now he was.

'Well done,' said Ross, coming up to me. 'You did great.' He gave me another hug, and it felt comforting. I saw Callum looking pale and exhausted. He'd heard for the first time what Dad had done, and it was clear he was wrestling to understand the life his sister had endured.

'Are you alright?' I asked, going over to him. He didn't answer, and I left him alone with his thoughts.

I noticed Barbara-Ann standing a little distance away, pulling nervously on a cigarette. I walked over to her, unable to keep my eyes off her, my sister.

'Hello, Barbara-Ann.' Now that she was up close the resemblance to our father was unmistakable. The commanding presence she had, that I'd noticed in the courtroom, was clearly inherited from him. Unlike him, though, she had a softness to her. She emitted a positive energy, suggesting she enjoyed life. That was not from Dad, so she must have inherited that from her mother. Her voice cracked as she spoke, a telltale sign of a life spent around cigarettes and alcohol. Maybe she'd followed her mum into the pub trade.

'Hello, Nicola,' she said it with a smile on her lips, as if she were as amazed as me at having a sister. 'I always wondered what you'd be like.'

'You knew about me?'

'Yeah, word got around that Dad had moved on, found a new wife and family.'

'Why didn't anyone tell the authorities?'

'Good riddance to him, that's what they thought, and they were right. Behind bars is where that bastard belongs.' I felt the earth slip from under me again, for here was another part of my life about which I had no idea.

'I didn't know about you,' I said.

'No, well, you had enough to be thinking about.'

'Is your mum here?' I looked around curiously.

'No, she passed a few years ago. She'll be watching, though, delighted you've done this.' We looked at each other for a while, both looking for something to link us, but apart from our abuse there was nothing. Barbara-Ann broke the silence by flinging her arms around me and squeezing tightly. 'You look after yourself,' she said, before joining her friends and family. I wondered if we'd ever see each other again.

Ross came back over. 'Come on,' he said, 'I'll take you for a drink. Our last one as mister and missus.'

He put his arm around me to lead me to a nearby pub, but before we left, I looked around for Callum. I spotted him across the street talking to a man and a woman. Even from this distance, the woman looked so like my mother that they could only be Elizabeth and Robert. I contemplated going over to say hello, but I figured Callum wanted some time alone with them, and, anyway, I didn't have the energy to make polite conversation with more long-lost relatives.

In the pub, we ordered some drinks and found a quiet table. It was all too much, and I burst into tears. Ross didn't try to comfort me, he just let me cry, expelling the adrenalin and emotion that had been coursing round my body looking for a way out. It felt good to cry, and eventually the tears turned to laughter.

'It's over,' I said.

We sipped our drinks without saying much until I became aware that Ross was distracted and asked him what was wrong.

'Nicola, there's something I want to tell you.'

'Is it Sam, is he okay?'

'Yes, he's fine. It's just that I want to let you know I've started seeing someone.'

I gagged, my whole body rejecting what he'd told me. I shut my eyes to shut him and his words out, to give myself space to think. I could either rail against him, which I had no right to do, or take the news graciously. I tried to be gracious.

'I see, that's wonderful news. What does Sam think of her?'

'He's not met her yet and won't for a long time. I just wanted to let you know.' I glanced over at him and I could tell he was embarrassed. 'I don't know why, but now that I know you're alive and well, I've been able to move on a little bit.'

'I see,' I said again. 'That's wonderful news.' If I said it often enough, perhaps I would believe it. 'What's her name?'

'Fiona. I'm sorry Nicola, maybe I shouldn't have said anything. I don't want to upset you, you've enough on your plate, but I thought I should tell you myself.'

'Yes, thank you for telling me. Listen, I'm knackered, I'd better go. I'll see you at the hearing.'

I left my drink and headed out the door, hoping Ross would follow me out and say it was all a bad joke. But he didn't. As ridiculous as it sounded, I'd half-thought that once the court case was over, Ross and I might be able to move forward together, divorce hearing or not. I still thought of us as a family unit, just one that didn't live together. But now there was Fiona, a woman who might usurp me, not only with Ross but, more importantly, with Sam. The thought terrified me. I hadn't worked this hard to get my life back on track to have some other woman take my place. I stormed back into the pub.

'Who is she?' I demanded. Ross looked around self-consciously.

'Someone I met at work.'

'Do you love her?'

'That's none of your business.'

'None of my business? You're my husband, don't forget that.'

'I've never forgotten that. You're the one who forgot, you're the one who left, you have no right to play that card.'

'Sam is my son, I'm not having some stranger come and take my place.'

'For God's sake, Nicola,' he said. 'Nobody is going to take your place, okay? We've not been seeing each other long, but I like her. I wanted to extend you the courtesy of letting you know before Claire or anyone else told you.'

'Claire knows?'

'Of course she does, she's one of my oldest friends.'

'She never said anything.'

'I asked her not to. As I said, I wanted to tell you myself.'

'Right, okay then.' My anger passed, but I was still feeling stroppy. 'Ross, I'm sorry, I'm sorry I overreacted. Of course, you must move on. You took me by surprise, that's all. I'm sorry.'

I left feeling foolish.

Chapter 38

I hadn't intended to go line dancing that night, but, after the stress of the court case, I wanted to be around people who weren't part of my sordid past. I wanted to be with those who knew me in the here and now, not who I used to be. Class was fun, and I laughed more than I had done in a long time, all too aware that I was feeling a little delirious.

It was busy that evening and, for whatever reason, everyone seemed keyed up. Mags and Roy had sold their house, they were downsizing and using what spare money they had on a round the world cruise. Another woman, Sharon, who I didn't know very well, had just found a new job. All this good spirit raised the energy of the group, and the evening flew by in a flurry of shuffles and claps.

I joined the other Tappers in the Bruce Arms, feeling newly energised with the exercise. I walked the short distance to the pub with Alan and we made idle chit-chat. Alan was easy and amiable company. He told funny stories about his colleagues at the surveyor's firm he worked for. 'Do you like your job?' I asked him.

'It's uninteresting, easy work,' he said, 'but it's essential income for the company and it keeps me busy. We're the bread and butter part of the firm.'

'What do you do for the firm?'

'I'm in valuations. Every year commercial properties need to be valued so that property owners know how much their assets are worth. Dull stuff, but I work with a nice crowd. What about you, what do you do?'

'I work in a hotel in the city centre,' I told him. 'There's a mix of tourists staying for a week or so and business people who come just for a night or two. The café and restaurant are busy with business meetings and lunches. At weekends, we get shoppers looking for lunch or afternoon tea. It's hard on the feet, but I enjoy it. There are no deadlines or stress.'

'And you've always worked in hospitality?'

'No, in a previous life I was a librarian at Glasgow University. That was a good job. It was busy, I liked my colleagues, and I enjoyed being around the students. I admired their youth and vitality. I loved how carefree they were.'

'What made you leave?'

'I had a baby and wanted to stay at home with him. When it came to getting back into the job market I wanted a change, something different. Talking to you now though, I miss it. I miss the smell of the books, the feel of them in my hands. Most people thought shelving books was boring, but I used to find it really relaxing, a time not to talk to anyone, just switch off for ten minutes, you know, recharge my batteries.' We'd reached the pub and our conversation ended.

Everyone very quickly became quite drunk, not least myself. I was in the mood for celebrating. I was on a high after the stress of the past six months, the euphoria that the world knew the truth about my father and that soon I would know if I would have any access to Sam.

There had been times, usually in the early hours of the morning, that I'd begun to question myself. Was it possible I'd made the whole thing up, or imagined it, or had it been someone else entirely who had carried out these abominations? Now that Dad had been found guilty, I could lay these fears aside and put them down to my father's brainwashing all those years ago.

I gravitated towards Roy and Mags, whose company I loved. I liked to hear about their week, how full their days were, their amusing family stories. I secretly wondered what my life would have been like if they'd been my parents. I imagined a childhood full of laughter and fun, of day trips out and visitors calling by. Roy and Mag's life centred around their family. They spent a lot of time with their now adult children, doting on their grandchildren. It wasn't without a little wistfulness that I listened to them, wishing my parents had been this loving.

'I envy the closeness you have with your family,' I said before I could stop myself.

'We are close,' said Roy, 'but it isn't always peaceful. Mags and our daughter, Sadie, have had some right old ding-dongs in their time.'

'Sadie would never admit it,' said Mags, 'but she's just like me so it's no wonder we clash every now and again.'

'What about you?' Roy asked, 'are you close to your parents?'

'No. I don't speak to my dad and my mum passed away recently. She fell down the stairs.' What with the events of recent months, and the alcohol, I burst into tears.

'Sweetheart,' Mags put her arm around me, 'I'm sorry to hear that. Were you close to her?'

'No. I'm sorry,' I couldn't stop myself crying, 'here I go again. I've done nothing but cry recently.'

'It's not surprising, you're grieving. That's nothing to apologise for.' Roy passed me a tissue.

'It's not just that, my whole life has been thrown in the air recently and it's only just hitting the ground.'

'What do you mean?' Mags asked.

'It's my fault that my mother died, I'm sure of it.'

'I thought she had a fall?'

'She did, but only because she'd been arguing with my father. I know he was angry with her because of me and let her fall down the stairs.'

'I don't understand,' said Roy.

I told them all about the court case with my father and how he had admitted to letting Mum slip out of his hands and to the bottom of the stairs.

'Oh, sweetheart,' said Mags, 'that's awful.' She put her arm around me.

'Added to that is the fact my soon-to-be ex-husband has started seeing another woman.'

'Divorce is never easy, of course you're upset,' said Roy.

'Do you want to talk about it?'

I told them about my breakdown and disappearance. I told them about Sam and how I'd thought Ross and I might get our marriage back on track.

'As time went on, I realised too much had happened between us and we couldn't recapture what we'd once had.'

'Did you still want to get back together?'

'No, but the fact he's moving on has left me emotional. I know it's what he needs.'

'Maybe it's what you need too?' suggested Mags.

'Maybe.'

'Oh, sweetheart,' said Mags, 'what a tough time you've been having. I wish there was something we could do to help.'

'You have. This group has been a lifesaver for me. It's a chance to forget all the other stuff.'

'And here we are making you talk about it.'

'Listen,' said Roy, 'you just let us know if there's anything we can do for you. Anything.'

'Thank you.' I smiled, feeling better for just having talked about it.

In a slightly drunk state, I found a seat next to Alan. I thought again how amusing and easy-going he was, and tonight, I noticed how blue his eyes were. It must be the wine, I told myself, I'd never noticed them before.

'Your Behind the Back step is coming along,' I said, 'I still can't get the hang of it and end up turning in the wrong direction.'

'You're doing just fine,' he replied with a smile.

I had always suspected Alan was interested in me, but hadn't encouraged him. But I did enjoy his company and, I couldn't deny it, his attention. It had been a long time since anyone had flirted with me. Mags's earlier words sprang to mind. Perhaps it was time for me to move on too.

I grinned at him. I don't really know why. I think I wanted him to say something nice to me, something to make me feel special and add a bit of excitement to my evening. The devil on my shoulder was egging me on, reassuring me that a bit of male company would be nice for an evening. My guardian angel on the other shoulder reminded me that I was not in a good place to begin any relationship and was, in fact, still married.

'What?' Alan asked in response to my grin.

'Nothing,' I said, letting common sense take over. 'It's been a good day, that's all.'

'What happened today?'

'I got some good news, news I've been waiting a long time to hear.'

'What good news is that?' I contemplated telling him, but decided tonight was not the night to divulge something so personal to him.

'What's new in the exciting world of valuations? Any exciting portfolios come your way?'

'You might laugh, but yes, we did get a big new client this week.'

'And who's that?'

'I'm not at liberty to say,' Alan said with mock seriousness.

'Ooh, it's like that, is it?' I teased.

'Yes, it is.' Alan looked at me intently for a moment, long enough for me to read his thoughts. I blushed, out of practice at flirting with men with attractive eyes. I tried to think of something to say, but came up blank so got up and left the table. I found Gavin and his partner, Mike. There would be no flirting with these two. It was safe ground. I didn't talk to Alan for the rest of the evening, but every so often we caught each other's eye and I would blush afresh.

At the end of the night I swayed myself to the bus stop, giggling at the simple pleasure of being alive and feeling that, for once, things were going my way.

'Goodnight.'

It was Alan who interrupted my reverie. I thought he might stop and talk to me until my bus arrived, but he didn't. He kept on walking.

'Night,' I called after him. I watched him walk to the end of the road until he turned a corner, disappointed he didn't look back. If he was trying to play hard to get, I thought, it was having the desired effect.

Chapter 39

One week later, I was back in court, this time for the divorce and custody hearing. Because our separation was amicable, it was considered prudent to try to agree everything in one day.

I met Kwame on the steps outside. We'd had only one or two meetings since he first agreed to take on my case. The time between that first meeting and now had passed so quickly, my entire world had changed.

'Congratulations on your father's conviction,' he said earnestly. 'Did it give you the peace you were looking for?'

'I think it will. But what I need now is to be with my son.'

'Let's see what we can do today then,' he said in a reassuring tone. When we went inside, instead of entering a courtroom, we were led to what felt like a meeting room. Ross and his solicitor, Simon Clarke, were already there. In contrast to the high drama of my father's case, this felt like a formality, a verbal and then a written agreement that Ross and I wanted to dissolve our marriage. All the time my stomach churned like a spiraling tornado, not butterflies gently fluttering. I felt sick with nerves. I held myself together as best I could when signing the divorce papers for, although it was the only way forward, it wasn't the path I wanted to take. I was still grieving for what could have been.

'Now,' began Simon Clarke, 'let's move onto the custody arrangements.'

'Before we do that,' said Ross, 'can I have a private word with Nicola?' Simon Clarke and Kwame looked at one another, confused. 'Please.'

Ross looked at me for confirmation this was okay and I nodded. Simon and Kwame stood up and silently left the room. Again, my stomach lurched, and I had to take a deep breath. I didn't know what Ross was going to say but after everything we'd been through together, I didn't think it would be good. When the door clicked shut I turned to Ross and waited. He looked at his hands, at the ground, the ceiling and finally at me.

'We've been through a lot, haven't we?' he said.

'Yes,' I said quietly, wondering where this was going.

'I feel like I've lived a thousand lives since you walked out all those years ago.' I saw it in his face. He looked older. His hair a little grayer, a few more lines around his eye. I noticed, too, that his face had softened and when he looked at me, his eyes were gentle. The anger had gone. 'I didn't think I could ever forgive you for what you did but...'

'But?' I stared at him, barely breathing. I didn't dare hope.

'Since you got back, I feel like I've really gotten to know you. All the secrets you were hiding, were ashamed of are out in the open. I can't believe you lived with it for so long.' Still I watched him, willing him to say what was really on his mind. He put his hands on the table and leaned forwards. 'But you did, and that took courage. Real strength. When I watched you in the courtroom, as your life was put on display, I saw you all over again. I saw the woman I fell in love with all those years ago. I saw your optimism, how hard you'll fight for what you love, your dignity through it all. I realised I still love you.'

'Do you mean that?' I wasn't ready to believe it was true. I'd not long left any hope of reuniting with Ross behind me. Could he really have had a change of heart?

'I do. There's never been anyone else for me but you.'

'What about Fiona?'

'She's a lovely woman, but she's not you. Do you think we could, you know,' he glanced around the room, 'put this behind us?'

I was up and out of my seat before he'd even finished his sentence. 'Yes,' I said, crashing into his arms. 'There's nothing I want more.' I felt Ross' arms around me, squeezing me tight, holding on to me as if he too couldn't believe this was happening. I tightened my grip on him, never wanting to let him go, thankful for the miracle the universe had thrown me.

'It seems my client has had a change of heart,' said Simon Clarke, surprising me. I hadn't heard him or Kwame come back into the room. 'Does this mean you've reached an agreement?'

'Yes,' said Ross. 'We've agreed to give things another try.'

Kwame looked at me, his smile broad and genuine. 'I think my client agrees to this.'

The four of us left the building, Kwame and Simon rushing off to their next clients. After all, we were only one of many families.

'What happens now?' I asked Ross.

'I guess it's about time you and Sam got to know each other again.'

'I'd love that.'

'Why don't you meet us in the park after school?' Ross pulled me close and kissed me gently. I cupped his face in my hands, so grateful to feel his skin under mine, to know that we were about to embark on the next chapter of our life together. 'I love you Mrs Ramsey.'

'I love you, Mr Ramsey.'

Chapter 40

The closer it got to half-past three, and I was due to meet Ross and Sam at the park, the brighter the world around me grew; the sky got bluer, the clouds whiter and the grass greener, as if I had landed in Technicolor.

Eventually, the hour arrived, and I hurried to the park where we'd agreed to meet. I'd walked so quickly that I was a little out of breath when I arrived and had to take a moment to compose myself. I heard him laughing before I saw him and when I did, my whole body relaxed. He was even more picture perfect than I remembered. My eyes welled with sheer relief at Sam being there. At the back of my mind, I'd worried Ross was playing a trick on me, or that I'd only imagined him asking if we could try again and be a family.

Having hurried all the way there. I now hung back, hesitating before making my way to them, unsure of how Sam would respond to me; I'd deserted him after all.

'Hi,' I called as I made my way over. Ross smiled and walked towards me.

'Hi,' he said, taking my hands in his. 'Are you ready?' I nodded and followed him to the climbing frame where Sam was clambering about. 'Sam, come on down for a minute. Sam, this is your mum.' Shyly, Sam hid behind his father's legs. 'Say hello.'

'Hello.'

'Hello, Sam,' I said, trembling. I wanted to reach out to him, grab him, and hold him close to me. I wanted to smell his hair, his skin, look into his blue eyes and read his thoughts, see what damage I'd done to him. But I held back. I clasped my hands together to stop them from leaping out of control.

'It's a long time since we last saw each other. Do you remember me?' He shook his head, smiling but still hiding behind Ross. 'Daddy said you might like to show me your trains.' I pointed to five or six trains positioned on a nearby bench. 'Are these the ones you brought with you?'

'Yes.'

'Will you show them to me?' And that was it. The ice was broken. We went over to the bench and Sam told me which ones were his favourites, their engines and the names he'd given them.

'I've been so looking forward to this afternoon,' I told him when he finished telling me about the last one. 'I'm so excited to see you, Sam.' He smiled, pleased and embarrassed at the same time. 'I've missed you. All the time I've been away, I've not stopped thinking about you.' I held Sam's face gently in my palms. 'I've never stopped thinking about you and I've never stopped loving you.'

'Thank you,' he said, looking up at Ross, unsure how to respond and falling back on good manners. 'Where have you been?' he asked. I'd thought a lot about how best to answer this question but had never come up with a suitable answer.

'Well,' I began cautiously, 'I got very ill and had to go away.' I was aware of Sam watching me, waiting for me to continue. 'It took longer than I thought for me to get better, but as soon as I was strong enough, I came back to see you. Do you understand?'

'What was wrong with you?' I looked to Ross for help but he offered none. He only shrugged his shoulders. I had to answer this one for myself.

THE DAY SHE CAME HOME

'I was very sad. I was sad because I couldn't look after you or Daddy properly. But I got lots of rest and now I'm better.'

'Did Daddy know where you were? Maybe he could have helped?'

'You know, you're right. Maybe he could have. But I was so sad I didn't think anybody could help me.'

Sam nodded, seeming to take in what I said, happy with my response for the moment. I was in a state of ecstasy. I was with my son, at the park doing normal family stuff. Although the sun shone brightly and the sky was a clear pale blue, the air was bitter and our breath moved like good spirits around us. We made up a game whereby we had to stay out of the cold shadows because the shadow monster lived there. It was safe in the light. Because it was so cold, there were only a few other children in the playground. Sam knew them and intermittently ran off to play. Ross and I walked the perimeter of the playground, trying to stay warm.

'How do you feel after this morning?' Ross asked.

'Excited,' I told him, taking his hand and smiling up at him. 'I know we can make a go of this. There's only ever been you. Been us. You and me against the world.'

Ross stopped walking and turned me towards him. 'No more secrets?'

'No more secrets.' I lifted my face to his, and he kissed me. I felt like a teenager again, excited and thrilled about what was to come.

'Careful up there, Sam.' Ross called over to our son, who was at the top of the climbing frame. Eventually, the cold air got the better of us and we persuaded Sam to leave the playground on the promise of hot chocolate.

'Can I get marshmallows with it?' Sam asked hopefully.

'Aye, okay,' relented Ross, 'since it's a special day.'

As we drank our chocolate, Sam told me about his friends at the playground, that some were in his class at school, but weren't his best friends. He was amazed I knew Claire, who he called Aunty Claire.

'Did you tell Aunty Claire where you were?' Sam asked. 'When you went away?'

'No, darling, I didn't. I didn't tell anyone.'

Sam thought about this for a moment, but didn't ask me anything more. I realised that he would have many questions for me in the following months as he made sense of who I was and what had happened. All too quickly, it was time to say goodbye. It again took all my restraint not to grab Sam and squeeze him fiercely. 'It was lovely to be with you today, Sam,' I said, kneeling beside him. 'We're going to see a lot more of each other now and become friends.'

'Why is that?'

'Because,' said Ross, 'your mum and I are getting back together. We're going to take things slowly so we can all get used to each other again. How does that sound?'

'Great,' said Sam, beaming.

'Give your mum a hug,' urged Ross and Sam reached out to me and I gave him a long bear hug, breathing him in and kissing him.

'Bye, Sam,' I said, reluctantly standing up.

'I'll call you tonight,' said Ross. 'We'll make plans.'

I watched them walk away, tears of happiness in my eyes. Sam turned around and waved.

'Bye, Mum,' he called.

'Bye, son.'

– THE END –

Thank You

Thank you for reading The Day She Came Home.

Reviews are crucial for helping new readers discover me and decide whether or not they want to take a chance on my books.

If you could take a moment to leave a review on Goodreads I'd really appreciate it. Even a simple 'I enjoyed this story' is fantastic!

Recommending my work to others is also a huge help, so if you liked this book, please consider spreading the word to others!

If you want to keep up to date with what I'm writing, and be the first to know about any new releases, join my mailing list, and receive the tiny, twisty, tartan thriller, All About You, as a thank you! http://books.emmadhesi.com/

My journey to publication hasn't been a straight line. It's taken me many years to return to my calling. I was once told that the job we wanted at eight years old is really the thing we want to do most in life. At eight years old I wanted to be an author, and the book that changed my life was Ballet Shoes by Noel Streatfeild. Oh, the magic of make believe!

Writing is a solitary life. As a young person, this was not for me. I lacked the maturity or confidence to sit down by myself for long stretches of time and put pen to paper (I still write longhand!). Prolonged periods of inactivity were interspersed with only short periods of intense writing.

At long last motherhood forced me to mature, and I waved goodbye to a busy social life and said hello to a life of early rises and bedtime routines. This cleared time for me to write more regularly and with increased intention.

After the birth of my second child, Post Natal Depression kicked in and took hold. As a coping mechanism, I journaled what I was going through, and often imagined what it would be like just to get up and walk away. Thankfully, I never took such drastic action myself, instead I created a fictional character who did, and followed her story.

That story became my first novel, The Day She Came Home. It has turned out to be a powerful way to share my feelings with other women struggling with PND and to help them know they are not alone.

Outside of writing, I love days out with my family. We're so enjoying being back in the UK. We feel like tourists, exploring Edinburgh and the rest of Scotland.

My husband and I have always loved travelling and now that the children are getting older, we hope to introduce them to the adventure that is world travel.

Here are some fun facts about me!

- I love genealogy and have spent too many hours geeking out on Census Returns, Death Registers and Ship Passenger Lists.

- I permanently borrowed a glass tumbler from Buckingham Palace – oops!

- My life hack guru is Gretchen Ruben, and she taught me I'm an Abstainer and a Rebel – it explains so much!

- The older I get, the more introvert I get.

- I am a "haggis curry". 50% Scottish, and 50% Indian.

- After travelling in South East Asia for many months, I determined to get my motor scooter license. I got it, but only just. I struggled to go any faster than 15 miles per hour, deemed slow enough to be a danger to other drivers!

Want to stay in touch? Here's how:
Website - www.books.emmadhesi.com
Instagram – www.facebook.com/emmadhesiauthor

Also by Emma Dhesi

Other books by Emma Dhesi include:

Belonging
More Than Enough
Follow Me

Printed in Great Britain
by Amazon